Also by
Christine Warren

Hard as a Rock
Stone Cold Lover
Heart of Stone
Hungry Like a Wolf
Drive Me Wild
On the Prowl
Not Your Ordinary Faerie Tale
Black Magic Woman
Prince Charming Doesn't Live Here
Born to be Wild
Big Bad Wolf
You're So Vein
One Bite with a Stranger
Walk on the Wild Side
Howl at the Moon
The Demon You Know
She's No Faerie Princess
Wolf at the Door

Anthologies

Huntress
No Rest for the Witches

Rocked by Love

Christine Warren

St. Martin's Paperbacks

This is a work of fiction. All of the characters, organizations, and events portrayed in this novel are either products of the author's imagination or are used fictitiously.

ROCKED BY LOVE

Copyright © 2016 by Christine Warren.

For information address St. Martin's Press, 175 Fifth Avenue, New York, NY 10010.

ISBN: 978-1-250-07737-0

Printed in the United States of America

St. Martin's Paperbacks edition / March 2016

St. Martin's Paperbacks are published by St. Martin's Press, 175 Fifth Avenue, New York, NY 10010.

10 9 8 7 6 5 4 3 2 1

With eternal thanks to my readers, who have gone with me on so many adventures. I love you guys.

Chapter One

Tsores zaynen far dem mentshn vi zhaver far ayzn.
Troubles are to man what rust is to iron.

Eleven fifty-eight P.M. Two minutes since the last time she'd looked.

Kylie gave in to the impulse to stick her tongue out at her phone while her foot jiggled relentlessly under the table. She had to beat back her impatience with a mental stick, but the specter of disappointment had started to polish a weapon of its own, one more the size of a cricket bat. As much as she would prefer to continue her lovely sail down Denial, after an hour and twenty-eight minutes, even she might be forced to admit defeat.

She'd been stood up.

Sort of.

"Stood up" was the most convenient term. She had arranged to meet a person of the opposite sex in a social setting at a designated time and place, but said person had failed to honor this agreement and had not shown up. In most cases, this would count as being stood up. However, in Kylie's case, she had no romantic interest in her missing acquaintance, and she felt more disappointment and curiosity than embarrassment at the situation.

Besides, at least she'd gotten a really good slice of pie out of her time spent waiting. Cherry streusel. Yum.

So she didn't feel the same way she would have if an actual date had failed to show, even though she'd had more riding on this meeting than the possibility of sexual attraction. She'd worked for months to create this opportunity, and she couldn't deny her disappointment in seeing it come to nothing, whatever it should have been called.

What term did you use to describe a covert meeting with a complete stranger that had nothing to do with sex or romance and everything to do with the exchange of secret information? And just to be clear, a "deep throating" was so off the table.

She set her phone down and reached for her cola. By now, the glass held nearly as much water as soda. The melted ice smothered the effervescent carbonation until she was left with little more than sweet, flavorless syrup. Maybe she should try making herself drink coffee again, though that would have been just as disgusting by now. Cold or watered down didn't really lean heavily to one side or the other. Tonight just didn't seem to be her night.

Kylie brushed off the negative thoughts. She'd never been the kind of girl to indulge in melancholy. She considered herself what her paternal grandmother had called a *vilde chaya,* a wild child. She was the kind of girl who saw what she wanted and went after it, doing whatever it took, even fighting dirty—or, especially fighting dirty—until she achieved her goal. Her goal now was to find a new way to track down her "date" and make sure that this time he couldn't ignore her.

Kylie hated being ignored.

Not that it happened often. Even her parents, who found her surprising, unpredictable, and wholly indecipherable, had trouble ignoring her. Of course, she'd made it easier for them when she'd moved to another state, but still. If Abraham Kramer and Constance Harding-Kramer couldn't manage to put Kylie completely out of their heads, some *schlub* with the vainglorious online handle of DrkMsgr sure as *shudden* wasn't going to do it either.

It had taken her months to find the stranger in the infinite space of the Internet, and she'd invested weeks more in grooming the connection. She'd chatted and swapped stories, offered advice and told jokes, slowly building their cyber connection behind her own mask as Wile E. Koyote. She'd felt perfectly comfortable in doing whatever she could to make that faceless presence trust her, because the information he had was just that important. He could change everything for her; she knew it.

Kylie felt a little bad about drawing in the stranger while harboring an ulterior motive, but not enough to shrug off the missed meeting. Yes, she had every intention of using this other person for her own purposes, but it wasn't like she was some kind of modern ax murderer, relying on the Internet to lure her victims to their doom. The person she was meeting would have walked away from their encounter unharmed, unhit-on, and perfectly safe. All Kylie wanted from him was information.

All she wanted was the truth about Bran.

The rhythmic jiggling of her foot stuttered, pausing

for a moment before resuming its hummingbirdlike flutter. The thought of him still hit her every time.

A year after Bran Powe had gone missing, Kylie had thought she'd come to terms with loss. She wasn't stupid; she knew that when people disappeared for so many months at a stretch, they weren't just out for a breath of fresh air. Something bad must have happened to keep him away from his friends and family. But even so, getting the call from his sister, Wynn, and hearing his death confirmed had hit Kylie like a physical blow.

Bran had been her closest pal since her freshman year of college. While the second of two spectacularly failed dates had made it clear that romance would never work for them, friendship came as easily as breathing. She honestly thought of him as the brother she'd never had, no matter how tired that cliché was. Losing him had felt like losing a tiny little piece of herself, and Kylie hated to lose even more than she hated being ignored.

For that reason (and because sitting still for a seven-minute yoga meditation was beyond her, let alone sitting the seven days of a shiva) she had spent the last six months obsessed with finding out the truth. She couldn't care less if she sounded melodramatic or halfway to crazytown; she knew there was more to Bran's story than anyone was willing to tell her. She knew darn well that nothing she did could bring her friend back, but she could at least find out what had really happened to him. As much as she loved his family, his sister Wynn's telephoned explanation that "they think he had a heart problem we didn't know about" was not cutting it with her.

Sure, Kylie knew that kind of thing happened all the time, but not this time. She didn't believe a word of it. Why, she couldn't quite say. Maybe she had heard something in Wynn's voice, or maybe the intuition she had learned not to ignore had sounded the alarm. She couldn't be certain, but either way, she knew there had to be more to the story.

She had dedicated the last six months to trying to find that "more." She'd pushed aside her work, her hobbies, her family and friends in pursuit of the truth, immersing herself in the world she knew better than anyone—the data.

Despite her legitimate professional accomplishments and the applications she had developed that left her financially set for life at the tender age of twenty-three, Kylie still considered herself a hacker at heart. If a fact existed in bits and bytes anywhere in the world, she could uncover it. Between the skills she'd learned and the talent that had always lurked inside her, she knew she could find anything, so she had begun by breaking into Bran's personal computer and online accounts and setting herself on the trail of the truth.

Tonight was supposed to have been a big leap forward. It would have been, if DrkMsgr had bothered to show up. She was convinced that he knew something about her friend, no matter how coyly he had danced around the subject. His knowledge of some deeper meaning behind the strange terms in Bran's files— words like "Guardian," "Warden," *"nocturni,"* and "the Seven"—had to be more than coincidence.

Kylie certainly didn't understand the references in Bran's journal entries and encrypted files. And why did an archaeology grad student need to encrypt his computer files, anyway? Especially when they made almost less sense to an outsider once the code was broken.

She had read through every word she could find, and all she'd gotten from his ramblings had been a massive headache and the vague impression that she'd just sorted through the background notes of an author's proposed series of horror novels. It had looked to her like Bran had been collecting information on demons. It was meshuga.

Part of her wanted to laugh at the crazy idea, but most of her couldn't manage the sound. Kylie didn't believe in demons, any more than she believed in heaven or hell or little cherubs with diapers and medieval weaponry being responsible for people falling in love. And it wasn't just because of her Jewish heritage. Heck, she only had that on one side of the family, but she still had trouble believing in anything she couldn't see and analyze and code into ones and zeros.

The little voice inside her head got a slap upside its own when it tried to remind her of all the things about herself that she couldn't explain so easily. About the way she didn't just read code, she *felt* it, as if it ran through her bloodstream in microscopic green digits alongside the red and white cells. About the way she occasionally caught sight of her reflection in a monitor and her eyes looked more green than brown, glowing with the light of an obsolete DOS system command screen. She wasn't the issue here; this was all about Bran.

Kylie looked at her phone and sighed. Twelve-fifteen. Damn it. If the stranger wasn't here by now, he wasn't coming, but if he thought no-showing would put an end to their association, he had another think coming. As soon as she got home and got back online, she would make that abundantly clear.

Frustrated, but glad to finally be moving again, Kylie dug out her wallet and left enough cash to cover her slowly nursed drinks and her single slice of pie. Then she added a supergenerous tip for the waitress who hadn't even tried to hurry her along in all the time she'd hogged the corner booth. No need for both of them to leave tonight's encounter dissatisfied.

The cool March air bit through her jacket and raised gooseflesh on her arms as she exited the mostly empty diner and began the brisk walk home. Her town house occupied the borderlands between Boston's Back Bay and Fenway, within spitting distance of her old stomping grounds around the university—a sound investment, or so her accountant had assured her when she'd purchased it eighteen months before.

At the moment all she cared about was that it wasn't too far from the meeting place to walk, because trying to catch a cab at this time of night in this neighborhood would be like waiting for the messiah. She didn't have six or seven thousand years to spare at the moment.

And besides, she'd been sitting still too long, bouncing foot aside. Even when she worked, she spent as much time out of her computer chair as in it. Kylie preferred to be in motion, given the choice. Tonight, she'd hoof it.

Sure it was late, and she had at least a dozen blocks to go, but in a city this size, the streets were never really empty, and Kylie had lived in the area long enough not to blink at the idea of making the short trip alone. She'd done it a hundred times before, and would do it hundreds more in the future.

She may have grown up in Connecticut, but since coming to Boston for college at the age of sixteen, Kylie had gone native in every way except for the accent. She still said "*Baw*-stun" instead of "*Bah*-stun," but aside from that, this city was her adopted hometown.

Leftover snow crunched under her feet as she cut across a small green square, her quick steps one short hop away from a jog. While the streets had been cleared days ago, the paths around the statue at the center of this minipark still sported patches of the icy white stuff. Apparently the gargoylelike hunk of granite that anchored the space didn't merit enough visitors for a thorough snowblower crew, and even in March, snow lingered. The piles of gray and white frost seemed determined to remind everyone in New England that the danger of the harsh winter hadn't completely passed, no matter what the calendar said.

As often happened during a Boston springtime, the weather today had run the gamut through all four seasons, starting with the frigid bite of winter, thawing to a morning spring and jumping to a midday summer. Now, the late night felt more like autumn, with a chilly breeze and the faint whiff of decay in the air.

Maybe if that thought had lingered for another couple of seconds—decay? Really?—Kylie would have realized how out of place it really was and been ready for the blow. Her luck wasn't that good, though, and her mind had already turned its focus on getting home and back online to see what had happened to DrkMsgr that made him bail on their meeting. When she sat in front of a keyboard, Kylie could see things most people missed, but in the real world, she occasionally overlooked the big picture.

Like the one where two ski-masked muggers converged on her from the sides and struck her hard enough to send her to the frozen ground with a grunt of surprise. They'd knocked out too much of her wind for her to manage a scream.

For a minute she honestly could not understand what was happening. It wasn't that she was naïve or anything, but she'd lived in Boston for almost seven years, and she'd never so much as had her pocket picked. And she was still in the Back Bay, for Pete's sake, one of the ritziest areas of the city. How on earth was she being attacked by a couple of escapees from a gangster movie?

Those thoughts flitted through her head in the space of half a second. Then a kick to her side sent the last gasp of breath choking out of her lungs, and the last functioning neuron in her brain snapped off with what she swore was a muffled squeak. *Emese meisse*—true story.

It sounded a little like the lab assistant character from *The Muppets*.

Come to think of it, she felt kind of like the victim of some weird experiment as her vision narrowed down to black. It almost appeared as if a vacuum had switched on, sucking her peripheral vision away, then pulling the central field in after it. She was left with nothing but blackness for a split second before the fireworks began, little sparks snapping and popping in the darkness.

Huh, hadn't she read about that happening in cases of severe oxygen deprivation? Too bad. Dying was so not on her to-do list for tonight, or really any night for the next eighty years.

Her lungs burned, every muscle in her chest straining for air. Still blinded, she could only feel her surroundings. Even her hearing had been compromised by the rushing of blood in her skull. Hard hands gripped her arms and jerked her from the ground. Unprepared for the movement, her head snapped backward, and her neck muscles screamed a protest. Funny how her attackers didn't seem to hear.

". . . her out of . . . wants to see . . . someone . . . fast."

Snippets of voices, male and menacing, sliced through the static in her senses. Fingers dug into her flesh and jerked, trying to propel her forward. Her legs buckled, sending her back to her knees, and curses rained down on her head.

". . . go! Now!"

Shouts and chaos took over then, an impression of movement and confusion. Kylie felt an actual drop of rain ping off her shoulder. No, wait; that felt more like hail, solid and hard and stinging even through her wool jacket.

The next shriek came wordlessly but pulsed with fear and panic. Oddly enough, it didn't come from her, even though her own chest had finally begun to ease, allowing her to gulp down a much-needed lungful of oxygen. No, girly though it had seemed, something told her the sound had come from at least one of her attackers.

What the heck?

It took a minute for her to realize that the roaring in her head had become an actual roaring, the kind that echoed through the night air and attracted attention from neighbors and passersby. Kylie had about two seconds to wonder where it came from before a different set of hands closed around her, and this time she didn't fall.

She flew.

Dag burst forth from his sleeping prison, bits of stone dropping in his wake like explosive shrapnel. What woke him he could not say, but instinct drove him straight from slumber to battle. His senses screamed at him to defeat, to destroy, to defend. Nothing in his surroundings registered but for a small female figure kneeling on the cold, hard ground while two human males attempted to drag her off into the darkness.

He would not have it.

His wings pumped the air, the huge, membranous spans catching the currents and sending the last remnants of sleep scurrying into the night. Already he felt strength and power heating his muscles, stretching his features into a fanged snarl and snapping his claws together in a definite threat. Not that the warning would do his enemies any good. Dag was a warrior too long denied a purpose.

Tonight, none would escape his wrath.

A battle roar shattered the hush of darkness. He took one long moment to savor the thrill of the fight, stretching into the sky before plummeting like an eagle onto his prey.

The humans screamed in terror, and Dag relished the sound. His talons dug into one man's shoulder, tearing through flesh and bringing hot, red blood pumping to the surface. One whiff was all it took for Dag to catch the taint. His enemy was not a simple human; his blood carried the insidious rot of the Darkness. *Nocturni*.

Knowing he faced his ancestral foe brought a fresh surge of rage and satisfaction. Perhaps this was why he had woken, perhaps he now faced the opening salvo of the war all of his kind knew to be inevitable. If that were the case, Dag intended to bring about a swift and brutal victory.

Using his rear claws, he shifted his grip on the demon's minion and gave one sharp jerk, breaking its neck with careless ease. His hands caught the second man before he could drag the female more than an inch from his fallen cohort. One talon, long and sharp as a dagger, pierced the vulnerable human flesh, stopping its black heart. When the second *nocturni* dropped to the ground, the female let out a cry, swaying on her knees as if about to fall.

Swooping in, Dag caught her in his powerful grip, but this time he tempered his strength, careful to keep his claws from biting through cloth and into flesh. Two powerful beats of his wings lifted them high into the sky over a city glistening with light and movement. He needed to move away from here swiftly before the noise of the brief skirmish drew more humans to the site. His kind had been summoned into this world to battle the *nocturnis* and their demonic masters, but they attempted to remain unseen whenever possible.

He glanced around quickly, noting both familiar and unfamiliar landmarks below him. He knew not how long he had slept since his last waking, but he could see that many years had passed him by. The small settlement he remembered had been called a city by its inhabitants even then, but it had paled in comparison to the older and larger European capitals he had known. Now, though, it appeared to have grown into itself, stretching much farther than the boundaries in his memories.

It took a moment to orient himself, but he recognized the closest building as the home of his former Warden. He did not doubt that the man had by now passed into the next world, but at least by sighting it, Dag knew where he was. He had not been moved in more than three hundred years.

The trip to reach the rooftop of the four-story mansion of the Houghton family could barely be called a flight. He hovered a moment over his old landing spot before recoiling in disgust. The detritus and building debris he might have ignored, but the sharp, sulfurous stink of tar could not be borne. He needed another spot to land out of sight of humans, and quickly, judging by the rate at which the rigidity of shock and fear had begun to leach from his human burden. She would not remain quiescent long.

Dag glanced around, his gaze finding a familiar sight in the crowded skyline. A church spire rose into the night, the open archways of its belfry providing an easy entrance and exit as well as an excellent vantage point from which to observe those passing below. He could reach it in moments and slip himself and his human charge inside before the chances of being seen became too dangerous.

Changing direction with a twitch of his wings, he covered the distance of more than a mile in seconds. He had to draw up and hover for a moment in order to set the human female safely on the floor inside the bell tower, because his full wingspan would never fit through the arched openings. With his rear claws free, he dug them into the stone of the portal and perched long enough to furl the appendages before hopping in after her.

Half a second after her feet touched the floor, her bottom followed. Her grunt nearly echoed in the cavern of the church bell, but she made no other sound, just stared up at him with wide, dark eyes.

Dag returned her gaze, finally taking notice of how tiny the female actually was. Oh, he had known she weighed so little he had barely noticed as he lifted her from the ground and flew her to safety; but he was a warrior, strong and hardened by battle. He could have flown a military tank that short distance.

No, the human wasn't simply light, she was little. He couldn't remember the last time he had encountered a human so small unless it was a child. This female, though, appeared fully grown, with mature curves visible even through her heavy garments. Still, the top of her head had barely reached his collarbone before she collapsed, even though he stood among the shortest of his kind. He doubted the human could boast so much as five feet of height. He literally was twice her size, but somehow she didn't appear to be afraid of him.

In fact, if he were forced to label the expression on her unexpectedly strong features, he would have to say she looked fascinated. She barely blinked, her gaze devouring him in long, thirsty gulps.

Those dark eyes dominated her face, wide and heavily lashed, tilted just the slightest bit at the corners. Her brows, too, were heavy, but gracefully arched and almost black against her fair skin. Her nose suited her face, strong and straight but not too large for femininity. It perched above a cupid's bow of a mouth now half open in astonishment. Her chin dipped toward her chest, a rounded point that indicated a mischievous and determined nature.

Overall, her face gave the impression of a lively spirit and a strong will, the type of human who spoke definitely and often. Thankfully, for the moment she remained silent, but he wondered how long that would last.

He'd grown accustomed through the centuries to attracting human attention, but mostly those who saw him felt either revulsion or terror at his appearance. Of all his brethren, his natural form appeared the least like those they were summoned to protect. His short, thick legs and arched back made him as comfortable moving on four limbs as on two, and his flat nostrils, heavy brow, and forward-thrusting jaw gave him a bestial, almost apelike visage. Add in the wings, the fangs, and the razor-sharp talons, and humans either loathed him or feared him. Mostly, he cared not which way they leaned.

But this female didn't try to scamper away the moment he gazed on her, and Dag found himself unsure of what that meant. How was he to act in a situation he had never before encountered?

He chose to glower, but then, he almost always chose

to glower. Settling back on his heels, he pressed his knuckles against the floor between his feet and ruffled his wings just to remind her of what he was. What he could do to her if he decided to name her an enemy.

"Now, human, I have saved you from the Order's attack dogs. You owe me a debt. To repay the value of your life, you will reveal to me if you are my Warden and what latest threat the Seven have brought from the Darkness. I am a Guardian, and I will do my duty to keep the Demons at bay."

If anything, the female went even more still. She seemed almost to stop breathing, and her dark eyes opened so far the whites shone in the dim moonlight. Her jaw fell another full inch, a look of utter shock suffusing her features.

"Warden?" she repeated in that unexpected rasp. "The Order, the Seven, the Darkness, a Guardian." She shook her head and scrambled suddenly to her knees, leaning forward to stare at him intently. "How do you know those terms? What do they mean to you?"

Dag felt his brows knit together as he stared down at the tiny human. "They mean everything. I am a Guardian of the Light, sworn to protect your world from the evil of the Seven Demons of the Darkness, and if you do not know this, then you cannot be my Warden. But if you are not, then tell me how I was summoned from my sleeping?"

"Sure, sure, absolutely. Just as soon as you tell me which rabbit hole I fell down, because all of a sudden I have the feeling that I am *very* late to the party."

Chapter Two

Dos lebn iz nit mer vi a kholem—ober vek
nikh mit oyf.
*Life is no more than a dream—but don't
wake me up.*

Kylie pinched herself hard enough to leave a bruise, but nothing changed. She still knelt in the bell tower of some ancient Boston church, and she'd gotten there by being flown in by a creature out of a Disney cartoon series.

Flown. As in picked up in a set of wickedly sharp talons, lifted clear off the ground, and carried through the air without the benefit of a cramped seat, an air-pressurized cabin, and a minuscule bag of complimentary pretzels.

If this turned out to be some kind of weird, mugging-induced hallucination, and she was really in a hospital bed somewhere having herself a nice little coma, she was going to be hella disappointed.

This was the most amazing thing that had ever happened to her!

You know, provided it was actually happening.

She shifted forward, easing an inch closer to the giant, inhuman creature that filled her vision, and winced when her muscles protested. She definitely felt like she'd just been attacked, and wouldn't she be pain-free if she were in a coma? If not, it sounded grossly unfair, so she was going to assume she was alive and the sight in front of her was real.

She wanted so badly to reach out and touch him, just to prove it. Her fingers actually twitched as she struggled to control the impulse.

"You speak nonsense, human. I saw no hole," the creature intoned, its voice so deep she felt it almost more than she heard it. It vibrated through the planks underneath her and up through her body like an earthquake. "You appeared to fall as a result of the *nocturnis'* attack, not because of some misstep."

Huh. Well, this was certainly proving to be an articulate monster, she decided with a blink, and that had to be more evidence on the side of reality. After all, given her tendency to abuse two languages—English and Yiddish—equally, why would her mind conjure up a figment of her imagination who spoke more precisely than she ever did?

And really, where would she have gotten the idea of being carried off from a random attack in a park by a living gargoyle? Even the statue she'd walked past hadn't looked like this. The gray stone of the carving had been weathered beyond belief, the features and details of the original nearly worn away by time and the elements. It looked more like a misshapen blob of natural limestone and not at all like this chiseled, three-dimensional work of Gothic art. When had she acquired the skill to think up a sculpture this vivid?

He looked like he should be perched atop a spire at Notre Dame. With his stony gray skin, animalistic features, and enormous batlike wings sprouting from his back, he defined the cultural image of a gargoyle. He sat crouched in front of her, and considering she'd bet that he topped out around seven feet when standing erect, she couldn't complain about his decision not to loom over her.

If her *bubbeh* had taught her better manners, she'd have thanked him. Well, okay, if the manner lessons had stuck with her, because heaven knew her grandmother had tried.

Muscles bulged and rippled every time the creature so much as drew breath. Muscles on top of muscles, so that he radiated the kind of power that could rend limbs from bodies or uproot ancient oak trees. He probably couldn't open a door without ripping the thing from its hinges, yet he had carried Kylie with care, not so much as pricking through her coat with the claws that looked like they came from some kind of predatory dinosaur.

Maybe that was why, when she looked at what should have struck her as a monster, she felt no fear. Fascination, curiosity, even awe, but no fear. So either she instinctively trusted the thing not to hurt her, or she was just seriously out of her mind. Even on her best day, that was a tough call.

Then her memory stirred, reminding her of the first words he had spoken to her, the words that had sounded eerily familiar. She'd read those words in Bran's notes, but what did they have to do with this impossible being? The tingling under her skin told her there had to be a connection. Nothing this unbelievable could be chalked up to pure coincidence, right?

She refocused on his words and watched him closely. "Okay. You used that word again. That 'nocturnal' word. What does it mean?"

"Nocturnis?"

She nodded.

"The *nocturnis* are the enemy," he growled, making the floorboards vibrate again. "They unite as the Order of Eternal Darkness, serving the Seven in their never-ending attempts to return to this world and seize it for their own."

The bell in Kylie's head went DING!DING!DING! and she shivered as if a cold wind passed through her. Neither reaction had anything to do with the bell next to her or the night air surrounding her, or from the fact that a living gargoyle stood between her and the only way down from the tower, a hatch above a narrow stairway. No, this was all from the pieces of an unknown puzzle suddenly beginning to come together. A few more, and she might even have a frame laid out to start filling in the picture of Bran's secrets.

"And the Seven are . . . what?" she prompted.

"The Seven Demons of the Darkness." The gargoyle's jaw worked, clicking his fangs together ominously. His eyes narrowed as he studied her. "Your ignorance of such things betrays you as an ordinary human, not a member of the Guild, but I do not have time to waste. If my slumber was disturbed, it can only mean that the Seven are stirring. I must find my Warden and assess the current threat."

He shifted as if to turn away from her. Kylie felt a surge of panic and reached for him. No way could she let this creature slip away from her, not after he'd come this close to answering so many of her questions.

"Wait!"

He ignored her, moving into the open archway and ruffling his wings in preparation for flight.

Hauling in a breath, Kylie took a gamble and hoped like hell she wasn't tangling herself up in a lie when she called after him. "What if I told you that I knew a Warden, and that I have information he was collecting on the guys you're talking about? What if I could get you even more?"

The creature hesitated and turned his head to gaze back at her over his shoulder. He didn't step down from the ledge, but he settled his wings once more against his back. "How did you come by such information, human? If you claim ignorance of so much more."

Kylie pushed to her feet and wrapped her arms around her torso. She told herself she felt cold, not vulnerable. "I said I had information, not that I understood it. I didn't know my friend was one—a Warden—until you mentioned them, and I guess I can't promise he was, but I can tell you for certain that he had a whole bunch of information gathered on all the things you just mentioned. Wardens, Guardians, *nocturnis,* demons. The whole shebang. I've been going through it for months without being able to figure it all out. Maybe you'd have better luck."

Now he did step back into the bell tower, but his expression and his whole demeanor had changed. For the first time, Kylie could see the ferocity of his shape and feel the menace in his hard, dark gaze. The black depth glittered in the night, seemingly backlit by a thousand tiny flames.

"How did you get this information, human?" he repeated, his lips curling back to expose long, gleaming white fangs.

She actually took a step back. Her. The girl voted most likely to spit in a golem's eye. "It came from a friend, like I said."

"And he simply gave you, an ordinary human, access to such powerful secrets?"

The low rumble of his voice sounded like an approaching storm. New Englander she might be, but Kylie had a sudden vision of tornados tearing across the horizon. She shook her head and retreated another step. "No, he didn't. But when he died, I took a look."

That provoked a snarl. "How did he die?"

"That's what I've been trying to find out."

"Explain."

He stopped moving forward, but considering he had her backed into the corner of the belfry a good four stories in the air, she figured he'd gotten her right where he wanted her.

She swallowed against the lump in her throat. "Bran Powe was my closest friend. A year and a half ago, he disappeared. Just vanished. No one knew what had happened to him, not me, not his family, not the police. No one."

Her hands shook as she told the story, but her heart had stopped fighting to beat its way out of her chest as she remembered how she'd gotten into all of this. When she remembered why.

"No one heard anything for a full year, and trust me, we were looking. Then, six months ago, I got a call from his sister. She told me he was dead, that his body had been found and that there were no signs of foul play. She tried to tell me that he must have had a heart condition that no one knew about, that his death had been tragic, but natural."

"You do not believe that."

"I don't."

He still watched her intently, but the snarl had faded, and his fangs no longer looked like they were five seconds from ripping her throat out. Hey, look at that. She really did remember how to breathe!

"I didn't even before I saw his notes," she continued, "which is why I looked into them in the first place. I don't know what I thought I'd find, but I figured maybe he'd gotten himself mixed up in something ugly, drugs or gambling or something. I never figured him for the type, but what else was I supposed to think? Demons and secret societies of superheroes somehow never even crossed my mind before I started digging. And then, I wondered if maybe he'd just . . . lost it."

"Lost it?"

"Went a little crazy." She felt bad saying it out loud, but she couldn't pretend she hadn't entertained the thought. The Bran she remembered had been as sane as the next person, but the impression left by his ramblings had made her wonder. He'd mentioned things that sane people just didn't mention. Who had computer files full of strategies to avert demonic apocalypse?

Of course, at that very moment Kylie was standing in a bell tower talking about those very same things with a creature she was pretty sure should not have existed, so who was crazy now?

The gargoyle scowled and Kylie reminded herself that if he hadn't killed her yet, she was probably safe. Maybe. "Most humans don't spend a lot of time thinking about demons, let alone collecting all sorts of information on them and how they and their minions want to take over the world. So I worried a little. So sue me."

"Most humans live in ignorance."

The sentiment might be harsh, but Kylie could see some of the tension ease from his muscles, and she hoped that signaled he no longer intended to rip her head off her shoulders. She was kind of attached to it. Before she could really relax, though, the creature shifted closer and drew a deep breath.

Was he *smelling* her?

Kylie bit her lip against the urge to voice that question. *Too soon,* she told herself. *Remember not to antagonize the monster. At least, not until he gets to know me better. By then, it will just happen naturally.*

She held herself still while he appeared to mull over whatever he had discerned from his sniff.

"If you do not serve the Guild," he finally ventured, "and you have no stench of the Darkness in you, how is it that you smell of magic?"

She squeaked, this time the sound escaping her throat instead of being confined to her brain. Again with the Muppet noises. "Magic? Me?"

He nodded, this time leaning forward until his head was just inches from hers. When he inhaled a slow lungful of air, she could see his chest expand. "Magic. You do not smell like a witch, though."

A laugh choked out of her before she could stop it. "What does a witch smell like? Eye of newt or toe of frog?"

He didn't appear to get the joke. "It depends on the witch. I have never met one who practiced an amphibian form of magic."

Oy vey. Did he always take things so literally? Kylie squeezed her eyes shut and raised a hand to rub against her forehead. She'd just realized how much it ached.

Come to think of it, just about all of her ached. Maybe that explained why she felt so *off* at the moment. She'd never spent much time in her life imagining how she would react if she were ever confronted with a mythical creature, but if she had, this wasn't what she would have bet on. She liked to think of herself as a scrapper, not as the girl who quivered at the prospect of a little gory disembowelment and some stilted conversation about witches.

Witches.

Her eyes flew open and her hand dropped so fast she nearly smacked her own ass. "I know a witch."

He rumbled something in response, but she had stopped paying attention. She was already dialing her phone. Witches knew about magic, right? So Kylie would bet her brownstone that one particular witch knew quite a bit more than that. After all, said witch had been related to a guy who collected information on demons. What were the chances she knew nothing about them herself?

The phone rang twice then a voice answered. "Hello?"

"Well, hey there, Wynn," Kylie all but purred, her eyes narrowed as if the other woman could see her accusatory expression. "How are you doing?"

"What's wrong?"

That gave Kylie pause. "Wrong? Why do you think something's wrong?"

"You called me Wynn."

"That's your name, right?"

"Wynn," the witch repeated. "Not Winnie-the-Pooh, not Pooh Bear, not Wynn-abago. Not even Wynneleh. You never just call me Wynn. Sooo . . . what's wrong?"

Kylie pursed her lips and tried not to pout. Trust her friend to seize control of the conversation just when Kylie was trying to exact a little revenge. Totally unfair. Time to regroup.

"Yeah, well, I have a question for you," she said, her

gaze still locked on the glowering gargoyle. "What's big and gray and stone all over and says I smell like magic?"

"Ohmygods."

"What girl likes to be told she smells, I ask you. Not, 'wow, what's that perfume you're wearing?' but straight up, 'hey, you smell funny.' It's not flattering."

"Oh. My. Gods!"

Okay, that was a somewhat more satisfying level of response. Of course, Kylie couldn't quite tell if Wynn was stunned, excited, or, you know, having an aneurysm.

"Personally, with those manners, I wouldn't have thought he was a friend of yours," Kyle continued, "but then, I wouldn't have thought Bran and you were big ol' demon hunters or some such, either. I guess maybe we shouldn't rely too much on assumptions, huh?"

"Knox! Come here! We found one!" The change in volume told Kylie her friend had lowered her phone to call out to her new fiancé. Who apparently knew more about all this than Kylie did. That grated. "Ky, I can explain everything, but first I have to ask. Are you okay?"

"Oh, you're totally going to explain, my friend, and you'd better make it good."

"I mean it, Kylie. Are you okay? Are you hurt? Where are you?"

The urgency in Wynn's voice made Kylie frown, turning some of her anger into concern. Just a skosh, mind you. "I'm fine." She waved her hand dismissively and her ribs protested. "You know, relatively," she qualified. "And I'm in Boston, natch, in a church, of all places. Nothing has caught fire yet, but I'm just in the belfry, so maybe it doesn't count."

A moment of silence. "You're *in* a church belfry?"

"Yeah. Flew here. Imagine my surprise."

Wynn cleared her throat. "Right. About that. You see . . ."

That was pretty much the point where the creature watching Kylie so closely seemed to lose his patience. "This witch you speak to, what does she know of the Darkness? Is she in league with the Order? How do you know you can trust her?"

In her ear, her friend let out an excited squeak. "Oh, wow, was that the Guardian? What's his name? Where did you find him? Can I talk to him?"

"Yes, let me speak with the witch, human."

Wynn babbled enthusiastic agreement in Kylie's ear, and the gargoyle held out his serving-platter-sized paw for her phone. Kylie shook her head and took a step backward. She always reacted poorly to high-pressure tactics. "No, you know what? Before you all have your little kaffeeklatsch, I think somebody needs to explain a few things to me. Beginning with *what the fuck is going on*?"

The huge gray creature actually winced, but Kylie had to admit that could be the result of her voice rising an octave and about twelve decibels rather than an attack of conscience. On the other end of the phone, Wynn mumbled something conciliatory.

"Kylie, I know," her friend said. "I know you deserve a whole bunch of explanations right now, but this is kind of a long story, and at the moment it's really, *really* important to make sure that you and the Guardian are safe first. Like, earthshakingly important. You shouldn't be out in public right now, especially since I'm assuming that one or both of you were just attacked by *nocturnis*."

That was disconcertingly accurate. "How did you know that?"

"Another part of the story. It just seems to be the way these things happen at the moment. I will explain everything, I promise, but first and foremost, you need to get somewhere safe. Can you get home? Fast?"

Kylie wanted to dig her heels in and refuse to move until she got the answers she wanted, but something in Wynn's voice made her grudgingly restrain herself. "I'm not all that far from my house. I don't think. I don't think he flew me more than a few blocks." She looked at the gargoyle, who shook his head. "Yeah, I can get home in a few minutes. But what about tall, stone, and grumpy?"

"He needs to go with you."

She knew Wynn was going to say that. That didn't mean she had to like it, did it? She just couldn't decide if her instincts were trying to tell her that sticking with the Guardian was the best idea ever, or the key to impending doom.

"Because you're the genius wunderkind they call Kyle E. Woyote, that's why."

"Really? You're gonna blow rainbows up my *tokhes*? Now, of all times?"

"If it will get you and the Guardian somewhere safe and private with a video-chat connection, I will blow rainbow-covered sparkly unicorn fairies up your butt, Ky. This is serious."

"You know how wrong that sounded, right?"

"Koyote, please."

Channeling the urge to scream out her frustration into a low, hissing growl, Kylie spat out her agreement. "Fine, I'll bring the thing—and I do mean The Thing, capital *T*, capital *T*—home with me, but I am calling you back the minute we get in the front door, Wynn, and I'm not going to be satisfied with simple explanations. I want everything."

"Oh, trust me, sweetie, there is no such thing as a simple explanation for this. You're going to get as many answers as you can handle, which will be about a hundred more than you're going to understand."

"Don't sell me short, Pooh Bear. I'm a genius, remember? I can understand almost anything."

"How about the end of the world?"

Chapter Three

Darf min gehn in kolledj?
For this I went to college?

He told her to call him Dag. When she tried to add Hammarskjöld or Nabbit to the end, he got cranky. As in, "bared his five-inch fangs and hissed like a frickin' cobra" cranky. Some people—er, mythological entities—had no sense of humor. He proved this when he mumbled something about teaching humans to hold their tongues around their betters.

On a night where the surprises just kept coming, Kylie got a biggie when her stone-faced companion deposited her at the base of the belfry and went from monstrous to monstrously hot in the blink of an eye. Actually, if Kylie had blinked, she'd have missed it, because one minute he looked like the gargoyle of her nightmares, and the next he looked like a former member of the BU hockey team—tall, muscular, human, and as if he'd taken more than one stick to his face over the years.

It took her a full minute to pick her mouth up off the

ground and another to catch a glimpse of the creature
he had been in the completely normal man standing before her. His features had been so animalistic in his
other form that she wouldn't have believed they could
translate into anything quite so attractive, if she had believed they could translate at all.

His prominent jaw, heavy brows, and nearly flat nose
had been refined into something completely masculine
and utterly arresting. They hinted at a mixed racial heritage that perfectly suited the golden hue of his skin.
No one should have that color of skin in Boston at this
time of year, all caramel and supercreamy latte, but it
worked on Dag. As did the height that skimmed just under the six-foot wire—more than tall enough for her to
have to look way up at him—and the musculature of an
athlete who believed all sports should be contact sports.

I'd make contact with that in a heartbeat.

She slapped her hormones back and threatened to
lock them in a cage if they didn't behave themselves.
Still, she couldn't argue with their taste.

His transformation from boogeyman to babe came
with a convenient set of clothing: worn jeans, battered
work boots, and a navy peacoat perfectly suited to
the weather. At least Kylie didn't have to worry about
him freezing to death as he trailed after her on the route
back to her house. That allowed her to worry about
other things, like how soon she could get the explanation she'd been promised, why she wasn't way more
freaked out by the adventure of the past few hours, and
where might be a convenient place to hide the bodies of
a gargoyle and a witch if they didn't make with the story
time, like, yesterday.

Sure, Kylie might be small, but she was sneaky,
smart, and mean, so she figured if she needed to make

a few bodies understand the inadvisability of messing with a woman with a high IQ, a nearly unlimited disposable income, and connections to the underbelly of the Internet, so be it. She had every faith she could come out on top.

Dag moved so quietly—eerily quietly—that she found herself glancing over her shoulder several times on the way home just to make certain he was still there. When she led him up the steps to her front door and slipped her key into the lock, she tried to tell herself that she had no reason to feel a twinge of regret that he hadn't disappeared on the way. She had a feeling at least half the story she needed to hear would turn out to be his, so better to have all hands on deck.

Even if a small place in the back of her brain did try to argue that a simple random mugging and a nice little coma up at Mass General might be an easier out.

Her house was dark and empty, not even her sometimes cat—a stray that came and went as he pleased and guarded his independence with tooth and claw—around to give the place a spark of life. It didn't usually bother her; to tell the truth, she didn't usually even notice. But something about bringing a stranger back to a house where she still had moving boxes in most of the rooms more than a year after moving in made her feel awkward for a moment.

Kylie reacted to her discomfort the way she always did—by lifting her chin and brazening her way through it. Fake it with authority was the family motto, after all; at least for their branch.

"Office is this way," she said, flipping lights on as she led the way toward the back of the house. "It's got the best setup for a video call."

Dag said nothing, merely followed her on those

unnervingly silent feet. She didn't even notice him looking around at the mostly undecorated and barely lived-in
areas of the house, and she stole peeks. Lots of them.

Investment value aside, the three-story-plus-basement
historic brownstone was wasted on Kylie. She used
maybe three rooms on a regular basis—her office, her
bedroom, and the en suite bathroom. Even the kitchen
only got as much use as required to unpack and serve
herself takeout. As she often said, she spoke two human
languages and coded in at least five more, but cooking
was not one of them.

The silence of the house stretched to include Dag,
since he made not a sound as she led him into her office off the kitchen. The real estate agent had described
it as a study filled with natural light and well insulated
to cut down on the noise from the rest of the house.
Kylie called it her Batcave. Or Acme headquarters, depending on her mood.

Her huge, battered desk barely took up a third of the
space in the room, so she had filled the rest of it with
books, equipment, toys, and other assorted things that
only existed to make her smile. Aside from her Aeron
desk chair, the only other seat in the room was a battered old armchair with faded toile upholstery and a
cushion permanently indented with the impression of
King David's feline backside. It also sported a layer of
his orange fur that would have made her grandmother
plotz.

She gestured to it with one hand as she set her keys
on the edge of her desk. Internally, she debated whether
a gargoyle could be allergic to cats, and whether she
should hope this one was. Petty, maybe, but she wouldn't
mind seeing the source of her discomfort in a little dis-

tress of his own. "Go ahead and sit. It will take me a minute to boot up and put the call through."

He obeyed without a word, relaxing into the seat without bothering to brush off the hair or remove his dark coat. Of course, brushing would have proven entirely ineffective, but the coat simply disappeared just before his butt hit the chair. Show-off.

Maybe she should get her nose checked out, because it seemed to her that if magic had a smell, Dag should be reeking of it. Funny, but all she could smell when she got close enough was stone and ash and warm male skin.

Damn it, at this rate she was going to need a whip and a chair to deal with her hormones. *Down, girls.*

Forcing herself to focus, she powered up her computer and busied herself shrugging out of her own coat while the password prompt appeared on the screen. As always, the steady light of the three monitors and the hum of the cooling fans on the CPU soothed her, and she found it a lot easier to ignore the gargoyle in the room now that she was back in control. Sit Kylie Kramer down in front of a computer with enough juice, and she could rule the world. At least part of it legally.

"Tell me something of the witch."

He issued the demand in a deep voice that reminded her of distant thunder and sweet pipe smoke. Kylie felt herself twitch at the sound, but hoped it would be disguised by the barricade of screens half blocking his view. Hey, a girl could dream, right?

"You mean Wynn?" she asked, stalling for time. She wasn't sure she was ready for more one-on-one time with this creature. Hopefully her friend would be waiting by the figurative phone.

"The witch. Tell me why you trust her."

Okay, that was an easy question to answer, and at least it took her own focus off herself, even if she could still feel the gargoyle's gaze pinned on her like a boutonniere. "Because she's family."

Dag frowned. "You share blood? Is she a sister?"

"No, and yes." Kylie pulled up the chat program and entered Wynn's number from memory. "Technically, she's my best friend's big sister, but I've known her for years. To me, she feels like family, related or not."

"And this other friend? If there is another with knowledge of my kind and of the Order, we should contact her as well."

"Him." She snapped the correction and stared at the central monitor while the connection formed. "And you'll need a Ouija board if that's your plan. Bran is dead."

For once, timing worked in Kylie's favor. The call went live before Dag could reply to her blunt words.

"Gah, finally! I was starting to freak out. You said you'd only be a few minutes. Is everything okay?"

"Wynn, relax. We walked through Boston, not Fallujah. We're fine."

"Sorry, it's just that this is really big news for us." The dark-haired witch looked sheepish as she shifted to allow another figure into camera range. "We were really getting worried that the Order had gotten to the other four Guardians before us."

"Yeah, so how about before you go any further here, you go back to the beginning for me." Kylie leaned back in her chair and crossed her arms over her chest. "Not only do I want to know what all this Guardian, demon, Order stuff is about, I also want to know what it had to do with Bran's death. And don't even try to sell me that *farkakta* story about a heart defect again, because I ain't buying."

"I'm sorry, Ky. Really. I felt horrible lying to you, but we don't talk about this stuff with outsiders. It's the rules."

Kylie felt a jolt. That stung, more than she had expected. "So now I'm an outsider?"

"Kylie, no. That's not what I meant, I just—"

Movement in her peripheral vision distracted her as Dag rose and rounded her desk to stand beside her. "I think the witch simply referred to the fact that you are not a member of the Guild, and therefore not normally privy to matters of our concern."

Wynn's face lit up, and she inclined toward her monitor as if to get a better look. "Was that him? Where is he?"

Dag leaned over Kylie's shoulder to peer at the screen. "I am here. You are the witch?"

"Um, I'm *a* witch; *the* witch is just a little too much pressure, to be honest."

Kylie shrugged, deliberately knocking into the Guardian with her shoulder. "And I'm still here. Or would you rather I gave you two some alone time to bond?"

"We three." The large man seated beside Wynn spoke for the first time. He had the same gravel bed under his voice that Kylie heard every time Dag opened his mouth. "However, I believe the best strategy would be for all four of us to remain in contact until we have finished our discussions and agreed on our next steps."

"Well, I, for one, am not stepping anywhere until someone tells me *the whole* farfoilt *story*."

Maybe it was the Yiddish that finally got through to Wynn, for after all that her friend had the decency to look abashed. "Right. On it. Introductions, then the story. Promise. Guardian, I am Wynn Powe, Warden to your brother Knox. Kylie, Knox is like . . . uh, sorry, I didn't catch his name."

Kylie pressed her lips together. Apparently Wynn had not met the love of her life at a store she supplied with bath products as the woman had originally said. "Dag. Dag, Wynn. Wynn, Dag. Story. Now."

"Absolutely. Just do me a favor? Try not to hate me or think I'm crazy until I get it all out, okay?"

And *finally,* Kylie got to hear the story. It sounded like a fairy tale, or a high-fantasy novel she'd glanced at while she wandered through the bookstore. Shelved somewhere between Terry Brooks and J.R.R. Tolkien.

Once upon a time, thousands of years ago, the world found itself faced with a great danger. Just as there is Light in the universe to give life and peace to all living things, so there is a Darkness that seeks always to devour goodness and to remake the universe in its image. Because Darkness, like Light, can never be completely destroyed, the only hope of keeping it at bay is to divide it and contain it, to keep it from pooling its power and devouring all that goes before it.

At the point where the world was most at peril in the face of this great evil, a group of immensely gifted magic users joined together to summon forth a power capable of defeating the Demons who make up the Darkness.

That power took the form of the Guardians—seven immortal warriors, one for each of the Demons they would combat. The mages did not create the Guardians but merely called them forth from the Light, fully formed and ready for battle. Their purpose became their titles, because they existed to guard humanity from the servants of evil.

The mages quickly realized, however, that the Seven

Demons of the Darkness could not be entirely destroyed. They were formed from the Dark itself, and so will exist forever in the same way that the Light will exist forever. In order to contain them, they were separated from each other to prevent them from feeding each other's power, and each was banished to a desolate plane where it was imprisoned for eternity.

Knowing of the potential for the Seven to return, the mages made the decision to remain united and thus formed the Wardens Guild in order to monitor the on-going threat from the Darkness. They gathered and shared their knowledge of the enemy, assisted the Guardians with the tools and support they required for battle, and monitored the activities of humans seduced or enslaved by the dark powers. The Wardens bore the ultimate responsibility for alerting the Guardians when they needed to rise up and face a renewed threat, and they also acted to send the warriors back to sleep when the threat was vanquished. Even during those periods of slumber, the Guild remained vigilant against the forces of the Darkness.

"A broch." Damn, Kylie muttered when Wynn finally wound down. "You guys were really serious about the demon thing."

"Deadly serious. But how did you find out, Kylie? Part of the job of the Guild is to keep the truth from the world so that humanity doesn't panic and start acting stupid. If random people are finding out our secrets, we might have a whole new problem on our hands."

Kylie's eyes darted to the side, her lips pursing. "I, uh, I don't think you need to worry about that, Wynneleh. It's not like it's the hot topic around the water cooler. I think you're good."

Wynn's eyes narrowed. "Kylie, what did you do?"

She sighed, big and loud, the way her *bubbeh* had taught her. "Come on, Pooh Bear. What do I always do?"

"You hacked into something. You hacked Bran, didn't you?"

"How else was I supposed to find anything out? You weren't talking, except for that meshuga about a heart attack. I knew you were lying to me, even if that is what the coroner's report said, too."

"You hacked the Cook County medical examiner?"

"Only a little."

"You know it doesn't help anyone if you go to jail, right?"

Kylie snorted. "Don't be insulting. You think I'm some kind of amateur?"

"Right. Sorry. For a second I forgot I was talking to Geekzilla."

"I prefer SuperGeek, thank you very much. I've got a thing for capes, and no desire to destroy Tokyo."

Beside her, Dag growled low in his throat and leaned toward the monitor. "This chatter is meaningless. We must focus on the task at hand. Brother, you must tell me why two of us have awakened at once. A grave threat indeed must stand before us."

"Graver than you think," Knox agreed, peering into the camera on his end. "And it is not just you and I who no longer slumber. Two others have stirred as well."

Dag said something brief and guttural in a language Kylie didn't recognize. She didn't need to in order to catch the gist. He wasn't saying how do you do. "Where have you gathered? I will join you at once."

"It's not that simple, big guy," Wynn broke in, laying a hand on Knox's arm as she spoke. "We aren't all in one place. Knox and I are here in Chicago, but Fil (that's Felicity) and Spar are in Montreal, and Ella and Kees have stayed in Vancouver. Mostly. For the moment, until we get a better handle on what's coming next, we've decided to monitor the situation in each of the cities where we've had incidents."

"Incidents?"

The witch nodded. "Kees woke first, in Vancouver. He and Ella had to face off against the first wave of *nocturnis*. From what we've been able to gather, they've organized themselves to go looking for the Guardians, hoping to destroy you while you're sleeping. In Knox's case, they succeeded. He was summoned to replace one of you the Order managed to blow up. But in between Kees and Knox, we got the really disturbing news. A sect in Montreal turned out to be sacrificing humans to feed to Uhlthor. We think it has already been freed and is gathering strength while the *nocturnis* work on releasing the rest of the Seven."

More of that unfamiliar language poured from Dag, and Kylie found herself wincing even though she still didn't understand a word of it.

"That's what really happened to Bran, Ky." Wynn's expression softened and creased with grief. "He . . . he was possessed, by the Demon. It took his soul. I had to—" She paused and drew a shuddering breath. "I had to release him."

They watched while Knox wrapped his arms around the witch, cuddling her against his chest as tears trickled down her cheeks. "Shh, little witch," he crooned. "You gave your brother peace. It was the greatest gift you could offer."

Kylie felt her own heart squeeze, but she knew pieces of the story were still missing. "But why would a demon go after Bran in the first place?"

Wynn lifted a hand to wipe her cheek, but she didn't

pull away from her fiancé's embrace. And Kylie would certainly be revisiting the idea of her friend's engagement to a member of another species at a later date.

"Bran was a Warden," Wynn said. "We've had Wardens in our family for generations, but Bran figured out something odd was going on in the Guild and with the Order. He got too close, and the *nocturnis* got ahold of him. They used him to feed Uhlthor's power."

"A Warden? You mean the magic guys from the story? Those are seriously still around?"

"You're looking at one."

"One of the few who remain," Knox added. "We have discovered that the Order has instituted a new strategy in this latest phase of the war. We know now that in addition to striving to free the Seven, they have been working for some time—perhaps even for several years—to weaken the Guild, thus minimizing the resistance they will face when they are ready to launch their primary attack. Hundreds of Wardens have been killed or simply disappeared. Some may have gone underground, but even we are having trouble locating them and making contact. Their headquarters in Paris has been destroyed. From what we can tell, none of the inner Council has survived."

"Yet only four of us have woken?" Dag shook his head, his expression both angry and aghast. "This sounds too far advanced for such a slow response. What has happened to our brothers? We should be awake and ready to strike at our enemies."

"Trust us, we're way ahead of you." Wynn's smile looked grim. "Ella, Fil, and I are actively searching, both for the remaining Guardians and any surviving Wardens we can find, but it hasn't been easy. When Knox said the Guild headquarters were destroyed, he meant it. It burned to ash, which is quite an accomplishment when you're talking about a several-hundred-year-old stone building. The fire destroyed the Guild's library and archives, as well as killed everyone inside. We're working blind while we try to locate the rest of you guys. We don't have the usual records to show us where you've been resting."

Dag scoffed. "A simple fire destroyed the Guild?"

"Simple, my ass. It was magical, without a doubt," Wynn said. "The Order was definitely behind it, and they were thorough."

"Thorough enough to have destroyed my Warden as well?" Dag asked. "If that were true, how is it that I have woken? With no Warden to issue the summons—"

"Oh, you've got a Warden, big guy. Don't worry about that." Wynn smirked. "As a matter of fact, you're standing right next to her."

"Her?"

"Me?" Kylie wasn't sure who sounded more shocked—her or the lump of lava rock hovering beside her chair. "Half an hour ago, I didn't even know what a Warden was, and now I'm supposed to play one on TV? *Ayn klaynigkeit.*"

Yeah, sure.

"Trust me, Ky. All three of us have stood right where you are, and it was just as big a shock to us," Wynn assured her.

Kylie choked out a laugh. "You just said you've got like a hundred generations of these Warden thingies in your family, Wynneleh, so tell me how that's the same as my not knowing magic existed before tonight."

"If you claim not to know magic, you are mistaken." Knox eyed her through the camera lens, his chiseled features serious. "A Warden must be gifted with power in order to be admitted to the Guild, and only those with the greatest abilities can summon a Guardian from his sleeping."

"Okay, *(a)* we just discussed that the Guild is now so much dust in the wind, and *(b)* I did no summoning of any kind. *Bupkes.* Whatever woke up Rip Van Winkle over here, I wasn't any part of it."

Wynn wriggled a little in her chair. "See, that's the thing, Ky. Knox is right. You must have some abilities you're not aware of, because every one of the Guardians who have woken so far have done it when a Warden near them was in danger, even if the Warden didn't know what she was at the time. Ella and Fil didn't know anything about all this before they got dragged into it, either. First time they ever heard the word 'Guardian' was when their Guardians started talking to them." She paused, her mouth actually curving into a smile. "In fact, now that I think of it, this conversation we're having right now is pretty much becoming a sort of tradition for our little underground army. Huh."

Kylie grunted. "Yeah, it's charming. Just like Shabbat dinner."

Knox leaned close to Wynn and spoke quietly, but his deep voice carried farther than he probably thought. "I do not understand many of the words this friend of yours speaks. Are you certain she makes sense?"

"I have wondered this myself," Dag threw in.

Wynn laughed and patted her Guardian's chest. "She's fine, big guy. When Kylie gets worked up, she starts to fling the Yiddish. Totally normal. Well, for her anyway."

"Yiddish? But this word means Jewish, and this language is not Hebrew, which I would recognize. It sounds . . . it sounds as if Germans and Russians were put in a pot and shaken until they couldn't remember their own tongues."

Kylie rolled her eyes. "Yiddish is the common cultural language of the Ashkenazi Jewish people of central and eastern Europe. It is also frequently spoken by Jews of that descent here in America as well as in countries around the world. In addition, it's used by plenty of non-Jews with fluent Jewish family members."

Dag eyed her curiously. "Then you are Jewish?"

"No. My father's a Jew, but my mother is just a capitalist."

Wynn laughed, but the Guardians looked even more confused.

Kylie had told this story a thousand times, so she sighed as she again answered the unspoken questions. "Jewishness varies depending on who you ask. Traditionally, and according to the Orthodox community, I can't be Jewish because my mother isn't. Judaism technically passes matrilineally. Also, since I don't actively practice, most Reform Jews don't consider me Jewish, either. They're liberal enough to say anyone with Jewish ancestry who practices Judaism is a Jew. Again, not me. But I spent a lot of time with my grandmother when I was growing up, and she was Jewish—my father's mother. She was also fluent in Yiddish, so I learned the language from her."

"And she uses it whenever she gets worked up, angry, frustrated, happy, you name it." Wynn grinned. "It's actually a pretty accurate emotional tell. Very useful."

Kylie glared. "You suck."

"Ladies." Knox cleared his throat, looking as if he were sorry to have spoken at all. "Let us focus on the matter at hand, shall we?"

"Right." Wynn nodded. "We need to find out what Kylie can do."

Kylie groaned. "Wynn, we've been friends for years. You know what I can do. I can finish a crossword puzzle in five minutes without thinking. I can write software, I can program apps, I can tinker with hardware, and I can hack into any computer this side of the galaxy. But that's it. I don't shoot lightning out of my fingertips, and I don't pull rabbits out of a hat. I'm a hacker, not Harry frickin' Houdini."

Dag rumbled, "Is that why your eyes change when you watch the computer?"

Kylie turned to frown at him, her stomach slowly twisting under her "Rock-Paper-Scissors-Lizard-Spock" sweatshirt. "What did you say?"

Dag gestured toward the setup on her desk. "Your eyes are brown when you are away from the machines, but when you watch the screens, they change. They develop a green ring around the pupil and glow with a strange light." He shrugged. "Perhaps it is a human disfigurement of some sort, but it looks more like magic to me."

Grinding her teeth together kept Kylie from either tossing her cookies or shouting a denial; she wasn't sure which would have come out first. No one else had ever noticed how her eyes looked when she worked, but then again, she usually worked alone. How had Dag seen it? It must be getting worse.

In the beginning, when she had first noticed the eerie light in her eyes, Kylie had only seen it when she was really deep into something complicated. She had to be concentrating hard and giving her skills a workout before that glow appeared.

At least, that's how it used to be, but she had seen it

more often in the last couple of years, almost any time she focused her attention on something electronic. Still, getting a freaky evil eye from time to time had nothing to do with magic, right?

"Oh, wow. I didn't know that was even a possibility. Can magic really work with technology like that?" Wynn turned to Knox, her expression excited. "Bran used to say that what Ky could do with a computer was magic, but I thought it was just a figure of speech."

"Perhaps not." Knox peered at the camera, his gaze thoughtful. "We tend to think of magic as something organic, something that comes from the earth, but in reality it is greater and more elusive than that. There have been tales of magic affecting machinery for centuries, since humans began to use it so frequently. Usually the two systems are viewed as opposing forces, disruptive and destructive to each other, but it is possible that your friend is able to harness her powers in a way that complements rather than contests the power of human technology."

"So she's like a cyberwitch." Wynn's eyes twinkled even over the remote connection. "Ha! Now who gets to call who names, *shiksa*?"

"Half *shiksa*. And like you needed an excuse before," Kylie grumbled, still trying to wrap her head around the idea that what she thought of as hard-earned skill might owe at least a little bit to some kind of supernatural power. She wasn't sure whether she should feel proud or embarrassed. Had she been cheating all these years?

"If this is the case, perhaps Kylie will be able to use her power to discover the things we have not," Knox suggested.

Wynn agreed enthusiastically. "That would be amazing. None of us is half as good online as the Koyote, magic or no. How about it, Ky? Do you think you can help us?"

"If I had any idea what you were talking about, I suppose anything might be possible."

"Don't pout. Knox is right. El, Fil, and I have been running into dead end after dead end." The witch sighed. "It hasn't helped that we're trying to do three things at once, even if we're all working on it together."

"We need to locate the three remaining Guardians, first of all. Dag is right that it will take all of them together to face whatever the Order has planned. Second, we want to locate any members of the Guild who might have escaped the Order's killing squads until now. Ella, Felicity, and I have learned a lot, first from some books El got her hands on, and my uncle Griffin has taught us a lot, too. He was a Warden back in the day himself. More Wardens means more information, and the more info we have, the better we can fight the Order. So finding the rest of the missing is important."

Since Bran had been one of those missing for more than a year, it didn't take a lot of work to convince Kylie of the importance of that task. She just nodded her agreement.

"The third thing is the trickiest, but maybe the most critical. For the last six months, we've actively begun looking for the Hierophant."

"The whosie-whatsie?" Kylie asked, tilting her head as if trying to hear more clearly.

"The Hierophant is the head of the Order of Eternal Darkness," Dag said, his voice a low rumbling of distaste and anger. "He serves close at the hands of the Seven and is privy to all their schemes and strategies."

Wynn nodded. "Not to mention being a first-rate schemer himself. He's basically the brains behind the operation, the head of the snake. If we can find him and take him out, we might send the *nocturnis* scrambling long enough to gain the upper hand."

"The Hierophant will also be close—physically close—to the place where the Demons are resting and trying to regain their strength," Knox added. "Finding him could lead us right to the Seven."

"So, do you think you can do that, Wile E. Koyote?" The look Wynn sent her through the camera was teasing, but earnest. "Can you do a little cybermagic and hunt down the Hierophant for us?"

Kylie lifted an eyebrow. "Are you giving me a choice here?"

"Sure. You always have a choice. This time, it's save the world, or go down as Demon chow." Wynn said it lightly, but her eyes weren't laughing. She meant every word.

Kylie threw up her hands and made a sound of disgust. "Well, since you put it that way . . ."

Chapter Four

A yid hot ahkt un tsvantsik protsent pakhed, tsvey
protsent tsuker, un zibetsik protsent khutzpe.
*A Jew is twenty-eight percent fear, two percent sugar,
and seventy percent chutzpah.*

By the time Wynn was satisfied that Kylie had a firm
grasp on the fundamentals of the situation, the night was
pretty much over. Literally. The sky had begun to lighten
to the dark blue-gray color that presaged the coming
dawn. Luckily, Kylie knew this time of day well. In the
long and dishonorable tradition of hackers and geeks
everywhere, Kylie operated on a night owl's schedule.
She often slept until noon and worked until dawn. Still,
this had been an unusually long night, no matter what
the clock said.

She stifled a yawn as she eyed Dag, trying to decide
what the heck to do with him. Wynn and Knox had
made it very clear that they expected her to keep him
close, but there was close and then there was in her
pocket. Frankly, Kylie didn't own pockets that big.

She did, however, own a guest room. Well, four of
them, technically, but only one of them sported an actual bed. She had no idea how Dag was going to squeeze

his ginormous frame onto the queen-sized mattress, but he'd have to figure that one out on his own. No way was she giving up her own bed for the gargoyle, even if it had been bigger. Luckily, she had the same size in the master bedroom.

"Come on," she said, leading the way out of the office and up the stairs to the second floor. She opened the door to the appropriate room and gestured him inside. "Sorry about the pile of boxes, but I haven't finished unpacking. At least there are sheets on the bed and towels in the bathroom. It's that door in the corner. You share with the room next door, but it's empty, so no worries. Sleep well."

"Where will you be?"

His words caught her before she could make it back to the staircase. She turned her head just enough to toss her reply over her shoulder. "Upstairs. Also sleeping. Good night."

Once again his footsteps were silent, at least until he hit the second step behind her. That thing squeaked when you so much as breathed on it. As soon as she heard it, she froze, then slowly spun to face him.

"Where exactly do you think you're going, Goliath?"

Dag scowled at her, although he did it so often she was starting to think that might be his resting face. "My name is Dag, impertinent human. I am concerned that if you should cry out, you would be too far away from me to hear. How would I come to your aid should you need me?"

She pressed a hand to his chest when he made as if to step forward, then cursed at the tingle of electricity that shot through her palm. "Trust me," she insisted, "I can be plenty loud when I need to, and if anyone shows up in my bedroom while I'm trying to get some sleep, you're definitely getting a demonstration of that. Now, once again, *good night.*"

Punctuating her farewell with a gentle shove—which didn't even rock him on his heels—Kylie turned and started back up the final flight of stairs. Every couple of steps, she glanced backward to make certain he wasn't following, no matter what her stupid hormones had to say. To her surprise, he let her go, but he watched her until she disappeared around the newel post.

Her skin continued to tingle for much longer than that.

Dag had slept for three centuries the last time he succumbed. He had no intention of closing his eyes again anytime soon. Instead, he took advantage of the human's retreat to reconnoiter around her home and gather whatever information he could. He did this for the sake of their security; knowing the building's entrances and exits made it easier for him to defend them. His burning curiosity to know more about the little female had nothing to do with it.

He repeated that to himself a few times, just to be sure.

He found her home to be spacious and structurally appealing, with lots of wooden surfaces and accents colored by the patina of age and stability. Given the small female's sharp tongue and impudent personality, he found the classic architecture mildly surprising.

He stifled the urge to examine the third floor, which she had indicated held only her private sleeping and bathing chambers. Somehow he thought that if she were to wake and find him prowling through her personal space, she might prove her screaming ability up close and personally. Instead, he first prowled through the level where she had left him before descending to the main floor and making a more thorough survey than he had managed when they initially arrived.

If her home provided any clues as to her character, then the small female appeared to be a study in contradictions. Most of the rooms in the large old house stood empty but for stacks of sealed brown boxes. Only about half of them could boast so much as a single stick of furniture. However, a few select spaces, like the office and the kitchen, brimmed with interesting and amusing indications of a female with an unusual sense of humor and a decided streak of whimsy. This did not surprise him, but the fact that he found such things appealing did.

On the wall of the impressively sized living room hung an enormous print depicting a vessel of some sort posed against a background of stars and empty space. To one side, glowing script proclaimed to any onlookers that someone associated "aim[ed] to misbehave." An oversized sofa in a nubby material the variegated color of beach sand and a low table looked cozy and inviting, but they proved to be the only fixtures in the room. The rest of the space appeared even darker and more barren in contrast.

He wandered through the main level, finding much the same scene wherever he turned. A room between the living area and kitchen sported not even a box, an echoing cavern between a high plaster ceiling and a gleaming hardwood floor.

Signs of life began in the kitchen, where at least most of the boxes appeared to have been unpacked. Plates, bowls, and drinking vessels in various bright hues filled the expanse of white cabinetry, and several sharp knives hung suspended by a magnet against the wall. A set of canisters on the marble counter depicted a frog-type creature playing a stringed musical instrument, an anthropomorphized pig in a dress and pearls, and a wide-eyed version of a child's stuffed bear in a polka-dotted bow tie. Despite labels claiming they contained coffee, tea, and sugar, he found each of them as empty as the next.

The office he had already seen appeared to be the room where she spent the most time. If he couldn't tell by looking around him, he would have known by the way her scent filled the air inside. Already it had committed itself to his sensory memory, unexpected and alluring, and in the enclosed space it teased him mercilessly.

Dag existed for battle, a warrior from the moment of his summoning to his last gasp of air. He had come into being for that singular purpose. Over the centuries it had offered him little opportunity to experience any of the softness of life, from the peace offered by nature's wonders, to the comfortable companionship of creatures not intimately concerned with the fight against the Darkness. Few humans and fewer human females had therefore ever entered, much less lingered, in his presence.

Still, he could remember no fragrance like Kylie's. Something inside him had expected sweetness, like sugar or honey, perhaps because of her sweetly delicate appearance. Then she opened her mouth, and he might have expected spice, the sharp bite of cinnamon, maybe, or a bittersweet clove note.

He got none of those. Instead, her fragrance reminded him of the desert, dry and fresh and ancient. Her sweetness came from the smoky depths of gum benjamin and blended with the buttery richness of cedar and the piquant freshness of frankincense. In fact, she smelled to him of the land her ancestors had called Holy, rocky and steep and unexpectedly bountiful. It made him think of a hot sun and warm breezes, of dark eyes and secret smiles.

And, now, it made him think of Kylie.

He should not waste his time dwelling on the human, he reminded himself. His exploration of her dwelling was meant to inform him of her character as it pertained to her role as his Warden. He needed to know if she was quick-witted or deliberate, steady or volatile, courageous or timid.

And hadn't five minutes of her company in the hell tower provided those answers already? His inner voice smirked. Dag ignored it.

The list of things he had chosen to ignore had grown impressively in the few hours since he had regained his awareness. He would ignore his strange fascination with the small human female who had spurred his awakening. He would ignore the oddity of a female Warden, the first in his many centuries of existence. He would ignore that each of his three woken brothers sported a female Warden whom they now claimed as mates.

Most of all, he would ignore the oldest legend of his kind, the one that told of a bond between a female of power and a Guardian like him that could free him from his endless pattern of sleeping and waking. A legend that offered him a life of his own, free to live according to his desires with a human female at his side to the end of his days.

Irrelevant.

Dag needed to focus on the matters at hand. After speaking to Knox and the witch Warden, Wynn, he understood what the low-level itch at the back of his neck signified. He could sense the threat from the Darkness rising, one greater than any he had faced before. In the past, he had woken to fight against the experimental pushes by the Seven, the subtle probes of their evil seeking a weakness in the prisons that contained them. When matters had become grave indeed, he had even fought beside one or another of his brothers, joining forces to defeat a stronger incursion. Never before had he known anything like this.

The thought of one of the Seven fully present on the human plane nearly staggered him. The last time such a thing had happened predated Dag's summoning, but each Guardian who ever existed came into the world with the full knowledge of his race, each individual's experiences cataloged and shared, almost like a hive memory. Each Guardian could access such knowledge at will, so he knew several of his brethren had died returning the Demon to its prison plane of existence. To know also that this time, the Guardians faced the added challenge of fighting without the full strength of the Wardens Guild behind them merely added to his concern.

His greatest worry, however, centered around Kylie herself. He understood that of the current female Wardens, only Wynn had previous knowledge of the Guild and its doings. From what she had told them, only she had any real experience in the practice of magic as well. However, Kylie not only lacked the training of a Guild Warden, she seemed surprised to hear her abilities classified as magic at all. How was such an innocent and unschooled human to face the concerted attack of a *nocturni* sect, let alone one of the Seven itself?

The answer, of course, was that she couldn't. Dag would need to remain vigilant, ready to place himself between the female and any harm that might come to her. Unfortunately, he somehow already recognized that doing so might see him incurring an extra level of harm himself—the first from the evil attack, and the second from Kylie herself, enraged at being thrust aside and prevented from fighting her own battles. Already he had noticed her stubborn independence and her sharp tongue, one he would not mind taming, given the correct opportunity.

Dag stood beside her desk and picked up a small, fur-covered object for a closer examination. It appeared to be a child's toy in the shape of a soft cat, pale gray with darker stripes. But when he picked it up, a recorded voice emerged from it and sang some sort of awkward lullaby. This was the female he was supposed to permit to stand beside him in battle?

What was it she had said several times over the course of the evening?

Oy vey.

A good five hours of sleep had been exactly what Kylie needed to face the day with renewed energy and a return of her normally optimistic attitude. Well, five hours of sleep and an ice-cold bottle of imported cola. Cane sugar and caffeine, baby—the breakfast of champions.

Especially when accompanied by a toasted onion bagel schmeared with a half-ton of creamy butter.

She had stumbled down from her rumpled bed, popped the top off her soda, and dropped her bagel in the toaster oven before her erstwhile houseguest made his first appearance. She wasn't sure if he'd been lurking in the living room like the statue he had started out as, or had been inspecting the water seal in her basement. Either way, she had the kitchen to herself one moment, and the next, blam! Instant gargoyle.

Okay, so he wore his human form, but still, his way of moving silently continued to creep her out, especially when she considered what a big guy he was. If *she* couldn't walk across the creaky old wooden floors in her supersoft fuzzy socks without making a huge racket, then he sure as heck shouldn't be able to pull it off. It just went to show that there really was no justice in the world (she had suspected this since she was five, and the kindergarten teacher had let Ari Milner play with the wooden blocks even though Kylie had *clearly* gotten to them first).

Luckily, she possessed decent peripheral vision, or she would have dropped her soda when he spoke and had to clean up shards of broken glass on an empty and insufficiently caffeinated stomach. "You yell 'Boo!' at me, and I'm so not sharing my bagels," she warned.

Dag paused. "What is a bagel, and why would I want a share in yours?"

A thought flashed in Kylie's head for a split second, just long enough for her to wonder if he thought she was sexually propositioning him. She had to bite the inside of her cheek to keep from bursting out with a belly laugh. Or, you know, jumping his bones.

"Oh, Goliath, you really need to get out more. Here, I got this." She pulled out another bagel and waved it under his nose. "This, my friend, is manna from heaven, the greatest gift my people have bestowed upon the earth. Watch and learn."

The second bagel joined hers in the toaster, and she leaned back against the counter to wait for the achievement of golden-brown deliciousness. Dag alternated between eyeing her and the toaster oven in silence. Not much of a talker, was he?

Despite her amusement at the idea that she had used

bread products as a tool of seduction, Kylie had to admit that her reaction to the hulking man-shaped monster in her house hadn't been some sort of post-traumatic stress. He really was just as hot as she remembered, which in itself felt totally weird; not because he wasn't human, but because he so wasn't her type.

Kylie knew her people, and she always dated among them. Her boyfriends, hookups, and crushes had always been geeks of one variety or another, either compunerds like herself, or sci-fi fanatics, or academic head cases like Bran. For heaven's sake, even with all the eye candy in the *Star Trek* movie remakes, her favorite of the group continued to be Simon Pegg. His character in another movie, *Paul*, was the closest she'd ever seen to her dream man on the big screen. So why did this giant, muscular, rough-faced, and gruff-voiced behemoth get her panties in a twist every time they wound up in the same room together?

Testosterone poisoning, her inner voice grumbled. *Only logical explanation. For pity's sake, open a window or something before you lose control and try to feel him up. Or worse.*

Her inner dialog had so distracted her that she nearly jumped out of her skin when the beep of the toaster cut into the silence. Cheeks flaming, she turned to grab a couple of plates from the cabinet, and hopefully a good handful of her rapidly disappearing self-control.

"I'd ask if you want butter or schmear, but since this is your first bagel, you get schmear," she babbled as she reached into the refrigerator. "It's only right to get the full experience. Well, fullish. I don't have any lox in the house. I personally find fish disgusting, especially for breakfast."

"Are you speaking this Yiddish language again?"

Kylie chuckled. "No, that was all full-on American." She thrust his plate at him and prepared her own bagel. "You want anything to drink? Coke? I have coffee, too. I don't drink it, but it seemed polite to keep it in case I ever got company. I have one of those little cup machine thingies."

Dag lifted his gaze from the white-topped brown delicacy on his plate to blink at her. His mouth opened and closed once before he actually spoke. "More American?" He sounded pretty unsure.

"Yeah, you sound like a man who needs caffeine, and you look like a coffee drinker to me. Hang on."

She flipped on the machine that lurked mostly abandoned on her counter, then rummaged through a drawer beneath it. It took a minute, but she finally found a K-Cup of indeterminate variety and fitted it into the brewer with a small grunt of satisfaction. Like she would know the differences among the twelve bazillion types of coffee in the world. Dag could take what she gave him and be happy.

A few moments later, she passed him a steaming mug of dark liquid, grabbed her own breakfast, and headed for the office. "Come on," she called over her shoulder. "This is a working brunch. We'll eat in here."

"I am unfamiliar with that term. 'Brunch.' Is it more of your Yiddish?" Dag settled in the cat's chair once again and sniffed his coffee before taking a sip. Kylie decided to interpret his ensuing grunt as approval, given that he went right back for more.

She had to laugh at his question. "No, brunch is about as Waspy as you can get. It just means a meal you eat sometime between breakfast and lunch, instead of having either of those individually." She took a bite of bagel and chewed while she eyed him. "You know, no offense or anything, but being a Guardian sounds like a pretty crappy job if you spend most of your existence encased in stone and never get to experience things like brunch and bagels."

Dag shrugged, eyeing his cream-cheese-topped food with obvious suspicion. "We are not encased in stone, as you say. We become the stone. And it is the reason for my existence. If I am not a Guardian, I am nothing."

She scowled. "That seems kinda harsh."

"It is the truth. Guardians are neither made nor born. We enter into this world fully formed, and only because we are needed to fight against the Darkness."

Finally giving in to the inevitable, Dag crunched into the chewy baked dough and grunted even louder than he had over the coffee. He eyed the treat again, this time with a great deal more respect. And greed.

Kylie's expression transformed into a grin. "Told you," she said before turning her attention to her computer monitor. Specifically, the one in the center. Her right foot began to jiggle with energy. "Okay, time to nut up or shut up."

She got a feeling that comment only sailed by because Dag's mouth was full, but she was already tapping away at her keyboard and picking up the thread of her months'-long correspondence with last night's no-showing informant. So far, he provided her most likely foot in the door to the world Wynn had described to her last night.

She looked up briefly when Dag spoke again, just long enough to notice that not even a crumb remained of his first foray into bagel nirvana.

"We have not yet discussed how we will proceed,"

he said, his serious expression somewhat marred by the glob of white cream cheese clinging to the corner of his lips.

Kylie bit back her smile. "You don't think so? Then what do you call that marathon video chat we had last night? A sewing bee? We went through this with Wynn and Knox. The rest of those guys are going to concentrate their efforts on locating the remaining Guardians and any surviving Wardens they can find. I am—I mean, we are—going to take over the search for the Hierophant. I can search in ways the others just don't have the skill set for."

He glowered at her. You know, some more. "I remember what was discussed a few hours ago, human. I referred to the fact that the other Guardian and Warden expect the two of us to work together, and we have yet to strategize between ourselves." He leaned back in his chair with his coffee in hand, his face somehow managing an expression of both stoicism and smugness at the same time. Impressive.

"I must wait until nightfall before I fly over the city," he continued, "to minimize the chances that I will be seen, but while the sun yet shines I can begin to search for any trail the *nocturnis* have left around the city. It may take quite some time, and I will expect you to stay close to me and follow my orders. You may still be in danger after the attack on you yesterday."

Kylie stared at him while he spoke, her brows gradually furrowing and her head tilting farther and farther to the side until her ear nearly brushed her shoulder. "It's like you actually think you're going to run the show here. That's so cute."

"Cute." Dag's features curled around the word as if it tasted putrid. "Female, your unthinking tongue will get you into much trouble one day. I am a Guardian. I have existed to fight this evil for more than a thousand years. I do not merely believe I will direct our actions, I know it. I will ensure it. You may have a human disregard for your own safety, but I am sworn to protect your race, and I will do this whether you like it or not."

She waved a hand in his direction and turned back to her keyboard. "Nice speech, Goliath, but in the present circumstances, I am way better equipped to find out what we need to know than you are. You think wandering aimlessly around the city is going to get you anywhere? Yeah, maybe in a couple decades or so. I bet you cash money I can put us on the trail of these nocturnal guys in less than an hour. How much you want to bet?"

"*Nocturnis.* You cannot even remember their name, and yet you think to defeat them by yourself? This makes your wager not only foolish but unwinnable."

"I never said anything about beating them up with one hand tied behind my back. I'm wily, not suicidal. I plan to stay as far away from Demons and demonic minions as I can during this whole shebang. But when it comes to finding things out, I've got the mad skills. I can locate these losers way faster than you can, that's all I'm saying. I'll point the can of whoopass, but you and the other winged warrior types can take care of opening it and spreading it around. Happy?"

Dag growled, his fingers tightening on his coffee mug until she heard the heavy stoneware begin to crack. He must have heard it too, because he abruptly set the cup down and rose to pace around the room. "Why can you not speak like a normal human? First you use your secret language, and then you insist on using words and phrases of nonsense. Even though I understand the words, your use of them together makes no sense. You deliberately attempt to obfuscate the truth with your utterings."

"Whoa. Calm down, Goliath. I'm not being deliberately anything. This is me." She raised her hands and pointed her fingers at herself. "What you see is what you get. The merchandise might be quirky, but it does not change based on customer complaints."

This time, the Guardian muttered something in that language Kylie didn't understand, and suddenly he stood before her not as an irritated hottie, but in the gray-skinned, bat-winged shape of his natural form. He leaned one hand on the floor in his customary crouching position and raised the other to his skull. "Your words make my head throb like a war drum. I lack the energy to maintain a human shape while you continue to speak."

For some reason, that stung. "Well, you don't have to be mean about it. I'm not trying to make your life difficult, Goliath. This is a bit of a shake-up for me, too, you know. Or did you not understand the part about how I was clueless about magic, Demons, Guardians, and Wardens less than twenty-four hours ago? You're not the only one dealing with a big pile of *drek* right now."

"My name is Dag!" he bellowed, his fangs exposed in anger, his wings stirring the air until the papers on Kylie's desk fluttered.

Her heart jumped, then settled back into rhythm. He hadn't precisely scared her, but she would admit to startled. Startled worked. "Sheesh, I know. I know. Note to self. Don't give gargoyles nicknames, especially of other gargoyles. You got it."

"How you made it to adulthood with that tongue still in your mouth is a mystery I lack the power to comprehend."

They stared at each other for a long moment, the silence punctuated only by the whir of her equipment and his agitated breathing. Kylie had to marvel over the fact that his monstrous form seemed to bother her not a whit, not even as worked up as he was in that moment. She wasn't afraid of him because of his appearance; in fact, she almost felt more comfortable with him this way. At least when he didn't look human, she wasn't constantly distracted by the hotness of his other form. Maybe now she could actually concentrate on her work, cut that hour she'd boasted about down by a few minutes.

"Look," she finally said, deciding someone had to crack the stalemate or they'd never get anything accomplished. "I apologize for upsetting you. I promise not to call you Goliath again, and I'll try to be as clear as I can when I talk, but I can't guarantee I can change a lifetime of speech patterns just for you. Sometimes my mouth starts running before my brain can catch up. Just ask my *bubbeh*—er, my grandmother. If I say something that doesn't make sense to you, ask me a question."

He huffed out a breath, and she almost expected to see smoke shoot from his nostrils, as if he were part dragon or something. "If the time we have spent together so far is any indication, I would never cease questioning you."

Okay, griping was easy to recognize and something she could totally deal with. She gave in to a grin. "Don't worry. We'll have you speaking modern English in no time. Then you can brag about being multilingual."

"I speak twelve languages. I'm just not sure yours is one of them."

Kylie looked up from her screen and goggled. "Twelve languages?"

"What you call English did not exist when I was first summoned into this existence, not even in England. They still spoke the earlier dialects, until they spoke French."

"Huh, I didn't think about it like that. I guess you're right, though."

"I speak the older dialect of English, this version you know, French, German, Latin, Spanish, Italian, Russian, Aramaic, Hebrew, Hindi, and Arabic."

Kylie blinked at him. "Wow. Remind me to take you with me next time I decide to travel."

Dag said nothing, just eyed her suspiciously.

Turning back to her work, she began scrolling through the files of correspondence she'd exchanged with the person known as DrkMsgr. There was a lot there, from e-mails to text messages to full-on documents when she had helped him with a couple of tech issues he'd been having. Until now, she had saved the data but she had left it alone. It was rude to dig too deeply into another person's identity until you had a good reason. Kylie figured a connection to the end of the world finally gave her a good reason.

They had discussed it during the call. Wynn agreed with Kylie that there was a good chance this DrkMsgr character had at least some knowledge of the Order and that he was worth pursuing as a lead. Kylie was about to pursue her *tokhes* off.

"How do you hope to locate the *nocturnis* on that machine? I do not think they would be so reckless as to create a—what is it called . . . a Web site."

Kylie snorted. "If only people really were that stupid. Though, actually, some of them are. But at the moment, I'm working on the theory that a demonic cult that's smart enough to have survived a couple of thousand years—"

"At least."

"Yeah, well, I'm going to give them credit for a bit more brainpower than the average *Necronomicon*-reading teenager. Groups don't last that long unless they're smart."

She turned to her secondary monitor and opened a new file. As she looked back and forth between the two screens, she caught the faint reflection of green light glowing from her eyes. Huh. Maybe she really did have some sort of supernatural power. Cool.

Of course, teleportation would have been cooler. She'd always wanted the ability to teleport. Think about it, no more airports. Ever. Hot damn!

She focused back on her task, for the first time neither ignoring nor attempting to stifle the strange light in her eyes. She also acknowledged the tingle that accompanied it, running down her arms and into her fingertips. Her typing went from rapid to blurred, it was so fast, as she mined through the data she had already collected and then took a metaphorical pickax to cut through to the layers beneath.

As usual, she lost track of time, but she didn't think it could have been more than twenty minutes before her eyes flashed with a burst of illumination and fixed on the information she'd been looking for.

"Gotcha, Mr. DrkMsgr dude." She crowed her triumph and sent her chair swirling in a celebratory spin. "What is that supposed to mean, anyway? Dark Messenger? Yeah, right. More like Dork *Meshugener.*"

Dag, who had spent the last however long alternating between peering over her shoulder and pacing around the room, paused beside her and leaned over the desk, wings fluttering. "What have you found?"

She leaned back and grinned up at him. "That guy I was supposed to meet last night, who said he had information on Bran and all the 'weird stuff' he was into—meaning, the Guild and all the rest? Turns out he's a fellow by the name of Dennis Ott, of 1273 East Adams Boulevard, Apartment B, Brookline, Massachusetts. We're practically neighbors."

"He is close?"

"Brookline is just a few miles that way." She pointed. "We can be making fun of him to his face inside thirty minutes."

Dag gave a growly rumbling sound, but Kylie recognized this one as less threat and more anticipation. "That, I understood." He smiled, fangs flashing. "Let's go."

"Yeah, um, just one thing."

"What?" His wings nearly vibrated his impatience.

She coughed to cover her grin and ran her gaze over his large expanse of bare, gray skin, all exposed but for the area under the gladiatoresque kilt he wore as his only garment. It seemed to appear on him automatically whenever he took his natural form. "Just, you know, it's kind of chilly out. You might want to put on a few more clothes. And a few less wings. Only a suggestion."

He cursed and in the blink of an eye transformed himself back into Hottie McHotterson, the dark-haired, dark-eyed bruiser in battered jeans and a BU hockey jersey. A classic O'Callahan #17. Was he an actual fan?

Her mind boggled.

"Better?" he growled.

And she was not answering that with a ten-foot pole. Instead, she grabbed her phone and pushed away from the desk. "Okay, let's roll."

"Roll?"

Kylie sighed. "Just follow me, big guy. For the moment, I'm driving."

"We are not in a vehicle."

"Argh!"

Chapter Five

Men zol zikh kenen oyskoyfen fun toyt, volten di
oremelayt sheyn parnose gehat.
*If people could hire others to die for them, the poor
could make a nice living.*

Kylie explained to him that Brookline was a separate
city bordering Boston to the west, but he could not
detect any demarcation between the two as she guided
the vehicle—it did turn out that she had one—along
the route to their destination. This second town appeared more like another neighborhood in the bur-
geoning city he knew rather than a separate entity of its
own. After all these centuries, the ways of humans
continued to baffle him.

"Okay, we just drove past the address." Kylie spoke,
drawing his attention back inside the cramped confines
of the automobile. He'd been concentrating on their surroundings in order to fight the odd distracting effect the
female had on him. "I'm going to find parking up ahead,
and we can walk back. It's that converted white Victo-
rian on the left."

Dag glanced back and saw the large house with white
clapboard siding and a wide porch on the front. It looked

in need of new paint, and he found the wires trailing toward it from a nearby pole to be both unattractive and potentially troublesome for creatures with wings. Otherwise it appeared ordinary and unassuming. He had difficulty believing one of the foot soldiers of the Seven lived inside.

"You are certain this is correct? I see no taint of Darkness about the place."

Kylie had half turned in her seat as she began maneuvering the vehicle between two others already parked at the curb. Apparently, she found she could spare enough attention from the task to roll her eyes at him. "What? Nocturna—*nocturnis* like to decorate the front yard with severed goat heads and human sacrifices on pikes? Somehow I can't see them wanting to draw that kind of attention to themselves."

He grunted, but didn't bother to protest or comment on her smart mouth. Again. But if she knew some of the things he had seen the servants of the Darkness do in the past, she would not be so quick to make fun. He refused to put anything past their evil minds.

He unfolded his large frame from his seat and extracted himself from the car, which the human had assured him was a perfectly normal size ("Not even a compact," she had scoffed). When he emerged, he felt a wave of gratitude for the freedom. His legs appreciated the chance to stretch themselves as he followed her down the concrete sidewalk to the front of the white house. Kylie approached the front porch, squinted up at some numbers beside the door, then shook her head and turned away.

"We have the wrong address?"

"No, but the numbers by the door are actual numbers, one through four. Our guy's address said apartment B.

I'm guessing that means basement, and I'm also guessing the entrance is going to be along the side of the house or out in back."

She led the way down a narrow drive beside the building, gesturing to a low jut of concrete blocks sticking out about three-quarters of the way along. "See? Basement entrance stairwell. Told you."

Her supposition proved correct. Rounding the low barrier, Dag found the awkward structure to be part of a retaining wall that supported a narrow stair dug into the ground. The tight path led to a white wooden door with two narrow panes of glass at the top. Kylie bounded down the stairs with no apparent worries and knocked before he could stop her.

Hissing, he grabbed her by the arm and hauled her away from the door. "What do you think you are doing, female?" he demanded. "Have you no sense of caution?"

She looked confused. "What do I have to be cautious about? We came here to talk to this guy, right? Well, it's a little hard to talk to someone if you don't, you know, meet them. That's how this visiting thing works. You go to someone's house, you knock, they answer, you have a conversation. Unless you're selling something, in which case they probably slam the door in your face."

"That is not how this works when the person you wish to speak to is a servant of the Darkness," he snarled. "What if he had warded protection on the door? You could have been harmed. Or what if instead of politely answering your knock, he opened the door only to hex you with a black casting? Until we know who this person is and what he is capable of, we will proceed with caution. Do you understand?"

"Please, I'm not deaf." She jerked her arms from his grasp and gestured toward the blank surface of the door.

"Nor do I appear to be injured or in danger of being hexed at any moment. In fact, I'm guessing the lack of an answer to my knock means that our friend isn't even home."

Dag battled back the urge to seize her again and shake her. Perhaps he could rattle some sense loose inside that head of hers. Instead, he turned his glare on the door. "Are you certain?"

Kylie shrugged. "Try it yourself."

He shouldered past her in the narrow space of the stairwell. The knock he gave packed a bit more force than the human's had. So much, in fact, that when his knuckles made contact for the third time, the panel shuddered and clicked before swinging an inch or two inward.

He took a single breath and froze.

"Wow, it must have been unlocked. Maybe he really is in there." She stepped forward, her face alight with curiosity. "Should we just go in, or—"

Her hand reached out to push open the door and made contact before he could stop her. She didn't press hard, but it was enough. The door swung halfway open, and the distinctive, sickly sweet miasma of death rolled out over the threshold.

"Don't," he snapped. "Wait here."

He could smell the blood and the taint of expelled waste that accompanied death, but no other fragrance greeted him in the small apartment. Instinct told him the killer was long gone, but he would make certain before he allowed the female to enter.

The body of a young man lay in the center of the main room, half on a layer of worn beige carpet, the other half sprawled over a grimy expanse of gray vinyl flooring. His throat had been slit in a stroke so deep the

white bones of his spine peeked out through the gaping
hole. Another, equally deep wound bit through his chest
from his sternum nearly to his pelvis. Blood pooled beneath the corpse, already congealed on the slick surface
of the tile and soaked deep into the pile of the carpet.
The male had clearly been dead for hours.

"Got in himmel."

Startled, Dag reached down and twitched the edge of
the man's clothing to cover the worst of the abdominal
wound. His gaze shot up to find the disobedient female
had not only *not* remained outside while he checked the
apartment, she had walked right up beside him and
stood gazing down at the dead body with an expression
of mixed horror and compassion. Her brown eyes had
softened, and she held a hand over her mouth that she
only removed to speak.

"Is that him? Is that Dennis Ott?"

Deciding it would be worthless to chastise her right
then, especially since his senses told him the danger had
passed and they alone occupied the apartment, Dag
shrugged. "I do not know, but who else would it be?"

Kylie finally lowered her hand and wrapped her arms
around her torso as if giving herself comfort. "I don't
know, either. A roommate? A friend? Lover? His feet
are bare, though—just socks—so chances are he lived
here. No reason otherwise for him not to be wearing
shoes this time of year. It's not like anyone in here has
been trying to protect the carpet. At least, not in the last
decade."

Dag nodded. "You are correct. I noticed the lack, but
did not consider the significance."

"Does he have any identification?" When he looked
at her curiously, her shoulders twitched. "Some guys

carry their wallets around all day. Maybe he's got a driver's license in his pocket."

From the way she jerked her pointed little chin toward the body, he gathered she had no intention of checking for herself. He didn't blame her. While he had seen death on countless occasions, he doubted this human had. She appeared too young and innocent to have encountered the sort of violence to which he himself had become inured. Mortals felt a natural reluctance to stray too close to the blatant work of death.

He crouched beside the body, careful to avoid the blood, and used his long reach to pat the pockets in the victim's black denim jeans. In the first two he found nothing, but when he crossed to the man's left side, he felt objects in both front and rear pockets. From the back he withdrew a leather wallet, also black, the leather already soaked and stiffened by blood. He held it up for Kylie to take while he investigated the front pocket.

She took the item gingerly, two fingers very carefully plucking it from his hand by the driest corner she could find. Stepping around the blood pool, she set it on the edge of a small table and flipped it open. "It's him. Here's his license. It's got a picture."

Dag grunted and withdrew a key ring and a folded piece of paper from inside the worn jeans. The objects had been spared the worst of the blood spatter, the note hardly smudged. Uninterested in the keys, he tossed them onto the table near Kylie and unfolded the crisp paper.

Sally's
Alley 423
10:30 P.M.
Wile E. Koyote

He read the short note aloud and looked toward Kylie. She remained beside the small table, fiddling with the dead man's key chain and frowning.

"That's from last night," she said. "I'm Wile E. It's one of my online IDs, and that's the place and time we were supposed to meet. I guess now I know why he didn't show. And here I was mad at him for standing me up." The corners of her mouth pulled down, and her dark eyes took on a haze of guilt.

"He was already dead," Dag confirmed. He found himself trying to gentle his normally gruff voice. The female appeared distressed enough without thinking him annoyed with her. More annoyed than usual, that is. "We will have to find a new lead to pursue."

Kylie nodded, not looking at him. Her gaze had dropped to the tangle of keys and baubles in her hand. Instead of setting it aside and joining him in leaving, however, she blinked and peered closer at a thin rectangle of black plastic. Her fingers fiddled for a moment, and a small but powerful light shone briefly from the narrow end.

She made an excited sound. She enjoyed artificial light that thoroughly?

"I have one of these," she said, and attacked the complicated mass of metal and plastic until she had separated the miniature black flashlight from the rest. "I picked it up at a trade show somewhere. Some company had them for a giveaway. It's a mini LED flashlight on this end—" She pressed a small button on the side and the light shone briefly once again. "But on the other end, it's got a portable USB drive with a surprising amount of storage space."

Dag shook his head. "I think this is where I ask you more questions."

She gave a shallow snort. "It's so weird to be talking to someone who doesn't even get basic tech. I need to give you a crash course in digital living, big guy. It's an electronic archive, basically. A small device that stores large amounts of data so you can transfer it between locations and devices." She gazed up at him and lifted an eyebrow. "I wonder what was so important to Mr. Ott that he carried it around with him wherever he went?"

"Take it," he said, glancing around the space. "I am unsure it will prove to have any significance, as I see nothing to indicate that he was deep in the inner workings of the Order. But no other item appears important to our investigation."

Kylie looked dubious. "You can tell that just by looking around? Maybe he didn't like early demonic apocalypse as an interior decorating choice."

He wondered if he would ever get used to a human who questioned his every word or action simply on general principle. In the past, most of them cowered when they saw him, if they didn't run screaming in terror. But not this female. She made *him* want to scream.

"The Darkness is a pollution," he explained, struggling for patience. "Humans who have close contact with it over long periods of time are altered by it. They begin to carry it around with them like an illness, leaving traces of it behind. The places where they spend the most time are usually heavily contaminated with its stench."

She wrinkled her nose. "All I can smell is blood and general stink."

"Exactly. He was not working closely with the Order for long, if at all. He had certainly not participated in any of their darkest rituals. Those actions leave stains that cannot be disguised. Searching him out may yield us nothing we can use."

"Hey, we had to start somewhere."

"True, but we are finished here. Come. We should not continue to linger."

Kylie approached the door, giving the body and the blood pool a wide berth. "What about him, though? We can't just leave him here and pretend we don't know anything. He may have a family somewhere, friends who care about him. They deserve to know he's dead."

He led her outside, engaging the lock on the knob before pulling the door closed behind him. "This dwelling has other occupants. They will begin to notice the smell soon enough."

"Ew. It's still winter. That could take days. Besides, that's just wrong." She shook her head. "I'll send the police an anonymous tip when we get home. I can send an e-mail they won't be able to trace back to me. It's the least I can do."

The alley beside the house and the street out front were deserted as they walked back to the vehicle, for which Dag felt grateful. He hated when his work caught the attention of humans, especially ones who believed they had some sort of authority over him. They had no grasp of what he fought against, and never possessed the necessary training or skill to defend themselves, let alone to face what he and his brothers had been summoned to face.

Kylie's words stayed with him as he folded and crammed himself back into the passenger seat of her torturously small automobile. "Why do you say that? The least anyone can ever do is nothing. To do anything beyond is therefore not the least."

"It's an expression, Gol—er, Dag," she said as she engaged the motor and maneuvered away from the curb. "And it's true. Human beings should treat each other with respect and decency. Which means that if I know of someone who has died and needs to be returned to his family for a proper burial, then I make sure he gets found. It may not be the least that it's possible to do, but it's the least *I* can possibly do."

Her solemn expression and the firm set of her jaw gave evidence that she felt strongly about her words. Dag found that both surprising and fascinating. Through his long centuries of existence, he had dealt most often with only two types of humans, Wardens and *nocturnis*. The first fought evil and protected their fellow man as a sworn duty, not out of deep feelings for them, and the second quested endlessly for dark power, uncaring of who or what they destroyed in their endless and insatiable search. To encounter one who did right because it *was* right counted as a novel experience and made the small female even more interesting to him.

He would need to take care, he realized as they made their way back to Boston, not to let his fascination with the human get out of control. While his brothers might be willing to accept the risk inherent in taking to mate a female Warden who must stand with them to face the latest *nocturni* threat, to Dag the danger was simply too great. He had lived a thousand years with his duty as his sole companion; he could live a thousand more without giving in to the weakness of emotions. It would be better that way.

For everyone.

Chapter Six

"Odem yesoydoy meyofor vesoyfo leyofor," beyne
leveyne iz gut a trunk bronfn.
"Man begins in dust and ends in dust," meanwhile
it's good to drink some vodka.

The Guardian remained silent on the trip back to the
brownstone, but this time the quiet felt different. On the
way over, it had felt as if he were trying to conserve his
strength to deal with her; now it just felt like brooding.

Kylie didn't know what he had to stew about. Not
only had she totally behaved herself on their little field
trip, but she thought the thumb drive currently burning
a hole in her pocket had real potential to at least point
them in the right direction. Once they got home, they
could take a look and move forward from there. She just
wished she could offer him some reassurance more convincing than, "I've got a feeling." So far, he didn't seem
to find those words all that persuasive.

Maybe if she sang him the song from the *Buffy*
musical . . . But no, she wasn't that cruel, and she
couldn't carry a tune in a waterproof bucket.

In the end, she decided the only way to deal with
Mr. Grumpy Pants was to just forget about it. Don't

think about him or his moods and just go on with life the way she would on any other day. Or, you know, any other day when she was hunting for the leader of an evil cult bent on bringing about the end of the world. And who hadn't had one of those, right?

Because Kylie had a generous soul, she didn't ignore Dag completely. In fact, when she swung by her favorite deli to pick up lunch, she even got something for him, too. Pastrami, no less. If that wasn't the act of a selfless woman, she didn't know what was.

She also avoided chattering at him, since he seemed to have no discernible appreciation for the art of conversation. No, he appeared more inclined to take the strong and silent thing to a new level of macho. Honestly, sometimes she wondered about the toxic effects of testosterone in the bloodstream.

When they returned to the house, she headed straight for the office, where she settled behind her desk with a fresh bottle of soda, a crisp dill pickle, and a monument to rye bread and the kosher deli tradition. Dag hovered in the doorway and scowled. It made for a change of pace from the glower.

"Do you never consume a proper meal?"

Kylie paused with half of her sandwich halfway to her mouth. "Do you never take the stick out of your butt?"

He reared back, his expression going from cloudy to tornado warning. "What are you suggesting, human?"

"It means relax, which is some advice I highly suggest you take. You look like a fault line about to crack." She took a huge bite of meat and bread, and stared at him while she chewed.

"And you appear not to be taking our mission seriously," he accused, dropping his own lunch beside hers. Presumably to add greater emphasis to his looming and scowling. "Do you fail to comprehend what is at stake here? Do I need to explain what will happen to you, your family, your friends, your *world* if the *nocturnis* succeed in freeing the Seven from the prisons in which they have been bound?"

Kylie washed down the pastrami with a hit of cola, her own expression turning grumpy. Not only was the Guardian a bad influence, but now he was talking down to her. She hated being talked down to. It went on the list right next to being ignored and losing.

Okay, fine, she had a pretty extensive List. Capital *L*.

"Look, brick boy, I comprehend everything just fine," she snarled, leaning back in her chair, her jiggling foot going still in a sure sign of irritation. "But I also comprehend that pacing around every second of the day grumbling about what might happen isn't a very effective strategy for stopping those things from happening. We have a plan, we have the first clue we were looking for, and we know what our end goal is. To my mind, that means the best strategy is not to get all pissy with each other, but to concentrate on the task at hand until we decide what the next task is. You think you have a better idea?"

"Yes. I will rip the heads of the *nocturnis* from their bodies and throw them into the fires of hell."

"Okay, first of all, ew. And second of all, go for it, stud." She opened her eyes wide and pressed her fingertips to her open mouth. "Oh, wait, that's right. You can't. Because you don't even know where they are. Which brings us back to my point; that the best thing we can do is follow the clues that lead us in their direction. Once we find them, you can get to ripping. I'll avert my eyes."

Kylie watched as the gargoyle struggled with his

anger, his hands balling into fists and the muscle in his jaw twitching like a Mexican jumping bean. She continued plowing through her sandwich, and her foot resumed bouncing. What could she say? She had a weakness for good pastrami.

Abruptly, Dag let out a muffled roar, flashed a bit of fang, then relaxed. "I do not like waiting," he admitted, grabbing the white takeout bag and dropping into King David's chair like a pouting toddler. "And inaction annoys me. To have been denied more than paltry resistance by the *nocturni* scum who attacked you yesterday, and then to be faced with no real target to pursue today has put me out of sorts. Without a battle before me, I am rendered useless."

Okay, that she could understand, even relate to. Kylie hated feeling like her hands were tied, too.

Like she said, it was a big list.

"I get it, but I'd hardly call you useless," she said, crunching into her pickle. She chewed a minute then elaborated. "Of the two of us, you're the only one who really understands what we're up against. I couldn't have gone into Ott's apartment earlier and known right away that the *nocturnis* were gone and that he wasn't very high up in the chain of command. That was all you."

Kylie paused and frowned. "That does bring up a good question, though. It's been bugging me since we first talked to Wynn and Knox. I get that in the cases of the others, the *nocturnis* knew about them beforehand— where the other Guardians were and that the other girls had magical abilities. But I can't figure out why anyone from the Order would go after me. I mean, I didn't know about you guys ahead of time; I didn't really even think of my skills as anything other than nonmagical; and they might have known you were a Guardian ahead of time, but they didn't attack you. They attacked me. What's up with that?"

Dag unwrapped his sandwich, his expression thoughtful. "I had not considered such a question, but perhaps the answer lies in the clue you believe we have collected." He gestured to the thumb drive she had dumped on the desk in her hurry to get to lunch. "If the dead man was indeed a member of the Order, perhaps he was the one who brought you to their attention. If you indicated curiosity about their business, you may have piqued their interest."

"I suppose you could be right." She wrapped up the second half of her sandwich and set it aside. No one had a stomach big enough to finish one of Saul's finest in one sitting. "And I guess that means it's time to get back to work."

Kylie took a long swig of soda, cracked her knuckles, and reached for the thumb drive, plugging it into a free USB port. When her machine recognized the device, she scanned it for viruses (because hello, not stupid) and found it clear. "Okay," she muttered to herself. "Let's see what this puppy has to tell us."

A few key strokes should have brought up the file structure, but instead she got a password prompt. "Security, huh?" She grinned. "Well, we'll see about that, now won't we?"

Rising to her feet, she pushed her desk chair out of the way and crossed to the closet. Dag watched her over his partially devoured lunch. "What is wrong? I thought you were examining the device."

"I am. I'm running a cracker on the password right now," she answered, pulling a large, inflated yoga ball from inside the closet. "But if this turns out to be half the fun I'm hoping for, the chair isn't going to cut it. I'm going to need something bouncier."

His expression told her she continued to baffle him, but then, she baffled most people. Returning to her desk, she positioned the balance ball in place of her desk chair and settled herself on top. The way it bounced and rolled beneath her turned her habitual fidgeting into something productive and worked her core muscles at the same time. Win-win.

Her decryption program continued to buzz through its routine. She knew it could take a while to run through all the possibilities, but waiting patiently so wasn't her shtick. She considered herself a woman of action. Plus, hadn't Wynn and her other new friends decided that her tech skills had a little extra oomph behind them compared to those of the average bear? Maybe she should try to really test that theory.

While Dag continued to plow through his pastrami— wow, he was actually diving into his second half, even with the added challenge of a bag of chips on the side— Kylie took a deep breath and cautiously turned her mental focus inward.

She didn't like to think that she lacked any kind of self-awareness, that she might have missed such a significant part of herself as a latent paranormal ability. It rankled. Then again, how many people in this world actually had paranormal abilities? Didn't it make more sense for a person to assume they got things done based on skill and education rather than on a bippity, a boppity, and a boo? Logically, why would she have chalked her talent for computers up to anything different from any other techhead in the world? She shouldn't have.

But then again . . .

Instinct had always gotten Kylie further than anything else when she ran up against a roadblock in her
programming. Sure she had studied and experimented,
taken classes and read books and learned from other
geeks along the way, but when push came to shove,
Kylie always did whatever her gut said would work best.
And her gut had never failed her.

Right now, her gut was telling her to single out that
set of bits right there. Good. Now rearrange the first and
last sets. Okay. Shuffle three places to the left. Aaaan-
nnnd . . . twist.

The encryption broke.

Usually, when big things happened on a computer,
you were lucky to get a new screen popping up. Maybe
a beep. On really big occasions, possibly a screen flicker.
What you didn't ordinarily see was a flash of red light
and a slowly building swirl of smoke the color of burning charcoal.

Nope, Kylie could honestly say, it was a first for her.
Dag, however, seemed more familiar with the spectacle.

With a battle cry that made the plaster walls of her
office shake, Dag leaped from his chair, spilling the
remnants of his sandwich all over the hardwood floor.
In the blink of an eye, he had transformed into his
natural shape, wings half spread in the confines of the
indoor space, his fangs exposed in a feral expression of
hostile rage. His black, glittering gaze was fixed on . . .

The smoke?

Kylie shook her head, wondering what the hell was
happening. Her wondering only lasted about four seconds, though, because that was how long it took for the
smoke to condense and take shape.

The shape of a demon.

Well, she was calling it a demon, anyway. If this

wasn't what the Guardians meant when they said the D-word, she didn't want to meet a real one. Ever.

Tumbling backward off the ball, Kylie scurried crab-like away from her desk and the giant, noxious thing that currently perched atop it. If her first impression of Dag had been that he looked like the monster from a childhood nightmare, this thing made her rethink that assessment. It shot straight into the realm of night terrors, and if any child on earth had dreamed up something like this, the future of the human race had come into serious question.

It looked not remotely human. Where a hard look could pick out the human in Dag's gargoyle face—and the gargoyle in the human—this thing stood so far removed from her species as to have evolved from an entirely different evolutionary tree. Maybe on another planet.

Where the trees were carnivorous.

Black and hulking, it shone head to toe, or possibly just top to bottom, with a slick, sickly sheen, like an oil spill over black water. The weird texture of its hide meant she couldn't tell if it sprouted fur or some sort of intricate scale pattern. Or both. Or neither. Three glowing red eyes peered balefully from its erstwhile face, the color reminding her of the pool of blood surrounding the body of Dennis Ott, only lit from behind with a malevolent glow.

It hunched over on itself, making its size difficult to discern, but its mass proved intimidating enough given that she couldn't quite identify any real body parts or limbs within the seething maelstrom. One minute she thought it a roiling ball of tentacles, like an H. P. Lovecraft story come to life; the next it looked like some kind of satanic vision, with squat goat's legs and overlong, claw-tipped arms alternating with gigantic clawed pincers along an articulated torso. Then she blinked, and she saw nothing but more swirling smoke, an evil genie popped unexpectedly from an unrubbed bottle.

Maybe her human mind just wasn't equipped to grasp its true form. What Kylie did grasp was that it was evil, and it wanted her dead. You know, after it fed on her immortal soul.

It gargled at her. She didn't know what to call the sound. Part chitter, part growl, part unholy whine, she could only say that it simultaneously made her want to run far, far away, and to cover her ears, stay right where she was, and vomit. She figured it was what the inventors of the bagpipe had been trying for.

Before she could follow either course of action, Dag struck. He repeated that structural integrity-compromising bellow and leaped at the demon like a wolf on a wounded caribou. The creature shrieked right back and twisted, focusing its burning gaze and noxious smell on the Guardian.

Had she mentioned the thing stank like a landfill inside the pit of hell in the middle of August? Because it did.

Kylie backed up against the wall because she couldn't think of anything else to do. Part of her screamed at her to run, run like a gazelle, and get the hell out of Dodge while the creatures before her battled it out. That part made some very compelling arguments. Still, another part of her hated the idea of cowering in the corner like the dumb blonde in a cheesy horror movie, and wanted her to charge the forces of evil with a crucifix and a chain saw. Being neither a Christian nor a lumberjack, however, she did not own either of those things.

She also didn't find the idea of getting in between the

two combatants a very appealing prospect. They tore at each other like a couple of wild dogs, teeth snapping, claws slashing, making noises she knew for certain could never come out of a human throat. Becoming collateral damage from a wild swing of a claw or a misplaced kick to the spine seemed somewhat inadvisable for a woman pretty anxious to make it to her next birthday, which was only a couple of weeks away.

Come to think of it, maybe she was thinking about her eightieth birthday. She'd kind of like to be around for that one as well.

The sounds of battle continued as the two inhuman creatures fought for supremacy. Just when she feared her desk was about to become the first casualty of war, a blur of black rose high in the air and then went sailing across the length of the room to leave a dent the size of Detroit in her library wall. Damn it, couldn't they be more careful?

Not that she didn't cheer a little inside when she realized that Dag had been the one to send the demon sailing, but did he have no idea of how hard it was to find a master plaster worker in this day and age? It wasn't the expense of the repair she minded but the logistical hassle.

The Guardian quickly followed his prey, leaping from the desk and landing directly on top of the battered dark entity. With a thunderous roar, he raised one arm high, then slashed downward, punching a hole straight into the demonic figure's torso. Or where a torso would have been on a human. When Dag drew his hand back, a shriveled black mass about the size of a steroidal grapefruit shuddered and smoked in his palm.

The demon shrieked in pain and outrage, but Dag simply drew back his lips and snarled. Then he took the nasty lump between two powerful hands, dug in his talons, and ripped the thing apart like a warm dinner roll. Immediately, the entity blipped out of existence, and the remains of the black mass burst into flame, then drifted to her floor in a pile of ash.

"*A feier zol im trefen.* A fire should meet him," Kylie muttered, then shrugged. "I suppose where he's going, that's pretty darned likely." She pushed herself to her feet and dusted off her hands. She really needed to settle on a cleaning service to start coming in regularly. "I have to say that's the first time I've come across that particular security measure. I don't think it came from McAfee."

Dag spun to face her, his hands still coated with the ashy remains of the demon, his mind still clearly in battle mode. The bared fangs gave him away real quick. "Are you hurt?"

He practically spat the question at her and looked about three seconds away from stripping her down to check for himself, but she'd heard adrenaline could do strange things to a person, so she didn't snap back. She did, however, put a couple of extra cautious feet between them.

Then she waved a dismissive hand. "I'm fine. You know, as fine as someone can be after discovering the code they just cracked had backup security in the form of a slavering demon."

"That was no Demon." Dag slowly straightened, shifting into his human form. His eyes raked over her as if trying to determine if she'd lied about some injury, but really she was fine. "If a Demon had entered this room, you would not be leaving it. Facing it alone, I might not, either."

Kylie felt a roll of unease. "Seriously? What do you call that thing if it's not a demon?"

"It was a *drude.* Technically, I suppose your kind might call it a demon, as it is a creature born of the darkness, but it resembles a true Demon in the same way a garden lizard resembles a dragon. There is no comparison in power between them."

"*Oy,* well in that case, what are we waiting for? Let's find some Demons. They just sound like fun!"

Dag opened his mouth on a glower, then closed it with a snap. "I think perhaps you used the rhetorical device of sarcasm to express disdain for this idea?"

"Ding, ding. Got it in one."

"I would prefer you to speak directly, and with a little more respect, human. You have a bad habit of treating serious situations with inappropriate levity."

"I see the stick is back," Kylie muttered under her breath as she moved to retrieve her balance ball and return it to her desk. When she'd jumped off, the thing had rolled nearly out the door.

As she settled warily back in her spot she raised her gaze to Dag. "Now, I'm no expert on black magic, but I am an expert on hacking, decryption, and cybersecurity, so based on timing, I'm going to say that there was a booby trap set on this drive. Break the decryption without a special *alakazam* thrown in, and some sort of latent spell is activated, summoning the demon. Sorry, the *drude.* Does that make sense to you?"

"I do not think you summoned the creature, and I certainly had no desire for the encounter, so I see no other explanation," the Guardian agreed with a *hmph.*

"Right. In that case, do you still want to tell me that following up on my informant and bringing back that thumb drive was a dead end, Mr. Pessimist Pants?"

Judging by his expression, Dag liked that nickname even less than Goliath, but at the moment, Kylie didn't care. She felt like she deserved to indulge in a good gloat, seeing as she'd been right and all.

He crossed his arms over his chest and did a fine impression of an unamused and potentially deadly disciplinarian. "That would depend on what we actually find on this device, would it not?"

"Shmulky," she muttered under her breath, turning back to the computer. What a killjoy.

Back to concentrating on her task, she finally pulled up the file structure on the drive and scanned through the titles. Several looked like word processing documents, a few pieces of electronic garbage, a subfolder of e-mail files, a single spreadsheet, and one video file. A picture being worth a thousand words, Kylie clicked on the video.

Her player program launched, and she found herself looking at a poor-quality film that appeared to have not only been filmed by a low-resolution cell phone camera, but that had also been recorded surreptitiously. Nothing else explained the positively painful angle of the image, or the obscuring black blob covering most of the lower left corner of each frame. Honestly, it was too poorly done to chalk up to mere incompetence. No one under the age of ninety was this bad with tech.

The sound quality sucked rocks of equal if not greater size. She spent a few minutes fiddling with light and sound settings, filters and resolutions, but there wasn't much she could do to make it more than marginally audible and visible. She waved Dag over and started the clip from the beginning.

"What do you have?"

"You know as much as I do. It's a video. It was on the drive. Now, watch."

He stood behind her balance ball, and both of them

turned their attention to the monitor. The first few seconds amounted to a lot of shaking and shifting, obscuring both the picture and the sound enough that Kylie couldn't even make out what they were watching. Gradually, the camera holder seemed to relax a little. The shaking didn't stop completely, but she figured he (or she) was just one of those guys (or girls) with a shaky hand, because it settled into a low vibration while the sound began to filter through the speakers.

Kylie could see now that the recording showed a portion of a somewhat crowded room. The lights were dim enough that she couldn't guess at its size or shape, and she realized the only illumination came from actual burning candles. What? Were these jokers some kind of reenactment group obsessed with the Revolutionary War era? It wasn't like Boston didn't crawl with those suckers.

Couldn't be, she decided, because at least a few of the figures on the screen wore thoroughly modern clothing, including the tall one standing in what should have been the center of the frame. The rest of those gathered seemed to be arranged around him, so she guessed this was the guy everyone listened to.

The man wiggled into and out of focus in the poorly framed shot, but Kylie could make out enough to see that he was above average in height and had an average-to-lean build. He wore a gray suit and a bloodred tie, and looked pretty slick, like a lawyer or a businessman, well groomed and well dressed. Pretty ordinary, really. So why was everyone so interested in what he had to say?

Darn it, if she was sitting here watching secret video of an Amway rally, she was going to be really pissed.

The video continued to roll, and for whatever reason,

the microphone finally managed to pick up enough of the speaker's words to provide an audible sound track. Still, she had to lean forward and strain to listen.

"*. . . Masters are unhappy with your current efforts. They have waited too long to be restored to freedom and to take Their rightful place as rulers of this wretched world. And you, children, have failed Them. Each one of you, with each day that passes, you continue to fail Them.*"

Kylie got a bad feeling. She twisted her head to look up at Dag. "Um, are they talking about who I think they're talking about?"

Dag hissed and nodded. That so hadn't been how she wanted him to respond.

"*. . . failures of late cannot be tolerated. I have visited the circles in question and made the displeasure of the Masters clear, but Their restlessness grows. They hunger, my friends, and it is our duty to provide Them with what They need to grow strong and join us in the physical realm.*"

"Which is exactly what we don't want to happen, right?" Kylie murmured.

"*We have been blessed with the presence of Lord Uhlthor now for many months, but His strength is still low, and much was expended in His war against the cursed Guildmen last year. We cannot allow these sorts of setbacks to continue.*"

Kylie shuddered. "So Wynn and Knox were right. That was what killed Bran, that Uhlthor guy. He really is out of jail or whatever."

Dag nodded, his eyes narrow and jaw tight. "So it appears. This confirmation is grave news, but it does offer proof that the Demon is not yet at full strength."

"Why do you say that?"

His gaze shifted to her, fire burning behind the ebony surface. "Because we still live."

And there he went again, demonstrating what a smooth talker he was. Be still, her beating heart.

Or not, since that was what they were all trying to prevent.

The video rolled on.

"Our efforts to weaken the Guild have brought some success, allowing us to summon the first of our Masters from His prison, but the latest reports are disturbing. We have been told that three females previously unknown to our sources within the Guild have appeared and succeeded in waking three of the Guardians. And I need hardly tell you that our Masters find this news greatly upsetting."

She hoped it gave them heartburn. The literal kind that Dag had recently inflicted on the *drude*.

"This is disturbing indeed, but it answers many questions I had over the destruction of the Guild headquarters," Dag murmured, his gaze still fixed on the screen. "Such a feat should never have been possible. If somehow the ranks of the Wardens were infiltrated by the *nocturnis*, it would make the accomplishment much easier to believe."

"Sounds like you were right, then. Do you think that's also how they were able to get to so many of the Wardens? And why the ones who left have been so hard to find? If they really are in hiding and other Wardens had a part in the threat against them, they probably don't know who to trust anymore." She took his grunt for agreement. "We need to let the others know about that as soon as possible."

"Finish this first."

". . . and so when we return, I will share with you all

what the Masters have decreed you might do to aid Their cause and momentarily sate Their hunger. It will require organization and effort, as well as total dedication to our cause, but when we succeed we will not only have restored the Defiler to power, but have freed His Sister from the torture of Her foul prison."

Kylie groaned. "Why do I think he's not talking about some random blonde out at MCI Framingham?"

"Another of the Seven," Dag bit out. "Shaab-Na. The Unclean. It is often referred to as female."

"Oh, goodie."

There was a knocking, shuffling sound and the video cut off abruptly. Kylie cursed and retrieved the file structure. "Crap, that's it? That was the only video. What the hell was their grand plan? What kind of grand plan ends up summoning and feeding Demons to begin with?"

Dag pushed away from the desk and stalked over to glare at the cindered remains of the *drude* left on the floor. Kylie had the feeling he was wishing he could put the thing back together just so he could rip it apart again. Hell, she would even have brought popcorn this time.

"The only way to restore a demon to power, or to lend it enough power to escape from the prison to which it has been banished, is to feed it." His tone was flat and hard, like the pedestal on which he had so recently perched. About as warm, too.

A queasy feeling churned in her stomach. "And Demons eat souls. Right?"

He nodded in a single jerk of his chin.

"Um, not that I really want to know the answer to this question or anything, but how do you feed someone's soul to a Demon? Even more, how do you feed it enough souls to accomplish what those dybbukim were talking about?"

Dag wore an expression of disgust and barely controlled anger as he shook his head. "There are too many ways. A Demon needs only to lay its hand on a human to grasp its soul, and it is the work of seconds to devour it. Sacrificial rites can also channel the soul into an object that stores it until it is given to the Dark one. There are also spells that can trap souls as they depart from dying humans and hold them for a Demon to ingest."

"Okay, so that's three things I never want to see happen." Kylie shuddered. "But it sounds to me like freeing a Demon or giving one enough power to make it strong again would take more than just a couple of souls. At least I hope so. Didn't Wynn say they figured the first one got released when an entire village was slaughtered somewhere in the Middle East?"

"She did," Dag said, looking less kill-y and more thoughtful for a moment. "The Order would need to take that into account."

"Which means they must be planning something big."

Oh, how Kylie hated having to say that. Big sounded really, really not good in this particular context. Like, big plate of challah French toast? Awesome. Big sacrifice to some batshit idiots' demonic overlord? The opposite of awesome, to the nth degree.

"Indeed. We must warn the others immediately."

"Warn them of what?" When he growled at her, Kylie bounced twice on her balance ball and contemplated using a third one to launch herself straight at the grumpy gus's head. Somehow, she restrained herself. "No, seriously," she said. "Warn them of what? That the Order is planning something big? Um, from what I remember of our last conversation, I think that's exactly what they warned *us* about, so I hardly think they're unaware. Until we figure out *what* the plan is, as well as other piddling little details like who, when, and where, we have no new information to share."

The glare he shot in her direction could have peeled paint, which made Kylie doubly happy that she rarely bothered with makeup. His lip curled back, revealing a long fang he should not have been carrying around in human form. *Pfft.* After the last eighteen hours it was going to take a lot more than that to scare her. She'd pulled on her big-girl panties.

Which looked exactly like her other panties, but with a tich more "fuck you" in the elastic.

"What?" She knew she shouldn't taunt the poor Guardian, but somehow she just couldn't resist. This was probably why her *bubbeh* always told her to stay away from tigers with tails. "You know I'm right. You just hate when that happens. Well, get used to it, snookums, because otherwise you are in for a bumpy ride."

He stalked over to her. Her grin lasted about three of his long strides. By the fourth, it had slid somewhere into her stomach along with about a billion gypsy moths. That was also when his big, rough hands closed around her and drew her to her feet.

"I swear by the Light that I will find a way to teach you to hold that tongue, female," he growled and hauled her against him. "Beginning now."

In one fell swoop—and boy, did she have a new and much deeper understanding of that expression now!— his head dipped and his mouth settled over hers with angry determination. Less than a heartbeat later, her smile waved good-bye to the moths and dove right into those panties of hers, proving once and for all that she was, indeed, a very big girl.

Oy, for a thousand-year-old stone statue who'd barely

had time to kill things between naps, let alone to date much, the man could kiss. And kiss. And kiss.

He ate her up with more relish than the bagel and the pastrami combined, seeming to feast on her like Shabbat dinner. His lips felt hot and firm, demanding a response that she had no trouble giving him. She could lose her mind in this kind of kiss, hungry, possessive, and oh so deep.

He entered her mouth and dove straight for her soul, teasing it out with little nips of his teeth and a wicked, taunting tongue. He stroked and sucked and ate at her until she moaned and clutched at him like a drunk on a bender. The comparison seemed apt, given the way her head spun, her balance deserted her, and her skin felt flushed with heat.

More than the kiss had her thoughts in a whirl. Until a few seconds ago, Kylie had been pretty well convinced that Dag hated her, that he tolerated her only because Wynn and Knox had insisted they work together and because he found it unsporting to kill defenseless humans. He certainly spent enough time looking at her like he found her to closely resemble a particularly annoying sort of insect. Like a flea with a vaudeville act, or something. But if this was how he kissed women he hated, she figured the ones he liked must spontaneously combust before he got within ten feet of them.

About three seconds before Kylie figured her socks would start smoking, he finally pulled back and stared at her. It took a few seconds for her eyes to uncross and focus again, but when they did, all she could read from his expression was the same shock and confusion she felt herself. Was a kiss that good a novel experience for him, too?

Dag snatched his hands from her and stepped back, leaving Kylie swaying on her feet like a birch tree in a windstorm. No lie. She actually had to reach out and put a hand on the desk to steady herself while the big lug just stared at her as if she'd been the one to knock him over the head with a lust hammer. How unfair was that?

When the room stopped spinning and her fine motor control finally returned, Kylie cleared her throat and opened her mouth. "Dag, I—"

"I will check security outside. No more *drude* will surprise us this day," he grumbled approximately one-half second before he fled out the door like a scared little girl.

Oh, hell, who was Kylie kidding? She didn't blame him a bit. A few minutes alone to regroup sounded like a mighty fine idea to her. As did a stiff drink, a slap upside the head, and a long, cold shower.

Groaning, she dropped back onto her balance ball, overshot her mark, and landed *tokhes* over teakettle halfway under her desk. Make that two stiff drinks. And she'd pour herself one in just a minute.

Right after she got the feeling back in her legs.

Stupid gargoyle.

Testosterone, she reflected as she stared up at the underside of her desk drawer. Forget the demons; testosterone would be the real death of them all.

Chapter Seven

A klole iz nit keyn telegram; zi kumt nit on azoy gikh.
A curse is not a telegram; it doesn't arrive so fast.

As if the scent of her hadn't been enough, now Dag had
to contend with the taste of her as well. And it was nothing but his own thoughtless fault.

He could not even conjure himself a worthwhile excuse. One moment they discussed the task they had set
out to accomplish, and the next she once again gave vent
to that sharp, impudent tongue of hers, and his control
snapped. He could think of nothing more than silenc-
ing her, of demonstrating to her once and for all that as
a Guardian, he bore the responsibility for the success or
failure of their endeavors, and therefore he would rightly
make the decision of when and how to move forward.

Unfortunately, his unruly instincts had ceased caring
about moving forward on the quest for the *nocturnis'*
defeat. Their only concern had become imprinting his
claim on the young female's smart and sassy mouth, as
well as a host of her other more intriguing bits and
pieces.

This weakness displeased him. A Guardian, like any warrior, must live by his strength, and emotion was a creature's greatest weakness. If he allowed himself to feel affection for another, it set the stage for worry to creep in at a critical moment. A worried warrior could not focus all his attention on his foe, and this opened him to the attacks of his enemy. Even rage could blind a Guardian in a crucial moment, but love was the greatest vulnerability a creature could have.

Love.

He tried to push the word from his mind as he circled the three accessible sides of Kylie's semidetatched home. One common wall shared with the neighboring building gave him pause, but short of knocking on the door and demanding its occupants move out and allow him to take over their space, little could be done to address the concern. He would need to keep a close eye on the situation.

Yet another thing emotion made all the more difficult. How was a warrior to give his full attention to his duties when his thoughts constantly strayed to an aggravating female? He could overlook some subtle threat and thereby place not just himself but all of humanity in jeopardy.

No, a Guardian must remember the stone in which he slept and keep that cool, firm resolution in mind in the face of even the most extreme temptations. Especially when the temptations tasted of mint and spice, butter, herbs, and endless pleasure.

At the end of the deep, narrow alley beside the house, Dag paused and drew in a deep breath. He held it in for a long moment, then let it out slowly and allowed his head to fall back to his shoulders as he struggled to regain the equilibrium that had deserted him for the first time in his long memory. The battle raged within him for endless minutes before he felt his control return. Of course, how long it would last in the face of his female's confusing chatter and wicked impertinence remained to be seen.

No, he would remember his duty and not allow his instincts or his inclinations to threaten his balance. It would be a simple matter of focus and discipline.

Too bad his female seemed incapable of either of those herself.

After a brief pause to assure himself of a cool head, Dag reentered the front of the house and returned to the office. As he'd predicted, Kylie once again sat at her desk, bouncing atop the ridiculous sphere she used in place of a proper chair. She didn't bother to look up when he stepped in the room, merely kept her gaze on her computer monitors and continued with the muffled clatter of rapid typing.

She thought to ignore him? Indignation threatened to rise, but he shoved it down and stomped on it. No emotion, he reminded himself. Her strategy was a sound one, and he would do well to emulate her. Repeating those words to himself, he turned to the only other chair in the room and found it already occupied.

No *nocturni* or human visitor had snuck past his notice, Dag observed, but Kylie had acquired a guest regardless. A large, orange tomcat sat half curled on the battered toile cushion, one hind leg stuck in the air while he industriously cleaned his short, sleek fur. When Dag approached, the animal didn't even bother to pause in his ablutions, just fixed unblinking yellow eyes on the stranger and continued to lick.

"That's King David." Kylie's voice broke the silence, her tone even and carefully neutral. "He comes and goes as he pleases, but when he's here, that's where he sits."

Dag took that to mean that he himself could either stand or go to the devil because the cat was staying put. He supposed that summarized the nature of cats, but it also indicated his little female might have been just as put out by that unplanned kiss as he had been. How he felt about that, he couldn't decide.

He glanced around the space and caught sight of the closet door. If he remembered correctly, Kylie's perfectly serviceable desk chair should still be inside. Crossing to the small space, he pulled out the rolling seat and positioned it beside the cat's current perch. It lacked the toile chair's soft cushions and well-broken-in cozy comfort, but at least it saved him from standing around like a fool in the queen's court.

He wondered if his female realized the significance of giving her cat the title of King. Wouldn't that make her a monarch in her own right? She seemed to have no trouble acting the part.

For several minutes he simply watched and waited, dividing his time between Kylie's green-ringed eyes and King David's furry yellow coat. Both ignored him, even after the cat completed his bath and settled into a sphinx-like pose to relax. It seemed cat and mistress had something else in common—neither appeared particularly impressed by his presence.

After nearly twenty minutes, it became clear to Dag that Kylie had no intention of speaking to him unless it became absolutely necessary. He could only hope that if a demon suddenly appeared at his back, she would at least put aside her irritation long enough to warn him to duck, but just then, he preferred not to chance anything.

When he finally broke the silence, his voice sounded unnaturally harsh, even to his own ears. "Have you found anything else on the device?" He winced when he heard himself, but it was too late to alter what was said.

Kylie stilled, her fingers freezing a hairsbreadth above her keyboard, her gaze still fixed on her screen. It appeared as if she debated the merits of responding to his question or continuing to ignore him, and Dag honestly had no idea which she would choose.

Of course, when she eventually made her decision and turned her dark gaze on him, relief failed to flood through him. She looked at him as if he emitted some sort of odor offensive to her senses.

"I've found several things," she said, her voice still tight and flat, as if she spoke to an irritating stranger. "As I mentioned earlier, there are a number of files saved on the drive in various formats. However, the footage we already viewed was the only video file. I'm afraid we won't get any more information of that kind from this source."

Dag nodded, trying to prevent a frown from pulling at his features. It took a second for him to realize why she sounded so strange to him; it was the lack of spark in her voice. Without the undercurrent of energy and impudence in her tone, she simply didn't sound like Kylie. She sounded like a recorded message.

Something told him not to point that out, though. He thought he remembered seeing a pair of scissors in her desk drawer. Better to be cautious.

He rephrased his question. "What have you found of importance?"

Her lips pursed briefly, then she bounced a few times on her ball and seemed to thaw a bit. He only wished he knew exactly what had precipitated the change so he could do it again in the future. He had the feeling this would not be the only time he angered her.

"I was really hoping for another video, so I checked for hidden files first," she said. "Nada. It's a total WYSI-WYG. I don't think Ott was as tech savvy as he liked to think. Or else he figured the *drude* would eat anyone who tried to get into his files, so why bother being sneaky."

Dag swallowed a sigh and reached for his calmest, most level tone of voice. "Nada?" he repeated. "Wizzy-wig?"

She blinked at him, her expression remaining blank for an instant before realization hit. She truly was unaware of her automatic use of slang and phrasing someone not from her own culture might have trouble understanding. At least he knew now that she didn't do it to torture him.

Or rather, she hadn't done so just then.

"Sorry. I didn't find anything buried or hidden," she explained. "What you see is what you get with this particular drive. So, next I started weeding through the files. E-mails are copies of his conversations with me. He didn't keep as thorough a record as I did, so that's pretty useless. The spreadsheet he set up was the first thing that really caught my attention."

She turned back to her keyboard, set her fingers flying and opened a new document on the screen which she angled to allow him to see it. He had noticed that she used the small palm-sized device next to her typing surface sparingly and had asked her about it earlier. She called it a mouse, and said she could use keystroke shortcuts more efficiently most of the time. Now, however, she used the small pointer icon the mouse produced to highlight areas of the ledgerlike document for Dag to make note of.

"It looks like our friend Dennis was compiling a database of local *nocturnis*," she said, her voice taking on more of the animation to which Dag had grown accustomed. "He has a list of people, mostly men, but evil is apparently not Y-chromosome-linked. Each entry is listed starting with what he calls the person's handle. I can only guess he felt some kind of nostalgia for the days of CB radio when they used them. But I'm guessing a lot of the members of the Order chose to go by an alias rather than a legal name. A *nom de guerre,* I guess you could say."

"This has often been the case. In the past, it proved an effective disguise, as information exchange was much slower and a real identity much easier to disguise."

Kylie nodded. "Yeah, I can see that. Anyway, for some entries he does manage to list a real name. Unfortunately, a lot of them are only partial, either first or last. Usually first. I'm guessing he was trying to ID them all, but it was slow going, so he hedged his bets by also including a short physical description of each person. I'm not sure if that was to jog his own memory, or if he actually started it with the intent of handing it over to someone at some point, but it could prove useful."

"Provided the information is accurate. I would not put it past any member of the Order to create such a document and populate it with false information for the purpose of throwing outsiders off the track."

"I don't know. That sounds like a pretty elaborate red herring, especially when you're going to save the thing on a drive designed to ensure said outsider gets eaten the minute they try to access it."

Dag grunted. "Perhaps. But I find myself unable to trust any information provided by this source of yours. Why would a member of the Order agree to give its secrets away? To do so is not only a risk to the other *nocturnis*, but also a direct betrayal of their Demonic masters. To do so practically invites a hideous death. Why take such a chance?"

"I don't know the answer to that, but I thought Ott's death did look pretty terrible. I mean, we both assumed the *nocturnis* were the ones who killed him. Maybe this was the reason why."

"You could be right. The only way we will know for sure is to verify the information he has provided. Was he able to list full names for any of the *nocturnis* he mentions?" Dag felt a surge of excitement. Perhaps he could use a good hunt to distract himself from his attraction to the female.

"Three. I've already started basic searches on them to see what comes up. I'll let you know as soon as I find something."

He could almost feel his wings rustle with impatience, but he supposed he would have to content himself with her assurance.

"I was just getting ready to open the word processing documents when you came back," she told him. Her gaze darted to the side toward him, but she made no mention of why he had departed in the first place. Good. His control was already stretched thin at times, like whenever he inhaled too deeply and caught a whiff of her intriguing, intoxicating scent. Or whenever his memory strayed back to—

No. He cut that thought off without mercy. He felt no need to test his own resolve so soon. Better to give it time to harden.

Damn it. He had to avoid words like "harden." They proved deeply unhelpful.

Clearing his throat, he leaned slightly back in his

chair. Any increase in the distance between them had to help, right? "Proceed," he instructed.

She shot him a look he felt hard-pressed to interpret. Either she simply wanted to ensure she had heard him correctly, or she visually took his measurements for a funeral shroud. Fortunately, she chose not to enlighten him but went back to work instead.

While she sorted through more files, and he waited in his ergonomically correct yet still-not-as-comfortable-as-the-cat's chair, the feline in question woke from his nap and stretched. A yawn followed, as did the quick pass of a tongue over white whiskers, before King David climbed to the arm of his chair and peered closely at Dag.

The Guardian returned the steady, yellow stare and allowed the cat to assess him. In fact, he returned the favor. He recalled that Kylie had said the cat came and went as he pleased, actually a stray who paid her visits rather than a pet of hers, and its appearance backed that up.

Though the King looked strong and healthy, he also had the look of a cat who had faced a life less pampered than the average housecat. A small piece of cartilage had gone missing near the tip of one pointy ear, and an old scar cut across the cat's face, nearly carving one cheek in half. Whiskers had long since grown in on either side of the silvery line, but directly in its path, no hair grew at all. Large for a domestic cat, the feline likely weighed more than fifteen pounds, Dag estimated, all of it lean muscle.

Well, almost all of it. He imagined it gained at least a pound or two from sheer attitude, just like its mistress.

Whatever the cat thought of Dag, it neglected to share

that information. After a thorough survey, the cat pirouetted on the arm of the chair and leaped to the ground, padding silently across the hardwood floor to Kylie's side. Stretching up on its hind legs, the cat rested one paw against her leg and used the other to bat her arm in silent demand.

Without pausing in her work, Kylie lifted her right elbow up into the air to allow the cat a clear path into her lap. King David took immediate advantage of the opening, jumping up to circle twice before curling up on the female's denim-clad lap. Dag could hear the animal's satisfied purr from several feet away.

Then he heard the hitch in the female's breathing a second before she spoke. "Oh, wow. Dag? I think I might have a clue as to why Ott decided to turn against the Order."

"What do you see?"

"I think they killed his girlfriend."

Kylie had been about seven seconds from running after Dag when he reappeared in her office door. Luckily, the complete inability of her own legs to hold her up prevented that from happening.

It would have set a very poor precedent if she had gone searching for him and attempted to cajole him out of his snit. It might have led him to believe first of all that he held the upper hand in their relationship, which clearly could not be allowed to happen; and even more damaging, it might have indicated to him that he was in the right in this particular situation. Since there was not a right made of lefts in kissing a woman as some kind of twisted punishment, then running off as soon as she got all hot and bothered, Kylie had a duty to ensure he had no chance to interpret things that way.

The problem with this little strategy of hers was that Kylie's personality didn't lend itself to extended snits. Sure, she had a temper, but it tended to flare hot and fast and burn itself out before she had a chance to build up to holding a grudge. She occasionally thought someone deserved to have her carry one with their name on it, but quite frankly, she found it to be a big waste of energy. There were so many more interesting and entertaining things to do in the world. Why would she want to expend all that energy on hating someone when she could just ignore them?

With Dag, she only managed that for a few minutes. Her determination suffered its first crack when he looked as if he intended to evict King David from his chair. Considering that the cat had been sitting in the chair for way longer than the gargoyle, and that the cat hadn't pissed her off in the last few hours, no way was Kylie going to let that happen, so she had been forced to speak to warn him off such a stupid move.

The crack got larger when he managed to ask her the completely civil and surprisingly nonarrogant question of what she had found in the files. Given his history so far, she had expected him to demand that she tell him everything so that he could decide what was important or not, or to simply take over from her and pat her on the head like a good little human. If he had tried it, she had been fully prepared to bite his fingers off. She almost felt cheated when she didn't have to.

But the final crack in her armor of annoyance appeared when King David gave the Guardian his formal stamp of approval. Oh, it was a subtle thing, but the cat had taken a good long look at Dag and decided the warrior would be allowed to stay. From the King, that amounted to a ringing endorsement.

Okay, so King David left a lot of things to subtext, but given that he hadn't bitten, scratched, hissed at, or sprayed urine on Dag, his reaction to the giant male absolutely constituted approval. Other men and women who had ventured into Kylie's house hadn't fared nearly so well in the past.

By the time she had skimmed the contents of the first document Dennis Ott had written and saved on the thumb drive, most of her anger had dissipated. Honestly, she knew the kiss should never have happened. For all intents and purposes, she and the Guardian were co-workers, and even she knew that office romances were a bad idea. Better to keep things on a professional level so that everyone knew where they stood and no one got hurt.

But, damn it, she wanted to be the one to make that mature and logical decision. She didn't want it thrust on her when the one who kissed her went running from the scene of the crime as if he'd just eaten a piece of bad sushi. That was *not* how a woman wanted someone reacting to one of her kisses. She wanted him to burn for her, to be consumed with her memory day and night. She wanted a man to try and move heaven and earth just to keep her safe—

The words jumped off the page at her, and Kylie felt her eyes go wide. Bouncing twice on her balance ball, she called out to the Guardian. "Oh, wow. Dag? I think I might have a clue as to why Ott decided to turn against the Order."

"What do you see?"

"I think they killed his girlfriend."

Dag surged to his feet and shredded the distance between them in one long stride. "Show me," he rumbled.

"This document?" She pointed at the screen. "It's like

a diary almost. Entries aren't dated, but they're all written in the first person and appear to discuss both events in someone's life and that person's thoughts and reactions to those events. Some are only a few sentences, some several pages long. I started at the most recent and scrolled backward, but this name caught my eye." She highlighted "Annie Mulhollow" in a streak of yellow. "I recognized it. It's one of the three full names on the spreadsheet."

Dag pressed one palm against the desktop and leaned in to read the text that filled the screen. "But wouldn't that make the girl a member of the Order?"

"Here." Kylie scrolled forward. "Keep reading."

She followed the text right along with him, but she had already scanned ahead. Those speed-reading classes in grade school had certainly come in handy tonight.

The journal entry read like a cross between a memoir and a manifesto. It began with the story of two young college students, plagued by curiosity and a deep dissatisfaction with the average middle-class lives they had been born to. Although they had every advantage— loving families, places in a respected university, friends, and each other—they still felt as if they should have something more. That inner restless greed had made them the perfect targets for a charismatic upperclassman who promised them not only excitement, but the chance for power and achievement beyond their wildest dreams.

The young man, referred to only as Alistair, had introduced the couple to a secretive and exclusive world that operated in shadows, and whispered seductive tales of wealth, power, and influence that could all be theirs for the taking. All they had to do was join. All that was required was to do as they were told.

When it started, Dennis wrote, it had seemed like a joke, like something out of a movie, all Skull and Bones meets the Hellfire Club. Sure, there were weird, elaborate ceremonies where the established members chanted the names of "demons" and called on the dark ones to grant them power, but no one really believed in any of that stuff, and the benefits rocked.

The "club" provided more than illicit thrills, it chipped in to cover the shortfall when the university raised tuition for the spring semester and Dennis didn't quite have the money to cover the bill. When Annie's car got stolen and wrecked, the club bought her a new one, one ten times better than the one she lost. Plus, the booze and drugs flowed like water, and it was really good shit. Sometimes, after Dennis drank from the ritual chalice, he almost swore he could see the faces of the "demons" his new friends liked to talk about so much.

Everything seemed great, fun, awesome, until the night he and Annie were offered their initiations into the inner circle.

The description of what happened that night provided almost no detail. Indeed, the vagueness of it initially made her frown. Kylie's first question was whether he chose not to describe the event, or whether he could not, because he'd never actually been there. Within a few more sentences, though, she came to an entirely separate conclusion—Ott could not describe the event because what had happened scarred his psyche so deeply, his mind fractured and sealed off the truth in order to preserve the man's sanity.

During his initiation, the secret ceremonies he had previously watched with a cynic's amusement took on a new and terrifying seriousness. The demonic faces

Dennis Ott thought of as products of a drug-induced hallucination became frighteningly real as the cult's inner circle summoned a being they called Master to emerge from the depths and feed upon their offerings.

To the young man this now seemed less an initiation and more a human sacrifice, and he realized that tonight's ritual chalice—the one he and Annie alone had shared—contained a paralytic agent, rendering him unable to move as a creature from a psychopath's nightmares had appeared in a swirling mist above their heads. Its form had not been the scary part. It manifested as a humanoid shape on top, thick mist below, like a cartoon genie. Of course, Disney rarely made the smoke below one of their characters writhe like tentacles or doomed, tortured souls.

Animators also tended not to give their creations eyes that shone with malevolence and hunger, slick like fresh blood, black like old engine oil, and deep like the abyss of hell. If they had, the cartoon industry would have folded like cheap patio furniture.

The creature struck Annie first, lifting her into the nauseating parody of an embrace. It hovered with her high above the ground, opened a mouth full of multiple rows of sharp, blackened teeth, and let out a shrieking cry that seemed to rend the very fabric of reality. As the noise continued, a strange glow began to form over Annie's limp body and slowly spiraled into the Demon's gaping maw. The *nocturnis* continued to chant as the thing fed until the glow abruptly blinked out and Annie fell bonelessly to the ground.

That would have been enough trauma for anyone, but Ott's nightmare was far from over. If Annie had died in that moment, he would have raged and grieved and gone to his death cursing the Order for all he was worth, but things got even worse. Annie did not die. In fact, after a moment of still silence, she gathered herself together and rose calmly to her feet. She slapped at her clothes to remove the dust and debris, then turned and thanked the *nocturnis* for their services.

"Our Master will take the second now," she had said.

Kylie blinked and looked away from the text to meet Dag's gaze. "How is that possible? Can a human being survive having their soul fed to a Demon? Or did it possess her somehow?"

The Guardian's brow furrowed deeply. "It does not appear to be possession, as the author makes no indication that the Demon disappeared from view. If it had entered the girl's body, it would no longer appear to the others in its vaporous form. I am guessing that the Demon took her soul, but left her animus in order that she continue to serve the Order."

"Um, okay. What does that mean?"

"Think of a human as a nut," Dag suggested, which Kylie let slide because now did not seem to be the time for cracking jokes. And look, there went her subconscious anyway. "The shell is the body, the soul is the kernel, and the animus is the husk or bran that surrounds it. When a Demon consumes a human soul, it can devour the insides completely and feed off the animus as well, or it can leave the animus behind and eat only the meat of the soul. With an animus remaining in its body, the human becomes a *tsineh*. It walks and talks and functions much as it did previously, but with no soul it is entirely devoted to the needs and wishes of the Demon who devoured it."

"Oh, ick."

Dag made a noise of agreement. "The question, then, is how did this Dennis Ott avoid the same fate?"

"You're right. I'm guessing 'clean living' is not going to cut it as an answer."

They returned to the text. The answer quickly emerged as one of two options: either Ott's guardian angel deserved combat pay, a Medal of Honor, and an immediate seat at God's weekly poker game; or dumb luck really did favor the mentally challenged. The cops had busted up their party.

"Folg mik a gang," Kylie breathed. "You've got to be shitting me. How does anyone not made entirely of rabbits' feet and lucky pennies get that kind of break?"

Dag pointed at the screen. "Apparently, it happens when they brag to jealous acquaintances about the 'good shit' their private club provides them. And when they deliberately punch a police officer in order to be arrested and removed from the scene."

"Yowza. I suppose that's one way to get out of a sticky situation. Why were none of the others arrested?"

"I suspect that none of the substances found were illegal, either because they used more esoteric ingredients, or because they used magic to eliminate any traces of banned substances."

"Wow. Don't let that strategy get out to the world of professional sports." Kylie scrolled down the page, her gaze skimming over more text. *"Oy vey,* does that really say the guy had himself exorcised? As in, 'I need an old priest and a young priest'?"

"It appears so. That may explain the lack of a taint in the apartment, despite his initial involvement with the Order."

Kylie looked at him, curious about that statement. "You mean the Catholic stuff really works?"

"Not in the way you imply." Dag shrugged. "Any strong faith in goodness can work effectively against the

Darkness. Religious rituals and acts of faith are magical workings by another name. They possess power to affect the world. That does not mean that any one human religion has all the correct answers to the meaning of life. It merely suggests that if this man believed in the power of the Catholic Church to remove the taint of the Darkness from him, he may have influenced the efficacy of the ritual."

"All righty then."

Kylie leaned backward, suddenly remembered she was balanced on her ball, not sitting in a chair, and righted herself with only minimal flailing of the arms. At least she didn't accidentally elbow Dag in the crotch. Though on second thought, it did feel like a bit of a wasted opportunity. She also disturbed King David's nap, to which he reacted poorly. He jumped to the floor with a hiss and stalked away, the tip of his tail twitching all the while.

"Well," she managed. "I'm thinking that this maybe explains why this guy was willing to answer my questions about demons, Guardians, *nocturnis,* and Wardens."

Dag frowned thoughtfully. "Perhaps, perhaps not. It explains his separation from the Order and his negative feelings for it and all it represents, but does it fully account for his remaining alive past his release from police custody? Or his continued collection of information on the group and the decision to share it with a stranger such as yourself."

"Hey, I'm not that strange." She ignored his skeptical look, mostly because she'd seen it before when she'd said similar things to others. "But yeah, I can see it as a motivating factor. Someone sucks the soul out of the person I love, and I'm going to want to bring those sons of bitches down. And I'd take help from just about anyone who offered it."

He appeared unconvinced. "How did you offer to help him, precisely? I was under the impression that you merely asked questions and expressed an interest in certain concepts surrounding the struggle between Darkness and Light."

"Does all that cynicism ever give you heartburn?"

"You have already experienced one attack by a minion of the Darkness. Do you truly wish for another?" He stared at her with those burning black eyes of his until she wanted to check her skin for burn marks. "You are in danger. Until we know the source of the threat we cannot assess its gravity. Would you prefer to be taken unawares?"

Kylie glared at him. "I thought you didn't approve of sarcasm, Rock Hudson."

He ignored her and gestured to the computer screen. "We must assume that this human was intelligent enough to hide from the Order after he escaped their clutches. One who had seen so much of their operations would never be allowed to live unless fully indoctrinated and devoted to their cause."

"You're right." Kylie considered that, her lips pursing as she thought. "That makes me wonder if Dennis Ott was his real name or some sort of alias. If I wanted to avoid a group of crazy psychopaths who knew my name and all the other pertinent details of my identity, the first thing I would do is change my name. I'd also leave town pretty quick, but if he did want some kind of revenge on the Order, he may have felt sticking around offered him the best chance at bringing them down."

"He had no chance of 'bringing them down' as you

say. The Order predates him by thousands of years. If my brothers and I have not managed to destroy it by now, he had no hope of besting our attempts."

"So he was an optimist. A naïve, totally-out-of-his-depth optimist, but still. It doesn't really matter to us who he was before he got mixed up with the *nocturnis*, I'm assuming, but if you're interested, I can see if I can find anything on his real background."

Dag shook his head. "That is unimportant. What matters is that even though he made an effort to hide from them, the Order still found him and killed him. If he was equally careless in concealing his connection to you, it would explain why the *nocturnis* are already looking for you. If they believe he shared his knowledge with you, they will not like leaving a loose end untied."

Oh, wow. Kylie hadn't even thought of that. "Um, maybe I should stop procrastinating and go ahead and order that home security system I've had my eye on . . ."

"Any measures you take to increase the security around you are worth exploring, but relying on mundane human methods would be folly. I will begin regular patrols around the building and will take full charge of your whereabouts at all times."

She couldn't say she liked the sound of that; to her it smacked too much of the life of a prisoner. On the other hand, she liked the sound of dying from a knife to the throat and the gut even less. "I guess we'll be busy for the next little while, then, huh?"

"Very." Dag looked grim. "In addition to doing what must be done to increase your safety, we still have unanswered questions raised by the contents of this device. Who was the man in the video recording? Based on his words, both what he said and how he said it, I believe there is a possibility he may have been, if not the Hierophant, then one very close to the ruler of the Order."

A surge of excitement raced through her and Kylie sent up a quick prayer. "Oh, please let it be that easy!" She called up a new program and did a few quick fiddles, capturing a screen shot of the man's blurry image and saving it as a separate file. "I got the film as clean as I was able to, but I know a guy who's an expert with imaging. If anyone can do something to get a recognizable face from this *shmuts,* it's him. I'll shoot it his way and see what he can do."

The Guardian grunted his approval of the idea. "Good, but there is more. How are we to discover the details of this grand plan the *nocturni* mentioned? Clearly we must put a stop to anything that could raise so much power for the Seven. Both for the greater good, and for the sake of the hundreds of lives that would be lost."

Kylie sent her e-mail to Vic, the wonder imager, zipping through the ether, then returned her full attention to Dag. "No, you're absolutely right. Whatever it is, we need to stop it, which means first off, finding out what 'it' is. There are still a couple of files on here that I haven't gone over yet. It's possible they could tell us, or at least point us to where we can look for more info."

"Digging deeper only increases the danger to you, and by extension, the larger cause."

She scowled. Seriously, the guy was a bad influence. "Are you saying we don't look? That we just let it happen?"

"Of course not. But perhaps it would be safer if you did as the other man did not and left this city for a different location, one where you would be harder to find."

"That's a joke, right?" Kylie knew the answer to that, but he needed to hear how ridiculous his suggestion sounded. "First of all, no frickin' way. Second of all, what? You're just going to send me away somewhere where I *won't* have my very own Guardian watching my back? Are you going to paint a target on it, too?"

"Do not be ridiculous. You could travel to the home of the witch. She is your friend, and my brother would guard you just as I would. You would be safer away from here."

"I call that *blote*. Bullshit. All I would be is away. Safer's got nothing to do with it. If they want to find me, they're going to find me. If you really want to keep me safe, you'd be better off bringing Wynn and Knox here where they can both help guard me and maybe teach me to better guard myself. I'm a Warden now, right? Well, I'm not going to be a very good one until someone shows me how."

When he opened his mouth to protest, she bounced right up off her ball and got up in his face. Or as close as she could be from more than a foot below it. "And you can add all that fine, rational logic of mine to this: I flat refuse. You want me out of here, you'll have to drag me out, kicking, screaming, and plotting in my head the quickest way back. I don't like taking orders, and I *hate* being treated like a child."

Number five on the List, actually.

By the time she finished her little speech, she stood before him on the tips of her toes, leaning so close that her chest nearly mashed itself up against his. She had her shoulders pulled back, her eyes narrowed, and her chin practically pointed at the ceiling. Her hackles were raised, her back was up, and frankly, she was a little surprised that smoke didn't seem to be pouring out of her ears, because she was mad, she was determined, and she was all worked up into an epic case of *shpilkes*.

Then she blinked and got a good look at Dag's expression.

All of a sudden, the *shpilkes* became tingles and dropped down to concentrate in a very specific place—namely, right between her thighs. What did it say that every time the two of them worked each other up, Kylie's mind turned immediately to sex?

And her mind still lagged about three steps behind her body, it seemed, which for the first time in her life was working more slowly than someone or something else.

The tension between them could not be cut by a knife. Kylie guessed it would require a chain saw at the very least. Maybe a laser torch. Dag's black eyes had turned nearly red, so brightly did the fires that normally flickered within now burn. She felt pinned in place, breathless and aching, and damn him for being the cause of it all.

For the span of several pounding heartbeats, she waited for his hands to close around her, for his mouth to crash down once again and consume her the way he had just a few hours ago. She could feel the crackling energy of lust sparking between them and knew anything could happen at any moment. Any. Thing. At. All.

But she wasn't expecting the roar.

Throwing back his head, Dag released a roar even louder than the battle cry with which he had greeted the *drude*. This time, her plaster actually did crack, a small section of it raining down from the ceiling even as the Guardian spun and shot from the room faster than the sound could travel.

Kylie stood there and watched him go, a light coating of dust in her hair and a vow to get even growing in her heart.

So Mr. Rocks for Brains thought he could just walk out on her every time things between them got a little heated? Oh, he would learn the truth, and Kylie T. Kramer would teach it to him, one day very, very soon.

She hoped he took notes, because it was going to be a long and thorough lesson.

Chapter Eight

Di velt iz sheyn nor di mentshn makhn zi mies.
The world is beautiful but people make it ugly.

The second time Dag disappeared, he didn't return for hours. Oh, he didn't really *go* anywhere. Kylie could occasionally see him through the windows as he paced around the house, covering all three sides in a uselessly repetitive patrol. More than once she considered going online and buying him one of those big, furry hats the ceremonial guards wore at Buckingham Palace, but when she found herself fantasizing about places to put it other than his head, she decided against it. She doubted he'd stand still long enough for her to lodge it where she really wanted to.

In the end he stayed outside until she gave up and dragged her ass upstairs to bed way earlier than usual. Apparently finding a dead body, being attacked by a minor demon, kissing a gargoyle, and then doing hours and hours of esoteric research could really take a lot out of a girl.

The next morning set a new pattern for the week.

After informing her stiffly that he had indeed decided to summon Knox and Wynn to join them in Boston, Dag had spent the rest of that day and every following one performing a disappearing act that would have made David Copperfield proud. He never went far, but he always seemed to find something to do outside, in another room, or as far removed from her presence as possible. Kylie started to wonder if someone had tampered with her shower gel and slipped some *eau de skunk* in there while she wasn't looking.

The few times he did deign to speak with her, it always revolved around his "security" concerns. The first words out of his mouth every time he so much as glanced at her were to inquire whether she'd called the alarm company yet, until she did just to get him off her back. The man could teach her *bubbeh* about nagging.

It wasn't as if Kylie hadn't always intended to have a security system installed, she just resented being ordered to do it. In this day and age, property crime was a concern not to be taken lightly, and her lawyers kept telling her that a woman with her money needed to be even more conscious of personal security than the average person. Kylie tended not to think like that, because to her, the money wasn't a big deal.

Okay, so she was worth more at twenty-three (about to turn twenty-four) than most people were after a lifetime of work and savings, but to her the money that resulted from her work was a total afterthought. It was the work itself she cared about.

When she'd written the app that eventually earned her millions, she had just wanted to see if she could fix a tech problem that bugged her. She hadn't intended at that point to drop out of college, let alone to be bought out and eventually hired by the very company whose product she had improved upon; that had just happened. And for her, the money was convenient. It meant she could buy a house in a neighborhood she liked, that she could decide what to work on based on what interested her, rather than any other criteria, and it meant she could buy herself a few cool toys when she felt like it.

Really, though, Kylie was a woman of simple needs. She didn't care about clothes or cars or keeping up with the Kardashians. She had the taste and appetite of a thirteen-year-old (her mother disdainfully amended that to a thirteen-year-old hoodlum, meaning anyone without a trust fund), didn't travel much because she always had something fascinating to work on at home, and the only person she had to support was herself.

Still, every time she talked to her accountant or her lawyers, they felt the need to harp about the fact that her story of being not just a successful woman, but a wildly successful *very young* woman in a male-dominated field had earned her enough publicity that she needed to be cautious. If only they knew what she'd gotten into now.

So, installing a security system wasn't a big deal, and the long-term accumulated nagging meant she had already done all the necessary research and selected both the provider company and the system she wanted long before an actual threat had come on the scene. Her address and the cost of her purchase even assured that the company got her an installation appointment that very week, the day before Wynn and Knox were scheduled to arrive. Kylie just hoped she could learn to use the thing in time to let them in the house without sirens waking the neighbors.

The alarm company crew of four men arrived early on Thursday morning. Well, early for Kylie anyway, who still operated on hacker time. Having to drag her *tokhes* out of bed and be presentable for company by ten did not make her a happy camper. Nor did the way Dag appeared the moment the men arrived and proceeded to hover over her like a badly trained guard dog while the crew went about their work.

"Will you please lighten up?" she demanded as she leaned against the kitchen counter and sipped her soda. At that moment, two of the techs were working in her office, wiring the window alarm and laying the groundwork that would allow her computer system to sync with and control the security as a central hub. They had strict instructions to get everything ready, but *not* to touch her computers or other electronic equipment until she was present and could set up the interface herself. No one touched Kylie's babies but Kylie.

"No," Dag growled. "I will not relax until this work is complete and these humans have been escorted off these premises. I am uncomfortable with so many strangers in the house."

Kylie rolled her eyes. "You realize this was all your idea, right?"

"That makes no difference in my reaction to four strange humans wandering about this space unsecured."

"Well, admitting you're irrational is the first step, I hear."

The low rumble of his growl vibrated through the marble behind her. Kylie ignored it. Frankly, the last five minutes had encompassed more communication than he'd managed with her over the last five days combined. She might just as well have dragged his sorry-assed statue form into the house with her for all the company he'd provided. King David had offered her a better conversational partner.

Kylie looked over when one of the workers peered in

from the door to the hall. "Excuse me, ma'am? I need your approval before I drill to install the front door control panel."

"Right." Kylie set her soda bottle on the counter behind her and rubbed her condensation-covered hands against her jeans. "Coming."

Dag followed so close on her heels he might as well have asked for a piggyback ride. Just as she was about to turn on him and potentially take his balls for hackysacks, another worker approached from the office.

"Uh, I'm about to run the wire through to the computers, but someone said something about not messing with the setup already there. Do one of you want to supervise while I do this?"

The worker didn't bother to hide either his disgruntlement at his work being second-guessed or his boredom with the tedium of his job. Charming fellow. Beside her, Dag growled, crowding her back against the partial stairway wall as if unable to decide which of the jumpsuit-clad menaces from Beanpot Security and Electronics was the most likely to whip a demon out of his back pocket and wave it at her.

Oy, if she had to roll her eyes at him again, she was going to sprain something.

Patting his chest, she transitioned the reassurance into a quick shove and stepped away from him. "Okay, big guy. You go with the fellow by the scary front door, which I haven't been allowed within twenty feet of since the weekend, and I'll go back to the office to make sure Prince Valiant over there doesn't hurt my babies. If another *drude* materializes out of thin air, I promise to scream real loud and high-pitched so you can come save my delicate female *tokhes.* Okay?"

Not waiting for a response, because when one came,

she knew she wouldn't like it, she nudged the Guardian toward the front door and turned to head back to the office. As soon as Wynn arrived, Kylie was going to either enlist her help to stage a jailbreak, or have the biggest, alcohol-fueled bitchfest ever recorded. No other way could she think of to cope with Grumpy McGrumperson for another solitary minute. She'd lose her mind.

She stepped into the office behind the slightly stocky and visibly scruffy security technician and surveyed the scene. Ignoring the bare patch in the ceiling left the other day by Dag, the company seemed to have done minimal damage to the plaster. A couple of small, neat holes indicated where they had inserted wire and fished it through the walls, but overall, Kylie was pleased at the lack of significant destruction.

Not that the room didn't look like an electronics bomb had gone off in the middle of it, because it did. Bundles of wires and spools of cables lay piled on the floor, the desk, and most other available surfaces. Tools and equipment spilled out of a large open bag and sat piled near a partially open window, and three boxes of new components lay open in the middle of the floor.

In the midst of it all, Kind David lay in his fur-covered chair with his paws curled under him and his slitted gaze fixed on the scene. He must have decided the job required close royal supervision, because generally he never stuck around when strangers came to the house, especially not several of them at once. Least in sight was one of his favorite games.

"Okay," Kylie said, resting her hands on her hips and surveying the area around her desk just to make sure no one had gotten overexcited and touched her equipment. "Why don't you tell me where you're at and we can go from there?"

When the tech didn't answer immediately, Kylie looked up to find him standing not by the bundle of cable where she'd last seen him, but less than two feet away from her. He still had the cable in his hands, but now he held a length of it in between his beefy fingers like a garrote, and when her eyes met his, she could see the crazy in them. They looked black and cloudy and entirely glazed over.

He lunged at the same instant that she screamed and threw herself backward to escape imminent strangulation. She heard a loud crash from the hall, a curse from her attacker, and a fierce yowl from King David, but she had no idea which came first. Everything seemed to unravel into chaos and her only thoughts weren't even real thoughts; she operated purely on instinct, throwing herself on top of the balance ball that had been pushed aside near her desk, rolling off the top, and using her legs to propel it into the crazy technician's path.

The tech kicked the ball away, the force of impact sending the inflatable sphere of rubber bouncing off half the vertical surfaces in the room. Every time it pinged and ricocheted, Kylie felt the hysterical urge to giggle. It almost made her feel as if she were featured in one of her Coyote namesake's cartoons. Any time now, someone was going to come out with a "Meep! Meep!" and she was going to lose it.

With the giant ball out of his way, the tech moved faster, cornering her in the space below the other, unopened window and laying his length of cable against her throat. Before he could exert any pressure, though, a golden blur flew into the picture and plastered itself against the man's head. He screamed and jerked back, and Kylie could see an enraged King David hanging onto the technician's face with tooth and claw.

The cat had puffed himself up to nearly twice his normal size, and his tail whipped back and forth like a cobra on meth while he proceeded to try and dig his way inside her attacker's skull. Judging by the blood and screaming, he might even be making some decent progress.

And her lawyer had told her to get a dog. *Pfft.*

Kylie scrambled to her feet, preparing to dart past the fracas into the hall and immediately to Dag's side, when the mountain figuratively came to Mohammed. Dag appeared in the doorway, skin gray, fangs bared, and humanity nowhere to be seen. Since no other tech accompanied him, either he had already killed them, or seeing him in his natural form had scared the unsuspecting workers to death. In the moment, she didn't really care which.

She immediately threw herself in his direction, wasting no time in protesting when he all but shoved her behind him. That was exactly where she wanted to be, so he wouldn't be getting any arguments. Not about this. She even had the foresight to cover her ears when he let out another of his roars, although she did glance up at the ceiling to make sure she had time to dodge any falling plaster. Luckily, this time the ceiling held.

The tech finally managed to pry King David from his face and threw the feline across the room. The cat sailed into the open closet door and thumped hard against something inside. Kylie heard another yowl and cried out in response. *Oy,* but she hoped he wasn't seriously hurt. As soon as Dag finished kicking this *roseh*'s ass, she was taking a shot of her own and then rushing the King to the vet.

Just hold on a few more minutes, bubeleh, *and I'll*

get you all taken care of. I promise. She just wished the cat could read her mind.

Dag, it appeared, didn't need to. On this, at least, they seemed to be of one mind: stomp this *kuppe drek* into next week, then have cookies and milk.

It didn't quite happen that way, though, because the minute Dag laid a hand on the tech, the guy gave a high-pitched shriek, his eyes rolled back into his head, and he wilted like a debutante in a whorehouse. He collapsed into a heap, held off the floor only by Dag's claws fisted in the front of his jumpsuit.

Then, of course, Dag let go, and the tech and the floor got much better acquainted.

Kylie stared for a moment, half expecting the guy to jump back to his feet, grin and quip, "Just kidding!" and get right back to the fight. Didn't happen, though. He stayed unconscious, and Dag continued to look as if he'd just bitten into a knish filled with rancid earthworms.

Cautiously, she eased a few steps forward and peered around the Guardian to the limp figure at his feet. "Uh, not to be a kibitzer, but any idea what just happened here?"

Dag sneered down at the tech and clicked his talons together in a gesture of frustrated violence. "This one is no *nocturnis*. Just a filthy pawn in their games."

Kylie blinked at that assessment and quirked an eyebrow. "Really? So he tried to kill me just because he doesn't like to work on Thursdays? That seems a bit of an overreaction."

"The attack came from the Order, but they used an innocent to make it happen." His gaze scanned the room and caught sight of the half-open window in the corner. "They must have been watching the house. When he opened the window, they seized the opportunity to cast a spell. They hexed him, bringing his mind under their control and commanding him to kill you. And they nearly succeeded."

"They can do that?" Even Kylie thought she sounded horrified, but that was nothing compared to how she felt inside. "If they can force any innocent bystander to take a shot at me, I'll never be able to leave the house again. I won't be able to trust anyone."

"You can trust me." Dag closed the window, then returned to loom over her, his expression solemn, but lacking the deliberate blankness he had shown her for the past week. "I have sworn to protect you. You can trust Knox, as well. As a Guardian, he too would be able to break the hold of the Order on one such as this and end the spell. And if your friend the witch has even half the talent of a trained Warden, you can trust her, too. She will recognize the danger and act accordingly."

Kylie shook her head. "I wasn't thinking about you. About them. Of course I can trust them. But what about the other techs? Maybe you were right. Maybe letting them inside was a bad idea."

And didn't admitting that chap her ass a little? Kylie hated to think that Dag's paranoia had been closer to the mark than her own laissez-faire confidence. It would be a long time before she felt comfortable allowing another worker into her house. Maybe she could learn to view those cracks in the plaster as character features.

"No." She could hear his reluctance to admit it, but he forced the word out nonetheless. "The system is a good addition to ensuring the security of the house and everyone in it, especially with the others coming. If these humans did not come to install it, others would

have. It must be done, and none of the others were af-
fected by the hex."

"How can you be sure?"

He hesitated, and for a moment, Kylie almost thought
he looked . . . sheepish?

"When I heard you scream, I became concerned for
your safety, so I gathered the other three and left them
bound in the empty room near the kitchen."

"You tied them up and left them in my dining room?
Dag, one of them is going to get free and call the cops
on us!"

She hurried out of the room and headed in the direction of the Guardian's captives only to have him stalk
after her, shifting his form on the go.

"I made certain they were unconscious," he protested.
"I am not foolish."

"Oh, so you knocked them out and left them tied up
in my dining room. That's going to make the police so
much happier. Happy to add more charges, you *shlemil*."

"I do not know the meaning of that word, but your
tone indicates it was not complimentary." He followed
her into the dining room, but took her arm before she
could rush over and unwrap the still figures from about
three thousand feet of plastic-coated wire. "The humans
are unharmed and will remember nothing when they regain consciousness. Do you think that in the thousands
of years of our existence, Guardians have never had
to deal with humans seeing us and jeopardizing our
secrecy?"

Okay, that eased her panic. A little. "Fine, but they
still need to be untied before they wake up, right?"

"I can see to it in a moment. First, I need to know if
you sustained any injury."

Confused and impatient, Kylie shook her head. "I'm fine. King David—*A broch!* King David!"

Kylie tore away and flew back to the office, heading straight for the closet where the cat had been thrown. She found him struggling to free himself from a tangle of hoodies she had stacked inside for cold days. She reached for him, earning herself a sharp hiss, followed by a plaintive mewl when he realized who she was.

"Oh, *bubeleh,* I am so sorry," she crooned. "Come here, *boychik.* Let me see what that mean man did to you." The sudden dimming of the area told her that Dag had followed and stood in the doorway, blocking the light from the room. "The tech threw King David in here after he jumped on his face and nearly clawed his eyes out. I need to get him to the vet and have him checked out. If he's hurt, I'm going to rip that *nishtgutnik*'s *putz* off and feed it to him."

She finally managed to untangle the cat and picked him up, cuddling him briefly to her chest. He endured the affection for a moment, even head-butting Kylie's chin and purring before squirming out of her grip and dashing toward the nearest exit.

"*Bubbee,* wait," she called after him, scurrying to follow. Dag put a hand out to stop her.

"The cat seems fine. It moved with no sign of pain or stiffness and easily covered the distance to the door at a run. I believe it objects to the idea of a physical examination. Much like someone else I could name."

Worried and irritated, Kylie snapped her reply. "I already told you I'm not hurt, stone face, so lay off. I really don't think now is the time for you to decide you're ready to play doctor."

Dag stiffened beside her a split second before the unintended double meaning to her words registered with

Kylie. She felt her cheeks go hot and shouldered past him to return to the captives in the dining room.

She cleared her throat. "What I mean is, the guy barely laid a hand on me. I jumped out of the way as soon as I saw the look on his face, not to mention the wire in his hand. And King David attacked him before he was able to do me any harm. So I'm fine. No need for a physical exam. From a doctor. Or anybody else, really. I'm good. All systems go."

"You are babbling," Dag observed, his words thoughtful. "The idea of an examination makes you uncomfortable? This makes me believe you are being untruthful about your lack of injury."

"No, really. I'm not bleeding, I'm not limping, my pupils are evenly dilated, and I'm having no trouble breathing. Satisfied?"

"You cannot see your own eyes react to changes in light, so how can you be certain about their dilation?"

Kylie ground her teeth together. "Do you really think I got a concussion from running and screaming?"

"You are the one who raised the possibility, not I."

Oy gevalt! God give her strength.

She took a deep breath and tried not to push it out with all the hissing force she had built up. "For the last and final time, I am unhurt. If my status in this regard should change at any time, I promise on my grandmother's life that I will inform you immediately. Without passing go, without collecting two hundred dollars. Now, if you don't mind, I think the more important task at hand is to untie the guys in the other room before one of them wakes up and thinks they've been kidnapped by the crazy Jewish lady and the big scary guy who talks like he's definitely not from around here. Mmkay?"

Without waiting for his reply, she spun on her heel and marched down the hall and the devil take the hindmost. Her mouth twisted into a frown as she patted her hip and realized she had left her phone back in the office so she couldn't check the time. She needed to know exactly how many more hours it would be until Wynn arrived.

Then she needed to go online and see if there were any liquor stores in the greater Boston metropolitan area that either delivered, or were staffed by employees open to a little judicious bribery. This jailbreak/bitchfest was going to require something a whole lot stronger than the couple of bottles of wine she had stowed in the kitchen.

Like vodka, maybe.

Or tequila.

What was rotgut, anyway? Kylie had always been curious.

Or, hey, did anyone in Boston sell moonshine?

As soon as the workers had been freed, Dag found himself battling against the need to disappear somewhere far, far away from his little human female. He needed space, lots of space, and time away to deal with the reaction he had experienced when he realized she had been attacked once again.

The sound of her scream of mingled fear and anger would echo inside his mind for the next thousand years. At least. He had stood beside the male human, watching as he marked and cut the opening to install the high-tech security control panel near the house's main entrance. One moment, he had felt nothing but boredom and the restless need to hurry this process along so that he could clear the premises of the strangers he had been forced to allow within his territory. The next, his ears had registered Kylie's scream, and his mind had exploded in a white-hot lightning storm of rage and terror.

Someone was threatening his female. The creature would have to die.

For the first time in his existence, his change had taken him by surprise, muscles and tendons stretching and snapping as his body reshaped itself into his natural form without his choice or consent. The human at his side had uttered a hoarse cry, then promptly passed out at Dag's feet. The action had been enough to remind the warrior to first secure the area, but taking the three minutes required to capture and secure the three workers had nearly cost him his sanity. The moment he dumped them in the empty dining room, his instincts would no longer be denied. They drove him immediately to Kylie's side.

He barely remembered the sight that had greeted him as he flew through the office door. A red mist obscured his vision, and all he had been able to pick out was the sight of Kylie huddled in a crouch beneath the window. The fact that her eyes were wide and animated and that he could see the rapid rise and fall of her chest were the only reasons why the house around them remained standing.

The feral temper inside him had urged him to seize the male and rip his head from his shoulders. He wanted to taste the man's blood, to see the life drain from his eyes, and to know that the foul piece of shit realized that in seeking to harm Kylie Kramer, he had actually sought his own death.

It took a moment for the sight of the cat clinging to the human's face to register, and for a split second, Dag envied the cat the ability to sink the points of his claws into the man's flesh. He could almost feel the soft parting of skin and muscle, the click of talon against bone, but then the human wrested the cat from his head and flung it across the room. Dag had gotten one glimpse of the man's glinting, darkly clouded eyes in the instant before his fist grasped the front of the uniform jumpsuit, but as soon as it felt his touch, the spell on the man shattered. The demonic influence winked out, and left Dag holding a confused, terrified, and cowardly victim of the same attack that had threatened his female.

He threw the man down in disgust and hurried to Kylie's side. Where he, of course, was greeted not with gratitude, or even an understandable accusation based on his failure to prevent such an attack, but with calmly delivered questions and the sass to which he was quickly becoming accustomed.

This did not mean he approved. He disliked the sensation he seemed always to have in her presence of being somehow off balance. A new experience, it made him question his ability to anticipate danger—hadn't he missed the threat of the *drude* and again of the hexed worker until each had nearly succeeded in harming his female? How could he guarantee her safety if being near her created such distracting turmoil within him?

Definite turmoil. Among other things.

He struggled against a flood of unfamiliar emotion every time he drew near to the small human, unfamiliar for more than one reason. For centuries, he had believed that his kind lacked the capacity for the relentless current of feelings that seemed to plague the mortal world. He experienced only the emotions suited to his purpose—rage at his enemy, determination to win victory, hatred of the Darkness, loyalty to his cause. No other had been allowed to distract him, but he could not recall when anything had tried. Yet now, the addition of one tiny mortal female into his presence had shaken the very foundations of his identity. How could he remain a Guardian when all he truly cared about guarding now was Kylie?

Dag brooded over the question throughout the afternoon and long into the night. He sought meaning in the change and found his thoughts returning again and again to the same point, to the conclusion that he had avoided since that first conversation with Knox and Wynn.

Perhaps Kylie was meant to be his mate.

For centuries, the legend had mocked him. He knew of no Guardian in millennia who had been freed according to the stories of the first of his kind. It had become a fairy tale among the brethren, and Dag had dismissed it as easily as any other story meant for children and fools. He would live forever in service to the Light unless an enemy managed to destroy him first, in which case a new Guardian would be summoned. No other option existed, certainly not that a woman of power would come before him and free him from his magical sleep forever. It had seemed not just improbable but entirely impossible.

Until Kylie.

The idea that he could have been so wrong disturbed him. It pointed toward the kind of mistake that could get a human or a Guardian killed, and hadn't that very thing nearly happened twice? Perhaps the only way to combat the problem was to give in to it.

That idea had his instincts rumbling a satisfied noise that reminded him disturbingly of King David's loud purr. The instant that he entertained the thought, something inside him settled and he felt a sense of calm like nothing he had ever experienced. It was as if something had clicked into place within him, a piece he hadn't known was missing yet whose absence had kept the whole machine from operating at peak efficiency.

A fresh wave of energy flooded him, strength reinvigorated his body, clarity at once settling over his mind. It felt as if Fate had simply been waiting for him to see the truth, and now that he had admitted it, he could once again become everything he had always been meant to be.

Guardian, protector, warrior.

Mate.

A smile of satisfaction crept over his features, then just as quickly drained away. He had just accepted the fundamental truth that Kylie Kramer was meant to be his, but one question still remained.

How was he going to break the news to her?

Chapter Nine

Az men est khazer, zol khotsh rinen iber der bord.
If you're going to eat pork, get it all over your beard.

It took the security company a good half hour to regain consciousness and another few minutes for their brains to reset so that none of them spent too much time wondering where the last hour or so had disappeared to. Plus, Kylie needed some time to come up with an explanation for the scratches and puncture marks all over the face of the one who had attacked her.

Scattering pieces of broken glass beside him and leaving an exposed electrical wire hanging out of his hand turned out to be the best she could come up with. She explained that he had accidentally electrocuted himself, knocking over a vase that fell on his head and accounted for his wounds. The fact that he accepted this at face value made her wonder if the hex the *nocturnis* had put on him had left the poor fellow with permanent brain damage.

Even with the delay, the crew managed to finish the installation in one day, if you didn't bother to note that it was full dark by the time they cleaned up behind themselves, loaded up their van, and drove off into the night. Whatever the bill turned out to be, Kylie figured she still wouldn't be paying them enough.

Did they have a bonus clause in case of attack by evil Demon-worshipping magic users? If not, they might want to look into that.

Dag's first reaction to having the house empty again had been to prowl through every inch of it—from attic to basement and everywhere in between—checking the locks on each point of entry, be it window, door, or (probably) magical portal. Honestly, she wouldn't be surprised if he reacted to finding a mouse hole by demanding the rodent inside provide proof of identity and swear an oath that it was not now, nor had it ever been, a member of the *nocturni* party.

Kylie left him to it and took a few hours to play with the new toy, experimenting with camera feeds, security settings, and alarm tones before finally calling it a night. Another attack meant another early bedtime. At this rate, someone was going to take away her membership card to the UberGeek Society of Night Owls.

Of course, she wound up waking early, and by eleven found herself shuttling boxes out of the second guest room and into the smallest of the four. It was bad enough making an unwanted visitor sleep surrounded by the detritus of her long-ago move, somehow she couldn't live with making people she had technically invited—and one of whom she actually liked—do the same.

Dag found her there, shoving a stack of boxes into a corner where it would be out of the way until she felt like dealing with it. Which at this rate, should be right after her retirement.

"What are you doing?" the Guardian asked. "You are normally asleep at this time, or in your office working."

"Early to bed, early to rise." She shrugged. "I'm clearing the boxes and stuff out of Wynn and Knox's room so they don't feel too crowded. Once I set up the mattress in there, it started to feel pretty cramped."

That was the truth. Luckily, she'd had the forethought to order a bed for the couple as soon as they confirmed they would be visiting. It had been delivered the other day, before the security-installation debacle. At the time, she'd been preoccupied with combing through Dennis Ott's thumb drive with a fine-tooth comb, so she'd had them lean the mattress and box spring up the against the wall and hurried them outside just to silence Dag's grumbling. It had mostly worked, but it meant she had to deal with setting it all up today, since Wynn and Knox would arrive later in the afternoon.

Just so Dag didn't think she was a complete jerk, though, she added, "I've already removed the rest of the stuff from your room. Sorry. I should have done that sooner."

He shrugged. "It was only four boxes. They took up little space. How long will it be before the others arrive?"

"Their plane lands at two-twenty. I'm having a car service meet them at Logan, so by the time they get their stuff and drive out here, it should be about three-thirty. Which means I need to finish moving boxes and getting everything set up for them."

"I will help," Dag proclaimed, and turned to stride down the hall to the back bedroom. His own occupied the front of the house, but this one overlooked the small rear patio area.

Sighing, Kylie dusted off her hands and followed. When she stepped inside, she nearly ran over the large Guardian who had come to an abrupt stop just inside the door.

"What is that?" he demanded, pointing a finger to the middle of the room.

Kylie followed his gesture to the bed and frowned. "Um, it's a bed."

"Why is it so large?"

"Because there will be two people sleeping in it. Duh. I figured if Knox was even close to your size, they'd need the room to be comfortable. So I ordered a king size."

"Yet you left me with a tiny piece of furniture clearly inadequate for my frame. Was this some plan to cause me physical distress as a form of revenge?"

Finally understanding his attitude, Kylie rolled her eyes. "Get over yourself. You got the bed I had, plain and simple. A queen size is perfectly adequate for one person, even an escapee from steroid camp like you. I have the same size in my room upstairs."

"Adequate for some. You are less than half my size, little human. You could be comfortable on a chair cushion. I require more space than that." Without another word, the Guardian stepped forward, turned around, and flung himself backward onto the bare mattress. Stretching out his arms and legs, he easily occupied the whole space with a smug smile. "There. You see?"

Kylie just stared, wondering if maybe she'd been wrong about the possibility of a concussion after all. Or maybe she needed to revisit her original theory about the entirety of the last week being the product of a coma, hospital-grade drugs, and a vivid imagination. The only other choice appeared to be acknowledging that the Duke of Dour was actually smiling at her.

And being playful.

Her psyche couldn't cope. It went completely *fart-shadikt*. She may as well have been oxygen deprived all over again.

Crossing her arms over her chest, she took a cautious step forward and frowned down at him. "I'm not buying you a bigger bed. We don't even know how long you'll be here."

Something sparked in his black eyes, but he just kept smiling and ran a hand across the smooth fabric of the mattress. "But you bought Wynn and Knox a new bed."

"No, I bought them *a* bed. As in, first one. It was either that or make them sleep on the floor, and I'm not that bad a hostess. My *bubbeh* would never forgive me."

Dag's smile faded. "You speak often of your grandmother, but never of your parents."

The quiet observation caught Kylie by surprise. And here she'd thought he tuned out most of what spilled out of her mouth. "Yeah, well, I'm closer with her than I am with them."

"Why is that?"

The question still niggled at her, even though it had been asked before. Dag wasn't the first person to notice how tight she and her parents weren't. Still, she never liked answering it, so she gave her pat response. "Just different personalities. We don't really get each other."

And some of us never tried. But Kylie never said that part out loud.

The Guardian seemed to digest that answer, but instead of moving on, he reached out to grasp her hand, pulling her toward the side of the bed. "Explain. What is there to 'get' about being family?"

Whoa, he wanted to go there?

She shook her head. "I think some people related by blood aren't suited to be family to each other, and some people who meet by chance and start out as strangers can be better family members than the ones you're born with. That second kind, Bran was that for me. Wynn, too."

"And your parents were the first."

Persistent *nudnik,* wasn't he? He asked so calmly, though, and sounded so genuinely curious that she couldn't quite bring herself to just brush him off.

"Definitely the first." She sighed and perched warily on the edge of the bed. "They didn't have me until they were older than most first-time parents. Only-time parents, actually. They never intended to have kids. I came as quite the shock when they found out. I'm not sure they ever really adjusted to the idea. They had careers they both felt really passionately about. Maybe they just didn't have a ton left over, especially not for a precocious kid with a thing for electronics who didn't take well to being told to keep quiet and not bother the adults."

"What careers do they have that took priority over their child?"

"Mom's a finance type. CFO of a venture capital firm where I grew up, in Connecticut. Her head is always buried in numbers; and Dad is a law professor. Civil rights issues mostly. The needs of the many outweigh the needs of the few. Or of the daughter."

She delivered the line with a smile. After all, she'd been using it for years.

"I would think two such accomplished people would have been proud of having a child who succeeded in so much at such a young age," Dag said. He'd heard the story of her early acceptance to Boston University, of her big invention and sale, as well as of her decision to drop out and pursue her own interests instead of getting her degree.

Kylie grimaced. "I guess in some ways they are. Mom likes that I impressed the tech world enough to earn a big paycheck, at least, but she seriously balked at the dropping out. Dad, too. And he's always wished I would use my skill to do something more serious, something to 'better the future of mankind.' He thinks of that program I wrote as a toy. Like I said, they just don't get it."

"Unlike your grandmother."

The thought made her smile. "Unlike *bubbeh*. She doesn't really understand what I do either, but she's hella proud of me for doing it better than anyone else. I think she just never had any preconceived notions about what I was supposed to be, so she just sat back and watched what I became." Kylie thought back to some rather loud conversations among Esther, her son, and her daughter-in-law. Those made her smile turn a little toothy. "Plus, she was less than impressed with how my parents dealt with me. We ended up spending a lot of time together. She's kind of my hero."

"I would be pleased to meet her one day." His tone rang with sincerity and something else Kylie couldn't name, but it made her belly tighten and twist.

The way the long fingers still gripping her hand continually teased and tangled with her own made it plain hard to breathe. What was he doing to her? For the past week, he'd made it his mission in life to avoid her as if she were a bubonic plague carrier. Then yesterday they were forced back into close quarters, and he wakes up this morning wanting to get all friendly and cozy? The man changed moods like the Bruins changed forward lines—every forty seconds or so.

Needing to regain some of that space between them,

Kylie made as if to tug her hand away and stand. "Come on. There are still boxes to move, and they'll be here in a few more hours."

Dag tightened his grip and shook his head. "Later. Stay here."

She huffed impatiently and pulled harder. "Let go."

She didn't see him exert so much as an ounce of effort, but one minute she stood next to the bed leaning her entire body toward the door and the next she found herself yanked off her feet and lying sprawled over the chest of a very pleased-with-himself gargoyle.

"No," he eventually rumbled, black eyes glinting. "I do not wish to."

Panic warred with excitement in Kylie's chest, but either way, she used the surge of energy to attempt to free herself. "Dag, come on. We've got stuff to do. Let me go."

Another swift move had their positions reversed, and Kylie gazed up into a very smug, smiling face. "I told you, I do not wish to let you go, and as it happens I have a few ideas of my own regarding activities that you and I need to perform right away."

He actually wiggled his eyebrows when he said it, and Kylie found herself torn between amusement and panic as the pressure of his body on hers made perfectly clear that his innuendo had been entirely intentional.

How in the world had she gotten herself into this situation?

More importantly, did she want to bother trying to get out?

Her hormones cast their vote with a lusty, "Hello, sailor!" and tried to get her legs to spread wide and wrap themselves around Dag's waist in preparation for a spirited ride. Her brain, on the other hand, hauled hard on

the internal reins and shouted, "Down, girl!" as it attempted to seize control of the situation. It had some
serious concerns with this entire concept, beginning with
the whole different species thing, moving on to the way
he had barely spoken to her for the last week, and cir-
cling around to the issue of his immortal life span and
bad case of petronarcolepsy. Wouldn't she have to be
crazy to get involved with this guy?

Crazy-shmazy, her hormones shot back. Had she gotten a load of those muscles? Better to trace them all
with her tongue now and worry about the details later.
As in, sometime postcoital.

Confused and frustrated by the internal dialog,
Kylie banged her head backward onto the mattress, wishing fleetingly that it was made of concrete instead of
soft, cushiony foam and resilient pocketed springs. At
this point, knocking herself unconscious might turn out
to be her wisest move.

Then Dag snatched the decision right out of her brain
with a murmur of, "Beautiful Kylie," and the soft, intoxicating pressure of his lips against hers.

Oh, wow. She had almost forgotten just how good the
man tasted, and right now that felt like a tragedy. To forget the glory of this would be to forget how to breathe,
or the rich-spicy-nutty flavor of rugelach fresh out of the
oven. It would make the angels weep and God shake his
head. And, well, she couldn't have that, now could she?

So she let herself melt, because what else was there
to do? The past week was over, and now all that mattered
was the hard weight of Dag's body pinning her to the
mattress, and the soft, hungry pressure of his mouth on
hers.

Maybe it was the impression left by his last kiss, but
Kylie had expected that if they ever came together it

would be the same, fast and angry and almost violent, all need and speed. But this felt like something else all together. For the first time in her life, she felt entirely seduced, literally led away from all of her objections and hesitations and second thoughts. Every shift of his lips on hers, every stroke of his tongue, every nibble and nuzzle led her further and further down the path to surrender, and she felt nothing but peace with the process.

Well, peace and eagerness and searing, mind-numbing heat, because while Dag used none of the speed or force demonstrated in their previous encounter, his touch still made her burn.

She felt him in every cell of her body, from the roots of her hair to the tips of her toes, because every inch of her felt alive and alert in a way she had never experienced. When she gave in and wrapped her arms around his neck, her fingertips tingled as they sifted through his short-cropped, dark hair. She could feel the tightening in her chest as she breathed in his earthy, stony scent and the race of sensation that started between her thighs and shot up to dance across the back of her throat.

A groan escaped her, cutting through the quiet, and it took her a minute to realize she had made that tense, needy sound. Color flooded her cheeks and she tried to turn away from the kiss. Obligingly, Dag released her lips only to trail kisses over her jaw and down the sensitive line of her throat until she felt her eyes roll back into her head. That was not what she had intended.

Pressing her hands against his shoulders, she tried to shift him, but it was like trying to move a mountain. There wasn't a crowbar on earth big enough to shift a Guardian from where he wanted to be, but Dag pulled back to stare down at her, his black eyes burning with inner fire. It was like seeing the light of a hundred flickering candles reflected in a pool of black water, and she found herself hypnotized by it. The words of protest she had meant to utter fluttered away on a puff of air.

When she didn't speak, Dag shifted his gaze from her wide-eyed stare, over her flushed cheeks, and down to where she knew he had to see her racing pulse throbbing against the hollow of her throat. One huge hand came up, brushing the hair back from her face and then burrowing into the thick, dark waves to cup the back of her head.

"You're so tiny," he murmured, leaning close so that his breath caressed her cheek with warmth. "I forget how small your body is because the rest of you is so very large. Sweet little human, I don't want to hurt you."

And just like that, her hesitation melted away and her sense of Kylie came rushing back. He was right; no matter what her physical size, Kylie Kramer was a big girl, and she could take whatever Fate and a certain gargoyle decided to dish out to her.

Heck, if she liked the taste, she might even ask for seconds.

Feeling her lips curve into a smile, Kylie gripped his shoulders with small, strong fingers and tugged to bring him closer. "Don't worry, Rocky. I promise not to hurt you, either," she purred, and reached up to press her lips once more against his.

Dag felt the change in her, even if he didn't know what to attribute it to. In the end, it didn't matter. All that mattered was that the woman who had frustrated, teased, sassed, and aroused him for the last seven days was in his arms and returning his embraces with a fervor that matched his own.

What more could a Guardian ask for?

Skin, the voice inside him immediately replied. Lots of warm, bare, creamy skin. Dag saw no reason to argue with that kind of logic.

He held the kiss, savoring the way Kylie had taken control. Her tiny, white teeth nipped and nibbled at his lips, her tongue soothing the sensitized flesh with soft, fleeting strokes before darting within to tangle with his. Meanwhile, his hands slipped under the hem of her shirt, pushing the cotton fabric up to reveal the smooth, soft skin of her abdomen. As much as he wanted the garment off, the feel of her distracted him, and his fingers traced random patterns for several minutes before they could drag themselves back to the task at hand.

Her breath sped up, and he felt the tremor in her muscles as he skimmed his hands higher, dragging the shirt up and over her head before casting it carelessly aside. Then he couldn't help himself. He had to pull away so he could see what he had revealed.

The sight hit him like a punch to the gut. If he had known what she hid beneath her T-shirts with their silly sayings, he would have tried to keep her constantly naked. Her pale skin glowed like warm cream dusted with honey and looked twice as tasty. Helpless to stop himself, he dipped his head and pressed his mouth to the tempting sight, groaning when her scent and flavor flooded him, hot and sweet and fresh, so complex and layered that he knew he could explore it for a lifetime and never capture every nuance.

His body ached for release, but he savored the torment. Inside the heavy fabric of his jeans, he felt hot and heavy and unbearably restricted, and he knew he couldn't allow her to suffer the same torment. Pulling off her snug, worn jeans was the least he could do to make her comfortable. The fact that it exposed legs that looked too long for her modest height was entirely incidental, even if their softly rounded curves made him picture how they would feel wrapped around him, clinging tenaciously to his hips as he pounded into her.

By the Light, thoughts like those were not going to help him maintain his control, but then again, neither was the sight of the woman lying stretched out before him clad in nothing but scraps of turquoise silk and a shy, sinful smile. When he reached for her, he had to stroke firmly to disguise the shaking of his fingers. Him, a warrior, brought to a state of trembling by this little scrap of a woman. He could only hope his brethren never discovered the shameful secret or he would never live it down.

He slid his palms up the smooth curves of her hips, tracing the dip of her waist and the gentle flare of her rib cage until his palms cupped the warm, soft weight of her breasts. His fingers closed, kneading gently, and a soft sound escaped her, like a breathless hum, before she arched into his touch, inviting more. Dag could hardly refuse.

Her nipples drew tight beneath his touch, shrinking into little pebbles that he burned to taste. As if she read his mind, she shifted and squirmed and the tight band of her bra went slack. She shrugged out of the bright silk garment and let it flutter from her fingertips to join the rest of her clothes on the bedroom floor.

When he growled something indecipherable, even to himself, she just chuckled, her smile taking a cheeky turn. "What can I say? You were taking too long."

Well, he'd have to make sure he didn't make the same mistake twice, now wouldn't he?

His head swooped down and before the sound of her amusement had completely faded he drew the tip of her breast into his mouth and sucked strongly. A strangled cry escaped her, and he felt her hands fly up to cradle him to her. Her fingers tangled in his hair and the sting made him rumble in approval.

Her taste filled his head, the rough and smooth textures of her skin fascinating as his tongue drew circles around her hard nipple. Part of him wanted to savor this moment, to feast on her forever, his female eternally hot and soft and needy against his hands. Another part of him, the part currently protesting vehemently against the confines of his jeans, strongly disagreed. They could come back to this later, and then again and again and again, but now he needed to be inside her. He ached to feel her warm inner walls gripping his cock, driving them both crazy with desire. Savoring each other could wait.

With a thought, he banished his human clothing and grinned at the sound of her surprised gasp. All at once, they lay pressed skin to skin, only the flimsy scrap of her panties separating them, and Dag intended to take care of that quickly.

Shifting his mouth to her other breast, he scraped his teeth over the taut peak and felt her whole body shudder against him. His hand slid down, gripped the thin fabric at her hip, and twisted. The silk tore with a whispering snarl, and he tossed it away before going in search of his real prize.

His fingers feathered through the neat little nest of curls decorating her mound and then slid deeper to find her inner flesh slick and swollen with arousal. The tip of his index finger brushed absently over the little nub hidden in her folds, and Kylie jerked, a high sharp squeal escaping her. Fascinated, he repeated the caress, then again and again until her entire body tensed and shook beneath him.

Her pleasure made him feel like a god, as if he could take on all of the Seven at once and never taste the sting of defeat. As if he could rule the world, move the heavens, and balance the entire universe in the palm of his hand. He wanted none of it, though; all he wanted was Kylie.

"Please," she said, panting, fingers sliding down to grip his shoulders and urge him up over her. "Inside me. Now. I need you."

She sealed his fate with those words.

It no longer mattered what Fate had decreed, or what the Light had intended. Kylie was his, and he would wage war on the whole of the universe in order to keep her.

Dag couldn't wait another instant.

He no longer cared if his hands trembled or his palms went slick or his breath came too fast. He just wanted to be inside this woman, to feel her pussy gripping him, milking him, joining him in the ultimate pleasure. He needed to make her his.

One finger pressed deeper, slipping inside her to feel her still quivering, her body flooded with the moisture of her arousal. Feeling how much she wanted him, he couldn't wait another moment. Shifting to grasp her hip in one hand, he used the other arm to raise some of his weight off her and settled easily into the cradle of her thighs. He fit as if she had been made for him.

"Watch," he ordered gruffly, needing to see the hunger and emotion in those dark, coffee-colored eyes. "Watch me, beautiful. Now."

Fitting himself against her opening, Dag kept his gaze on hers as he pressed inside. She gave a soft, shuddering cry as their bodies merged. Every slick inch of her welcomed him with a tight embrace, and he continued relentlessly deeper until he could go no farther. Her muscles clenched around him, squeezing like a fist, and the sound of her breathing stopped for a moment as they watched each other at the perfect moment of their union.

He knew the wonder of it couldn't last. The hunger built too quickly, burning through the initial ecstasy of feeling her body welcome him. Now it clawed at his belly, demanding more. Demanding that he feed the beast and claim his mate until no one could doubt that she belonged to him.

Dag shifted, even that small movement sending shudders through them both. He settled his forearm against the mattress and slid his hand beneath her head until he cradled her skin in the palm of his hand. His fingers tangled in her hair and he leaned into her until his mouth hovered inches above hers, their breath mingling in hard, raspy pants. His other hand slid down her thigh to curl around the tender skin just above her knee. He used his grip to urge her leg higher until she clasped his rib cage with the smooth muscles, opening herself further. His cock slid just a fraction deeper, but it was enough to make both of them moan.

"Dag, please," she panted, licking her lips. Their mouths hovered so close together, he felt the swift pass of her tongue like the brush of a feather against his skin. "I need. I ache. So bad."

"Shh," he hushed her, tightening his fingers in her hair until he could see her eyes dilate at the little sting it caused and feel her pussy shiver around him. "I know, little human. Let me help."

Gaze intent on her sweet, flushed face, Dag eased into motion, pulling his hips back inch by inch until he almost left her, then sliding forward again with aching slowness.

"There," he crooned. "Is that better, little one?"

With a muffled shriek, his mate bared her teeth and dug her heel hard into his back. "If you don't fuck me right now, you big, boulder-brained *bulvan,* I swear by all that is holy, I will make you rue the day you were summoned."

The chuckle escaped him no matter how unwise, and when he grinned, he thought he might be flashing her fangs instead of teeth. She shredded his control that much. "Well, then," he said, inching her knee a fraction higher. "Let us make sure that does not happen, hm?"

Easing out, he teased her for a long aching moment, feeling the way her pussy clutched at the head of his cock, trying to draw him back inside her. When she pulled hard against his grip, thrusting her head forward and snapping at him with her even, white teeth, he gave a roar and let himself go.

Dag pounded into her, no longer taking the time to savor each thrust and retreat. Pleasure overwhelmed him, every breath, every shift, every tiny movement brought another wave of ecstasy. Kylie cried out her approval and thrust her hips toward him, meeting every advance with one of her own, demonstrating her displeasure at every retreat.

Their bodies struggled together, twining and writhing toward the same goal. Dag ground his teeth together, his breath forced out of him in animalistic grunts every time he thrust home. Kylie matched him with breathless, aching cries, each a higher pitch than the last until all he could hear was the puff of air that accompanied each exclamation.

The lure of climax loomed before him, taunting him, and Dag chased after it, dragging his mate along with him. Shifting his grip, he released her leg to reach between them and press hard against the slick nub at the top of her sex. Once, twice, he increased the pressure until he felt Kylie explode around him.

Her body clenched around his like a vise, her grip nearly painful for a moment as the pleasure raced through her. His name tore from her lips in a hoarse scream, and her whole body tensed before dissolving into a mass of head-to-toe shudders.

The repeated squeezing of her channel around his cock overwhelmed him. Offering a muffled roar of his own, Dag let the orgasm wash over him and poured himself into his mate's snug heat.

He collapsed above her, shifting when she grunted to protest his weight. He slid an inch or two to the side, unwilling to relinquish her warm embrace, but equally having no desire to suffocate her. They lay like the wounded after a battle, breathing heavily, weak and unmoving. One of his hands remained tangled in her hair, while the other cupped the curve of her hip and savored the damp satin texture of her skin.

Neither spoke. Whether because neither had the breath to do so, or because neither knew what to say seemed equally possible. Dag had no trouble identifying his feelings, but his grasp on Kylie's seemed much less certain. He had claimed her; she was his mate. He knew he could never let her go, but whether this news would thrill or horrify her, he had no idea. His little human rarely reacted in any way he had expected.

Case in point: knowing how much his small female loved to speak, he expected her to say something. Whether it would be a serious comment or a sassy quip, he did not even try to predict. But instead, she merely turned into his warmth and snuggled closer, one hand curling to tuck under her chin, the other pressed against the plane of his chest. When her mouth opened wide, the only sound to emerge was a huge yawn, one that would have done King David proud.

Then, like her cat, she drifted easily into sleep. Dag sighed out a laugh and cuddled her close, leaning down to press a kiss to the damp curls that clung to her forehead. Life with his mate would never be boring. It might be the only thing he felt certain of at the moment, but it would do.

For a start.

Chapter Ten

Shuldik iz der stolyer; ven er volt nit gemakht di bet,
volt ikh nit gekumen tsu keyn khet.
It's the carpenter's fault; if he hadn't built the bed,
I wouldn't have sinned.

The sharp rapping sound intruded on Kylie's sleep and made her frown. She felt too warm and drowsy to care much where it had come from, so she decided to ignore it and slide back into sleep. A few seconds later, it came again, this time louder, with enough force to shake the window in its frame.

Wait, window? Why would someone be knocking on her window? What was going on?

Sleepy and confused, Kylie tried to roll over, only to find the way blocked by a very large, very male, very naked body stretched beside her.

Memory came flooding back in full, unedited Technicolor. *Chub rachmones.* What had she done?

The gargoyle, obviously.

Okay, of all the times for her own brain to pick to snark at her, it had to settle on this one? Really? Throwing her arms over her eyes, Kylie lay still and wondered if it was too early to pray for death. Or too late.

Bam!rattle. Bam!rattle. Bam!rattle.

The noise came again, eliciting a snarl from somewhere to the left just over her head. She continued to ignore the world outside her own inner elbow and felt the mattress dip and shift as Dag rolled to his feet. When he roared his displeasure, the rattle sounded again and she finally realized the noise came from glass shaking in the windowpanes. Someone had been knocking on the window.

The second-story window.

Realization dawned, bringing with it panic, guilt, and a soupçon of outright humiliation. Kylie's gaze flew to the bedroom window to see a gray-skinned, fang-flashing face staring back at her. Since the face obviously belonged to a Guardian, and the only one she was acquainted with—intimately acquainted—clearly stood inside the room with her, she had no trouble guessing that Knox currently hovered outside the guest-room window, wearing an expression of mingled irritation and amusement.

With an *eep,* Kylie reached for a blanket to cover herself and discovered none to be had. She hadn't yet made the bed she and Dag had just, um, occupied. Groaning, she did the only thing she could, flinging herself off the far side of the mattress and hiding in the space between it and the far wall where no more strangers could see her bare tits and ass.

Oy to the ever-loving *vey!*

Knox tapped on the glass again, this time with much less force, and gestured at Dag to open the window. The latter complied with enough irritated force to have the old sash screeching in protest.

"Wynn is waiting below by the front door," Knox said the minute the barrier had been lifted. "No one answered our knocks, and she became concerned, so I agreed to look around for our hosts. It appears I have found you."

Kylie groaned and heard her grandmother's voice clearly inside her head. *"Dayn mazl, Got, vos du voynst azoy volt men dir di fentster oysgezetst."* You're lucky, God, that you live so high, otherwise people would break your windows. In that moment, Kylie's hand itched for a rock.

"We did not hear the knock," Dag bit out, and Kylie peeked over the mattress to see he had regained his natural form in response to the rude awakening. Too bad the other man was a Guardian, too, because she would have liked to see those claws of Dag's do some damage to the jerk's smug smile.

"I can see that is true."

Kylie groaned even louder and banged her head against the side of the bed. "Argh! Make him go away. We'll be downstairs to let them in in a minute. With clothes on."

Dag didn't bother to repeat her instructions, just slammed the window closed and turned to face her, spreading his wings to block the view from outside. "I take responsibility for this. I failed to properly protect you."

The statement made Kylie's brain shoot immediately to condoms, which they had so not used, and panic took over for a second. Then she invested a minute in relearning how to breathe, and reminded herself with a great sense of relief that she was on the pill. It didn't make everything better, but it helped a little. "Yeah, well, it's a little late to worry about it now, but hopefully it's not a big deal. I mean, I'm clean, and unless you've had way more free time while you were awake than I've been imagining, I'm guessing the chances of you carrying anything are pretty small. I mean, if those microbes can even live through the three-hundred-years locked-in-stone in the first place."

Dag's wings rustled, and his expression shifted from grim stoicism to clear confusion. "I do not understand what you speak of. Of course you bathe regularly, and what does my slumber have to do with any of this? I allowed an outsider to stumble upon us without knowing he approached, and I allowed him to see your nakedness. I should have guarded you better. The failure shames me."

Oh. So not the condom thing, then? Kylie felt her cheeks light up like a menorah on the last day of Hanukkah. "Um, yeah. Right. We were interrupted. That sucked." Feeling around on the floor beside her, her fingers brushed against a pile of cloth. It was her T-shirt. Kylie nearly wept with relief as she pulled it on. At least her tits were covered now. One—er, two—down, one to go. "But it's not like it was another *drude,* or another psychotic electrician, so that's a plus. No harm, no foul, right?"

Peering around the dim space—since Dag's wings continued to block the window's vantage point but also the light coming through it—she finally spotted her jeans and could have kissed them, she'd been missing them so much. She wriggled into those before she rolled to her feet and turned to face the Guardian. "It's not like I enjoyed being woken up and meeting Wynn's fiancé while nude and out of it, but I'll live through it. I think saying it 'shames' you might be taking things a bit too far."

She spoke the truth, but none of her words did anything to cool her blush or calm the twist of unease in her belly. Probably because none of them could change the fact that she'd just lost her mind and had sex with the worst excuse for a one-night stand in history—a non-human, immortal, shapeshifting, demon-fighting gargoyle whom she had met just a week ago. Dag might not be a bad Guardian, but she was definitely a bad Kylie.

Very, very bad.

She would have to come up with a suitable punishment on the way to letting her guests into the house. You know, as she should have done in the first place. Was it possible to draw and quarter oneself, or did that require a team effort?

She got halfway out the door before Dag caught up to her, placing a now-human hand on her shoulder. "Kylie . . ." he began.

"Not now." She cut him off and quickly scooted out from under his touch. "We can talk about . . . whatever . . . later. Right now, Wynn and Knox are waiting. Let's go."

Not bothering to wait for his reaction, she headed briskly for the stairs and jogged down before he could stop her. When she deactivated the alarm and swung open the heavy front door, she could feel him behind her, but she'd just have to find a way to ignore his presence.

Kind of like she'd now have to ignore the annoying smirk on her friend's pretty face.

"Well, hello there, Ms. Kylie." Wynn grinned, her singsong tone guaranteed to give her friend a migraine in under six seconds. "I think you were expecting us, or did the fact that we were, ahem, coming . . . slip your mind?"

Though never previously given to fits of violence, Kylie knew one more laughing remark from her friend would lead to a swift fist in the witch's face. "I hate you right now," she hissed, turning on her heel to stalk back to the kitchen, leaving her guests to make the best of her less than warm welcome.

Ikh hob es in drerd! To hell with it. She'd already used up all her warmth. In her cheeks.

She heard the rise and fall of voices and the rumble of luggage wheels on the hardwood following her down the hall. Ignoring them, she yanked open the fridge, grabbed herself a soda, and nearly sent the cap flying across the room from the force with which she wielded the bottle opener.

Wynn actually had to duck as she entered the room. "Um, we didn't mean to interrupt. You know that, right?" Her grin had faded, and now she looked concerned and a little bit guilty. "Knox told me what he saw, but it wasn't like we deliberately barged in."

Kylie lowered her drink with a sigh and let her shoulders slump. "I know. And I don't really hate you." She pulled one of the high stools away from the center island and climbed onto the padded seat. "At the moment, I think I just hate myself."

Her friend sat beside her. "Why would you hate yourself? Did you drug him? Was it sexual assault?"

Snorting into her cola, Kylie shook her head. "No, that's not how I would say it happened."

"Well, he's a Guardian, so I know he didn't assault you. These guys have a code of honor that makes jarheads and saints look like moral degenerates. So why the crazy over two consenting adults doing what consenting adults like to do?"

Kylie looked at her friend like the crazy had come from an entirely new direction. "Wynneleh, he's a member of another species!"

Wynn rolled her eyes. "Nominally. So yeah, Guardians

aren't exactly human, but it's not like you screwed a donkey, Ky. Get over yourself. Are you trying to tell me there's a woman on this planet who could look at one of our guys and not think they're damned sexy?"

"Oh, why am I bothering with you? You've already gone over to the Dark Side."

"Damn straight. And the cookies are awesome."

"Do you mind? I'm having a personal crisis over here. I don't know what I was thinking."

"Yeah, I mind, because I think a crisis is a huge over-reaction. I'm also betting that you *weren't* thinking at the time, which is just the way it should be. I sure as heck can't string two coherent thoughts together when Knox touches me. That's just the way it is between mates. Frankly, I count it as a pretty big perk."

Kylie held up a hand and cocked her ear. "Wait a second there, Pooh Bear. Mates? Where the hell did that word come from, and what is it doing in my conversation?"

"Our conversation. Don't be a greedy bitch. And what, you thought you and Dag were just good buddies?"

"Um, I thought we were about half an insult away from sworn nemeses. And I kept thinking that, right up until my pants fell off."

Wynn snorted. "All by themselves, right? Come on, Koyote. You heard about me and Knox, Fil and Spar, and Ella and Kees, and you thought every one of the new female Wardens turning out to be the mate of the Guardian she woke was just a big ol' coincidence? I thought all you geek types had to know about things like statistics and the laws of probability."

Stunned—literally; she felt as though she'd just taken a softball to the side of her head—Kylie thought back to her initial conversations with Wynn about the Guardian situation. She remembered their talk. She remembered the mention of those couples. She even remembered being informed of her new Wardenship, but she did *not* remember the M-word ever entering the picture.

And, oh yes, she would have remembered.

She pointed an accusing finger at her friend. "You never said anything about mates. You said the two of us would have to work together because he's a Guardian and I'm a Warden and those twains just meet like that. There was no mention of mating. Mating was never in the handbook."

Wynn pursed her lips and looked up at the ceiling. "You know, there really should be a handbook, shouldn't there?"

Suddenly two hulking figures stood behind them, one of them crowding close to Kylie and growling low in his throat. "What have you done to upset her?" Dag demanded, glaring at Wynn.

The witch glared right back. "Actually, I'm not the one who upset her, big guy. I think that honor goes to a little story you never bothered to tell her. I swear, what the hell is it with you guys and withholding vital information? You'd think having Ella and Fil both contemplating ripping your balls off would have taught you all a lesson on sharing means caring."

Knox gave his fiancée a hard look. "You believe I withheld vital information from you, little witch?"

Kylie had always dismissed Dag's claims that he ranked as one of the smallest of his kind, but after seeing Knox in person, she felt forced to reevaluate. The gargantuan man—even in human form, which she had to admit was a lot nicer to look at than the gargoyle side she'd seen in her guest-room window—looked to be in imminent danger of overflowing her kitchen. Her enormous, remodeled, showroom-ready kitchen her Realtor had described as the focal point of the house. In comparison, Dag's size seemed almost, you know, normal.

Wynn appeared neither intimidated nor particularly impressed. "No, you did not, but you didn't get a chance, did you? I knew it all right from the start, so hiding the facts never would have gotten you anywhere with me."

"I hide nothing," Dag cut in, his tone angry and expression stony. "But whatever I choose to do is no business of yours, witch. I can handle my life however I see fit."

"Um, excuse me?" Kylie found herself raising her hand in her own kitchen and tried not to think too hard about the implications of that. "Anyone care to fill me in on what the hell is going on?"

Wynn opened her mouth, Knox shook his head, Dag bared a fang, and the witch backed off, mumbling, "Apparently not," half under her breath.

"Dag is correct," Knox said, laying a hand on his fiancée's shoulder. "He has the right to conduct himself however he feels is most appropriate. And we all have more important matters to deal with. Perhaps we should simply agree to 'table' this discussion, I believe one would say, and focus on the reason why we have all come together here."

Kylie took note of the similarities in Dag's and Wynn's disgruntled expressions. Then she spied Knox's determination and realized no one was likely to explain what the heck had just happened anytime soon, so she bit back a growl and jumped off her stool.

"Fine," she said, setting her soda aside with a click. "In that case, I'll show you guys your room, and then I'm hopping in the shower. We can all use the time to decide what we want for dinner, and we'll start work when it gets here. Follow me."

She stalked toward the stairs, not really caring if they obeyed or not. The house wasn't that big. Eventually, they'd find the only spare room with a bed in it and put two and two together. With the mood she was in, Kylie would even let them find the bedding she'd piled on the nightstand and make their own damned bed.

She just hoped they didn't stumble across her torn panties in the process.

Crap, she swore as she picked up the pace and raced ahead to retrieve her discarded undergarments. *Next time, they get a hotel.*

Or, you know, I keep my legs together. Whatever works.

Kylie quickly discovered that her state-of-the-art shower-head lacked a setting for self-flagellation, so she turned it to massage and tried to content herself with a mild pummeling. Even the addition of the body jets and the cross-spray couldn't give her the beating she so richly deserved, but at least the water was hot. Didn't Christians think sin could be burned away? Wasn't that the whole rationale behind burning witches?

At the moment, Kylie entertained a fond thought involving one particular witch and a book of matches, but that was probably because she just wasn't a very nice person. Oh, she used to be, but that was before she got mugged by demon worshippers and entered the Fabulous Land of Make meBelievei'mcrazy. Now, she was finding out she had homicidal tendencies and the morals of a big ol' slut. Lo, how the mighty were fallen.

Good thing she was so short. It cut down on the trip.

A puff of cool air had her opening her eyes and frowning at the shower settings, but before she could even focus on the temperature gauge, a thickly muscled arm curled around her from behind. It pressed against her just below her breasts, a more effective restraint than a roller-coaster harness. She shrieked loud enough for her *bubbeh* to hear her.

In Connecticut.

"Hush," Dag said, hugging her to his naked body. "It is just me."

Kylie pressed both palms against his forearm and shoved. "Well, *just you* wasn't invited, bub, so get out of my shower!"

"No. You are angry with me," he said, "and while I deserve some of your ire for not protecting you better, I will not allow others to come between us. We must discuss what was said."

"I'm not interested in a discussion," Kylie said through clenched teeth. Not only did his arm refuse to budge, but the baseball bat pressing against her lower back told her the rest of him didn't want to go anywhere, either. "I'm also not interested in anything else you might be thinking about, so I repeat, *get. Out.*"

"I do not believe that statement to be entirely truthful," he purred into her ear. His second arm snaked around, and he laid his hand against her belly just above her mound. "Shall I show you why, little human?"

"If you think seducing me is going to do anything but make me *more* eager to rip your balls off, I have some very important information to share," she ground out, her teeth clenched together at least as hard as her thighs.

Dag's hands didn't move, but then, neither did the rest of him. Well, part of him twitched against her skin, but she didn't think he could help that. Those things tended to have minds of their own.

"If you will not be seduced, yet you will also not talk with me, what other choices have you left us? I will not allow you to think ill of me forever without allowing me the chance to explain my own actions. It would be unfair to expect as much."

Kylie tried again to push him away. He didn't tighten his hold, but he didn't budge, either. Maybe he really was made of granite. "Fine, you can explain all you want, but you'll have to do it later. Outside the shower. After we're both fully clothed."

One long finger tapped thoughtfully against her skin, low on her belly. Whether the gesture was deliberate or unconscious, it made Kylie's belly clench and her mouth go dry. She deliberately failed to take stock of any effect it might have between her legs.

"That seems inefficient." Dag leaned down to rest his chin on the top of her wet hair so that she felt entirely surrounded by him, yet curiously she felt more protected than threatened. "We are both here, and the nature of bathing ensures us of adequate privacy. Also, we should have nothing to hide from each other. We have been skin to skin already, so modesty is not necessary between us."

"Says you."

"What is the purpose of hiding from one another what has already been seen and felt by us both?" When Kylie didn't answer, Dag's hands gently urged her around to face him. "Do you feel there is some indecency in your lack of clothing? Because you cannot think that the sight of your body would do anything but give me pleasure."

Okay, so despite her embarrassment and lingering

irritation, Kylie couldn't deny a surge of pleasure at hearing that. Still, a girl had to make a stand from time to time. "This is not about whether or not we've had sex."

"Is it not? That was what you and your friend discussed when you were alone, is it not? And it made you angry. Even before Knox and I joined you in the kitchen, you had begun to grow upset with me. In fact, you were upset before you even left the bed we shared."

Given the way she'd jumped off said bed, muttering to herself in Yiddish, she supposed a denial would prove pointless. "I was . . . at myself. At my own behavior. I don't usually act like that." She looked down at herself and grimaced. "And I don't usually have conversations while I'm standing around in nothing but my business."

Dag's eyes twinkled. "What is the human saying? Ah, business is good, yes?" When she just rolled her eyes, he sighed and pulled her tight against him, so not even the water rolled between them. "There. Now I cannot see that you are naked, so now may we talk?"

"Oh, sure, because that"—Kylie wiggled her belly against his erect penis—"is not at all distracting."

"If I can ignore it, I do not see why you cannot."

"It keeps poking me!"

"It consumes blood supply meant for my brain. On whom, then, does it have a greater effect?"

"I can't believe I'm standing in the shower arguing about your dick." Kylie gave up and let her forehead smack against his hard chest. Almost as good as a brick wall. "Fine. Say whatever you think you have to say, then get out. Go."

At least she'd had the foresight to ensure the house had on-demand hot water, since the only thing that would make this discussion more fun would be the shower turning into an ice bath in the middle of it.

The silent pause told her he hadn't really expected to win that argument. She just hoped he was enjoying it, because from now on, she'd be taking no prisoners.

"I failed to properly protect you, and there is no apology sufficient for that oversight. I can only admit to my own deficiency and vow to you that I will not again forget my duty or my purpose. I swear to you that I will keep you safe."

Kylie shook her head without bothering to lift it. She didn't need to be distracted by the sight of his nudity. It was bad enough that she should feel it. Every glorious, muscular, rock-hard inch of it.

Down, she mentally scolded. *Bad hormones! Sit!*

"I already told you that wasn't a big deal," she mumbled. "You didn't fail to protect me from a threat, you just didn't answer the door when someone knocked. Big difference. I think we can both just forget about that."

She felt him stiffen—*his muscles, you damned endocrine system!*—before he spoke with obvious caution in his tone. "But if you were not upset by my lack of readiness to protect you, then your argument with the witch implies you regret our mating for other reasons."

"That's just the problem," she said, finally tipping her head back to meet his gaze. "When exactly did we mate? Because I don't recall that happening, or ever being put out on the table. Then all of a sudden everyone is just moving forward as if it's a done deal. What's up with that?"

His chest rumbled, enough that she could feel it against her skin. "The answer to that question would depend on one's definition of 'mating,' in order to determine what did and did not happen."

"When did you appear before a House subcommittee?" she snapped. "How about we stick to the communal definition everyone except for me seems to be going with? Because the only definition I'm familiar with is the one from *Wild Kingdom*. And there's no mistaking that *that* happened."

Still, he hedged. "That definition requires that I tell you another story of the origin of the Guardians and the Wardens Guild."

"I'm wet, and I'm naked. Do I look like I'm going anywhere?"

Dag sighed so hard she thought he might turn inside out. Seriously, it gave her grandmother a run for her money.

"Wynn told you of how the first Guardians were summoned to battle the Seven and to defend the human world from the Darkness."

Kylie nodded for him to continue.

"For hundreds of years they did this. Ages passed as they woke and slept and woke again, each time answering the summons of the Wardens and battling to defeat the enemy so that the human world could remain untouched. But the Guardians are not of this world, and as warriors, they felt little emotion toward it. They lacked a connection to give their duty a higher purpose. Over time, they began to wonder why they should continue to fight and bleed for a world they cared nothing for. And so, the next time the Wardens called them from sleep, the Guardians failed to respond. They ignored the summons and remained locked in their stone forms, eternally slumbering."

When she thought about that, Kylie couldn't say that she blamed them. Even to her, this whole nightmare of demons and Guardians, *nocturnis* and Wardens, it all felt like someone else's war to wage, even after she had personally been attacked. Twice. Honestly, the reason she had let herself get sucked in had been Wynn's end-of-the-world comment, because she lived in the world. If it ended, so did she. But for the Guardians, what did it matter if the human world kept on ticking? They only saw it when they had to risk their lives for it. After a few centuries, she imagined she'd be over that kind of system, too.

"The Guild panicked," Dag continued. "The threat of the Darkness had risen, and with no Guardians to battle the Seven, it appeared all hope of life was lost. They began to prepare for the worst. But then something happened they had not planned on. A woman appeared before them, a woman of power whose magic rivaled that of any of the Wardens but who had been turned away from a position in the Guild. She refused to believe that the Guardians would permanently desert mankind, and so she knelt before the statue form of a Guardian and she prayed that he would wake and stand against the Darkness.

"The woman called to him, and to the astonishment of the Wardens, the Guardian heard her call and answered. He woke and seized the woman, claiming her as his mate. He vowed she had been destined for him, and that for her sake and the sake of her people, he would again take up the struggle against the Seven."

Uh-oh. Suddenly Kylie forgot all about *Wild Kingdom* and started to feel a lot more *eHarmony*. Did he think this was Girl Scout camp? Because this was turning into the scariest story Kylie had ever heard.

"One by one, women of power appeared, and one by one each Guardian found his destined mate. Each fought for her sake to banish the Darkness once more from the world, and when the threat had passed, each one demanded that the Guild release him from his duty so that he could spend the rest of his existence with his chosen mate.

"From that time forward, my kind has whispered, but only a handful of additional Guardians have ever been said to have found their true mates. It has become a kind of legend among us, a fairy tale each of us has heard and yet none of us truly believed. Until now."

Kylie really wanted to blame the steam for the way her head was spinning and her heart had suddenly decided to sprint a hundred meters in 0.7 seconds. Oh, if only she could. "I—you—but what—"

Oy.

She took a deep breath and tried again. "Are you trying to tell me that you think I am some kind of sent-from-heaven perfect girlfriend, and we're going to live happily ever after together for the rest of eternity?"

Dag scowled down at her. "You do not believe me."

"Right now, I don't believe I'm not lying in a bed at Mass General in a drug-induced coma, so don't take it personally." Desperate for clothing and a little bit of personal space, Kylie finally succeeded in pulling out of Dag's embrace and shutting off the water. Hurrying from the enormous shower enclosure, she wrapped herself in a short, fuzzy bathrobe (okay, on her, it wasn't really that short) and bundled her hair into a towel with shaking hands. She wished it was from cold.

She also wished her *farkakta* hormones weren't pouting about the lack of shower sex. As if there weren't one or two things in this world just a teeny bit more important than orgasms. And no, she was not asking for a vote.

Dag followed her into her bedroom, hiking a towel of his own around his hips. "Why do you doubt what is between us?" he demanded, looking distractingly hot in the plush gray towel with droplets of warm water beading his skin. "Do not tell me that you felt nothing when we joined, because I will call you a liar if you make the attempt."

"Of course I felt something," she snapped. "I'm not dead. But hot sex is a long way from predestined mates, so don't look at me like I'm the jerk because your train left without me."

He blinked at her, dark lashes spiky with moisture, and she saw his frustration in the way his skin wanted to bleed from tan to gray. "Once again you try to confuse me with your speech. I thought we had gotten past such juvenile tactics."

"Juvenile? Just who do you think—" Kylie cut herself off and bit back what she had intended to say. "No, you know what? I am done having this discussion. I said we should wait, and that's what I'm going to do. We both need a little bit of time to step back and figure out where we stand. And don't tell me that you don't," she said, raising a hand to ward off his protest. "No. I don't care if you think you're fine just the way you are, because *I* need some time to think, and I'm darned well going to take it."

She stomped over to her closet and gave him her back as she flung open the door. "Now, if you don't mind, I'm going to ask you to go get yourself dressed and meet me downstairs with the others, where we will behave like civilized Jews, gentiles, and Guardians, order Chinese food, and do what we all came here to do."

Behind her, she could almost feel him vibrating with frustration, but when she finally gave in to the urge to peek, he had disappeared through the door to the second floor. When she heard that telltale step squeak, she threw herself back onto her bed and took a deep breath.

She had no idea what she was going to do. The word "confused" didn't even begin to describe her current mental state. She'd felt off-kilter since the first moment Dag lifted her off the ground, and it had nothing to do with being flown over the rooftops of Boston and deposited in a church belfry. No, the huge gargoyle's effect on her had nothing to do with gravity and everything to do with chemistry.

Yes, fine, she could admit it. They had something between them, something Kylie had never felt the likes of in her entire twenty-three (almost twenty-four) years. Oh, she had been in lust before, had even thought she was in love a time or two, but nothing compared to the feelings Dag stirred in her heart, her stomach, and in a host of other places she swore not to think about just now.

Maybe that was half her problem. Whatever Dag made her feel, she couldn't find the right thing to call it, not in English or Yiddish. And she suspected that if she spoke another language, she wouldn't find it in that vocabulary, either. All she knew was that the man drove her crazy in more ways than she wanted to count. That didn't mean she believed in the "destined mates" story; it just meant she didn't know what to believe.

And, yes, Kylie Kramer was a big enough person (barely) to admit that was the worst of it. For her whole life, Kylie had always known exactly where she stood, even when she didn't like the view. Now? Well, now, she wasn't even sure she had feet.

Closing her eyes and sticking her tongue out at the ceiling, Kylie gave in to her basest impulses and blew a long loud raspberry at the world. It even helped, at least a little.

Okay, she thought. She would give herself two more

minutes to kvetch, and then she would haul her *tokhes* out of bed, put on some clothes, and go order pot stickers. With enough meat, dough, and dumpling sauce, anything in this world became possible.

Even facing a witch, two gargoyles, and Seven Demons from hell.

At least she wouldn't have to do it on an empty stomach.

Chapter Eleven

Wen ikh ess, ch'ob ikh alles un dread.
When I'm eating, everyone can go to hell.

Kylie got her pot stickers. And her chicken mai fun, her beef with asparagus, and her vegetable spring roll. Actually, between her and the rest of their little group, the restaurant threw in free crab Rangoon, free hot and sour soup, *and* free almond cookies. Everything lay spread out on her giant coffee table like a three-day feast. The entire staff would probably be talking about the four people who ate like thirty, but whatever. Kylie never thought clearly on an empty stomach.

The food also served as a source of distraction, although by the time she had trooped downstairs either everyone had developed a conscience, or Dag had told them where to shove the knowing glances. Everyone seemed to be on their best behavior.

Dag finished relating the story of yesterday's security installation and the hexed workman who had attacked Kylie. Fortunately, he left out the mea culpas and kept things short, so she didn't feel tempted to shove her chopstick into his ear. Much.

"I'd say that answers the question of whether or not this Ott guy let Ky's name slip before they killed him," Wynn said with a wince. "They had to have been watching the house and waiting for an opportunity to have managed something like that. Definitely not a random-target thing."

"Yeah, I think we've pretty much come to that conclusion all on our own."

"The question is how much they believe she knows," Knox said, turning to Kylie. He and Dag had elected to sit on the sofa ("like adults," he had said) while she and Wynn sat tailor fashion on the floor of the living room. "That they will wish you dead is a certainty, but their level of determination to see it done sooner will depend on how many of their secrets they believe you possess."

"I'm not sure how we figure that out. Obviously, they know that I had contact with Dennis Ott, or whatever his name was when he was mixed up with the Order. But they didn't find the drive in his pocket, or I'm assuming they would have taken it, so they don't know that we've read his journal or seen that video."

"Speaking of, any word from your AV guy yet?" Wynn asked.

"Vic?" Kylie shook her head. "No, but it should be any day. He's squeezing me in as a favor, but I know he'll get to it as soon as possible. He likes me."

Dag growled at that, and Kylie ignored him. Well, she rolled her eyes, then she ignored him.

"The sooner the better." Knox set aside his water glass and wiped his mouth with a paper napkin. "If Dag's theory is correct, and the video actually shows us the identity of the Hierophant, we cannot have that information too soon."

"Either way, it's important," Wynn said. "But our real task now is figuring out the details of this big strike the local sect has planned and when it's going to happen. We can't let them raise enough power to return Uhlthor to full strength, let alone give them a shot at freeing Shaab-Na as well."

Kylie pushed away her plate and shook her head. "I've been over that drive with a fine-tooth comb. If Ott knew the details, he didn't save them on there."

"Which leaves us where?" Wynn asked.

"Nowhere very useful. Maybe you guys wasted your time coming all the way out here."

Wynn scoffed. "Wasted what time? It's a two-hour flight and, oh yeah, you're my friend, so it's such a hardship to see you."

"There is no waste," Knox assured her. "What the Order had planned here sounds bigger than what they attempted in any of the cities where we have faced them so far. It is only right that we should join forces and deal with this threat together."

"We merely need to discover the nature of it," Dag said. "Then together we shall defeat it."

Kylie nodded. "Okay, okay. Enough with the rah-rahs. What do we actually *do* at this point? I mean, where do we start?"

Before anyone could make a suggestion, someone knocked at the front door. This time, Kylie even heard it. "Hold that thought," she told them, pushing to her feet and hurrying to answer the summons. When she caught Dag following her, she felt an instant of irritation before logic kicked in. She didn't know who was on the other side of the door, she wasn't expecting any visitors, and she'd been attacked twice (three times, if you counted the *drude*) in the last week. Maybe having backup wasn't such a bad idea.

Too short to reach the peephole, she brushed aside the gauzy curtain covering the sidelight before she opened the door. When she saw who was on the other side, she nearly *plotzed*.

Brushing aside Dag's concern, she wrenched open the door. "Vic? What on earth are you doing here? You're supposed to be in New York!"

The genius of digital video she and Wynn had just been discussing stood on her front steps shivering in the chilly night air and looking decidedly sheepish. "Yeah, well, I came up to give a seminar this weekend, so I thought I'd bring you your clip. I should have called first, but I wanted to surprise you. Did I come at a bad time?"

Victor Gill could have posed as the poster boy for Kylie's People, the geeks and geniuses she had always befriended, dated, and slept with before her gargoylization. Standing on the short side of average at around five feet nine inches, he had a lean, lanky build, and the kind of casual, preoccupied appearance of someone who paid more attention to a computer screen than to clothes, hairstyles, or cultivating more than a passing acquaintance with sunlight. He wore dark-framed glasses over his exotic dark eyes, and the dusky skin tone of his Korean ancestry kept him from a kind of glow-in-the-dark pallor.

He hovered on the threshold and glanced behind her, eyeing Dag nervously.

"No. *Oy,* no, not at all. Come in." She stepped back and waved her friend inside, nudging the Guardian back with a (mostly) gentle nudge (kick) to his shin. "Are you hungry? We ordered Chinese, and I think there's enough to actually feed China. Let me get you a plate."

Vic hung back near the front door while Dag glowered. "I don't want to intrude. I mean, I really should have called first, but—"

"Don't be silly. It's so cool to see you." Kylie marched over to her friend and linked her elbow with his to drag him toward the living room. "That big menace in the corner is Dag, by the way. Ignore him. He's just grumpy because the restaurant didn't send enough duck sauce."

The grump in question protested his label with a snarl, because that was effective. Then he trailed after them, continuing to loom while Kylie introduced her friend to the group. Somehow, meeting Knox didn't seem to make him any more comfortable.

"Come on. Sit." Kylie urged him to a spot on the sofa opposite Knox and turned for the kitchen. "Just let me run and get you a plate. Be right back."

Vic jumped to his feet like someone had just goosed his ass. "No!" He seemed to hear the panic in his own shout and cleared his throat before repeating much more calmly, "No, really, Kylie. I—I can't stay." He pulled a hand out of his pocket and held out a small red thumb drive. "Here. I cleaned up your image and saved it on here. Although next time I see you, you're going to explain how you came across such crappy footage of Richard Foye-Carver at some kind of a candlelit social."

Kylie had reached out to take the drive, but when she heard his joking words, her fingertips went numb. "Richard Foye-Carver?" she repeated dully.

"Yeah, not exactly his usual photo op." Vic eased toward the hallway, keeping wary eyes on both Dag and Knox. "So, um, give me a call this weekend if you've got time for, you know, coffee or something. I'm speaking Sunday morning, but otherwise I'm pretty open."

In the corner, Kylie could see Dag's glowering expression and hear the subtle rumble of his muffled growl, but frankly, everything had sort of faded into the background with Vic's news. Her mind kept trying to wrap around it as she walked her friend to the door, but every time she thought she had it, the slippery nugget of information would slide away.

Pasting on a poor imitation of a smile, she waved to Vic as he jogged down the steps and out into the night. Then she closed the front door, reset the alarm with trembling fingers, and slowly made her way back into the living room.

Wynn was the first to voice her thoughts. "Did that kid seriously just say the video is of Richard Foye-Carver? You've got to be kidding me."

Oh, if only, Kylie thought, sinking back to her seat and gazing down at the small device in her hand. This opened an entirely different can of worms than the one she had been prepared for.

Richard Foye-Carver was a name most of the developed world would have recognized if they heard it. The scion of a wealthy family, Carver grew up in the world of international business and high finance, evolving over the years from young playboy to wealthy-in-his-own-right tycoon, to renowned philanthropist and human rights activist. He appeared regularly in news reports from one third-world location or another, shedding light on the sad plights of the world's poor and persecuted.

And Kylie was supposed to accuse him of leading a cult of demon worshippers who were attempting to bring about the end of the world.

She could hear her *bubbeh*'s voice. *A mensch tracht und Gott lacht.* Man plans, and God laughs.

But really, did He have to make everything quite such a comedy?

From the sofa, Knox scowled. "This name holds meaning for you."

Wynn snorted. "Yeah, a little bit. The guy is a famous international figure, known as being a champion of the little guy and an all-around pseudosaint." She gave a brief potted biography of the man, ending with the thoughts that had already run through Kylie's mind. "Not only would no one believe a word anyone spoke against the man, but getting near enough to stop him ourselves would be next to impossible. The man has his own private security team that's probably better trained and certainly better equipped than the U.S. Army, and he never goes anywhere that the press doesn't follow and film everything he does, darn near up to using the toilet."

"It's useless." Kylie slapped the drive down onto the coffee table and glared at it. "Finding out his identity is essentially worthless to us. Yeah, we know who he is now, but we can't do a darned thing with that information. We might as well not even have it."

Dag stepped up behind her and crouched, his big body nearly surrounding her. "I do not agree with that," he said, flicking the drive with one finger and making it spin. "You say it is impossible to get to this man, and I say there is no one who cannot be reached, especially when a Guardian is involved."

"And I'm saying we couldn't get to him if he were a normal human being without getting our heads blown off. That's without even adding in the dangers that come from him being able to use black magic on top of everything else."

He tilted his head a bare inch. "That does make things a bit trickier."

Kylie opened her eyes wide and turned to Wynn. "Their heads really are made of rocks, aren't they?"

"No." Wynn defended her fiancé and his brother, laying her hand on Knox's knees. "Well, maybe sometimes."

The big Guardian frowned down at his witchy mate. "You doubt my ability to assassinate one member of the Order? When I have another of the brethren at my side? I take issue with this insult."

"It's not an insult," Kylie said. "It's an observation based on known data." When both gargoyles would have protested, she held up a hand. "Give it a rest, guys. No one is questioning your kick-ass macho fighting skills. Chill."

Wynn murmured her agreement, and the Guardians settled back but continued to look disgruntled. Of course, they almost always looked disgruntled, so Kylie ignored it.

Along with the images that flashed through her mind of the one occasion when she'd seen Dag looking a long, long way from disgruntled.

She cleared her throat.

Now that the initial shock of Vic's revelation had passed, she forced herself to get a grip and do what she always did—figure out what came next. "Okay," she said, as her foot started bouncing under the coffee table. "We just need to regroup a little and figure out where we really stand. So what do we know?"

"We know the identity of the Hierophant," Dag snarled. "And we should do something about him."

"We *think* we know," Kylie corrected. "Nothing in the video or in Ott's notes positively IDs the figure giving the speech as *the* Hierophant. So all we really know with one hundred percent certainty is that Richard Foye-Carver is a member of the Order of Eternal Darkness."

"We also know that he's nearly untouchable," Wynn reminded the brooding Guardians. "But we also know about this big strike that the local sect is planning to launch."

Kylie nodded. "Right. I think it makes more sense to focus on that. I mean, the Hierophant has existed forever, right? I mean, there's always someone around who's going to step up and lead the *nocturnis,* whether it's Carver or someone else. While it's a nice idea that we could take him out and throw the whole nest of vipers into chaos, *(a)* we don't really know that would happen, and *(b)* it might not be enough to stop whatever they have planned."

"But if we concentrate on discovering that plan and stopping it . . ." Wynn followed easily behind her friend's train of thought.

"Then we accomplish two things at once. We keep the Order from channeling a whole bunch of power to the Seven—"

"Potentially freeing Shaab-Na on top of Uhlthor."

"—and we buy ourselves more time to figure out if there is a feasible way to take out the Hierophant without getting ourselves killed or put on the fugitive lists of half the nations on earth."

The Guardians exchanged a silent glance. Kylie could almost hear them whining to each other about how much it sucked when the "human females" stuck their noses into things. Especially when they made such good points.

"Fine," Dag snapped. He returned to his seat next to Knox, looking like a prince holding court. A big, battered, grump-ass prince with the ability to turn into a gargoyle and eviscerate errant nobles, but still. "But we do not know what the *nocturnis* have planned, nor when their strike will occur."

"And that's what we have to concentrate on finding out."

"How?" Knox demanded.

Kylie and Wynn exchanged glances, and the witch slumped back with a groan. "Don't tell me. More research."

"Hey, I thought you said you were getting good at it?"

"Doesn't mean I like it," Wynn grumbled. "And it doesn't mean I don't get to try things my way first."

Kylie raised an eyebrow. "Your way being . . . ?"

"I'll spell it. You still have that drive from your informant? Or the note? The note would be even better."

Kylie frowned and thought back. "The drive, yeah. I might have the note, too, but I'd have to look in the office."

"I may be able to do a trace, especially if it's handwritten, and find out where he was over the past few weeks. Maybe we can find the Order's meeting spot. Sure, it's a long shot, but it beats the alternative."

"Then I'll take the alternative," Kylie said. "I think I might have to go to the deep for this one. If the Order is going to have any online presence, or if its members are going to set up any online communication, it's going to be there. I don't think they're Instagramming ritual snapshots."

"The deep?" Dag asked.

"The deep Web," Kylie clarified. "The dark Web, the darknet."

They all gave her the same reaction—the blank stare. Really, dealing with geeks was just so much easier sometimes.

She tried to break it down for them. "Basically, it's all the places on the Internet that don't get indexed and aren't searchable on your average search engine. You can't Google it. It's only accessible to anonymous users—you know, theoretically—and it tries to keep the identities of its users anonymous through complex routing and other little tricks of the trade. But anyone who wants to discuss things that are illegal, immoral, or liable to cause one form of government authority or another to come after them, that's where they hang out."

"Sounds perfect for our little friends."

"Which is why I'll be taking a look. You just say a prayer for me that I don't stumble across anything too gross while I'm looking. Some of the shit people talk about down there is just nasty."

Dag watched her shudder and frowned. "And what will Knox and I do while you two search for the answers to this *nocturni* strike?"

Kylie and Wynn exchanged glances before Wynn turned to her fiancé and fluttered her eyelashes. "Sit around and look pretty?"

He bared his teeth at her.

"You guys are still in charge of security," the witch said, more seriously this time. "Plus, we're going to need someone or someones to scout out any places we think might warrant interest from the Order in terms of good target locations. I know Knox would prefer I not go out exposed like that."

"And don't forget," Kylie added, "I meant it when I said that when the shit really hits the fan, I am not going to be charging into battle armed with a laptop and a gaming headset. Wynn and I might be hogging the glory for the moment, but when it comes down to kicking ass and taking names? That is aaaallll you two."

"Three." Wynn grinned. "I've found out I'm pretty good in the buttocks-booting department."

Kylie laughed. "I'll take your word for it. But me? I'm really more of a central-command, support-staff, civilian-noncombatant sort of a girl. I'll just bring the popcorn."

While Dag took Knox to check the outside perimeter of the house (Knox already being familiar with it from his earlier flyby of the bedroom window. Thank goodness they'd been at the back of the house where no one could see his gargoyle ass flapping away), Kylie and Wynn took care of putting away the huge quantity of leftovers.

Although, come to think of it, the two enormous Guardians ate even more than she would have suspected. Stagnant like rock their metabolisms clearly weren't.

Kylie was sorting through a drawer full of reusable takeout containers looking for matching lids and bottoms when Wynn threw the first punch.

"So, did you and Dag get the whole mate thing worked out?"

Seriously, it hit like a fist to the solar plexus, one Kylie had not seen coming. She felt positively winded. "What?" she managed to choke out.

"When you guys went upstairs before dinner." The witch scraped rice into a plastic tub and had the chutzpah to smile at her. "It sounded like you could use some time to talk things out."

"You've got to be kidding me. You think an hour is enough time to deal with the idea of everyone in the world assuming I'm now the destined life partner of a hunk of limestone with an attitude? *Az a yor ahf mir.* I should be so lucky, but my mind isn't quite that flexible, hon."

"What does it have to flex around? And don't exaggerate. Me and Knox—okay, and Fil, Spar, Ella, and Kees—are not the whole world. We're six people."

"No, you're three people and three mythological creatures who should not exist in my version of reality. Four, when you add in Dag. You don't think this is the kind of news that takes getting used to?"

Wynn gave Kylie the same look her grandmother used to use when Kylie told her the half-dozen missing cookies had been too burnt to serve to guests. "You've had a week to get used to the fact that Guardians exist and Demons are plotting to enslave humanity. If you weren't capable of grasping it, I'd be visiting you in a psych ward by now, so don't give me that excuse. The new facts of life are not what's giving you trouble here."

Kylie pouted as she piled leftovers into the fridge. "Why should I not have a little trouble with all this? You had a big ol' head start when it happened to you."

"On the subject of Wardens, Guardians, and the Order? Yeah, I did. But when it came to mating a great big hunk of winged badass, I did not, and I'll thank you to remember that."

Groaning, Kylie climbed onto a stool and buried her face in her arms. "Wynneleh, it's just too much," she mumbled into her own forearms. "I don't know what to do with all this."

"Really? Because judging by the crack in the plaster behind the headboard in your guest room, I'd say you knew exactly what to do this afternoon."

"There are knives hanging right over there." Kylie glared. "Don't make me stab you."

Wynn laughed. "What? I'm not allowed to know you had sex? Or I'm not allowed to know it was good enough to crack your plaster?"

"Neither. Either. Both. Yes. No."

"Maybe?" Her friend's amusement rang clear, but at least she didn't laugh again. "Look, I'm not going to tell you that I took to this whole mating thing like a duck to water, either. I don't think any of us did, and it's natural to have doubts. It's weird, it's fast, and it came out of frickin' nowhere, am I right?"

"*Oy vey,* are you right!"

"Right. But this wasn't really nowhere. I know you're not really religious, and I'm all witchy-witchy-woo-woo, which you don't really get, but I do honestly believe that the Goddess, or God, or Fate or whatever you want to call it, has a hand in all of this."

"Is the hand attached to a mouth that can't stop laughing?"

Wynn snickered. "Maybe. But that doesn't mean it's wrong about all this. There's a reason why we—you and me and Felicity and Ella—why we've been able to wake up the Guardians, and why we've been able to do it now, when clearly the danger from the Order is building. There's a reason why the old Wardens have gone missing, and why what's happening now bears so many similarities to the legend of the first Guardians and the females of power." She paused. "Please tell me that Dag at least told you that whole story after what happened this afternoon. I mean, after we talked in here earlier."

Kylie nodded.

"Okay, so you know that when the old ways stopped working, that was when the women woke the Guardians and helped defeat the Seven. The Guardians couldn't do it alone; they needed the special bond they had with their mates. They drew strength from it and that strength was necessary to their victory. So maybe the same thing is true now. Maybe we're necessary to help Dag and Knox and the others keep the Order from winning."

Kylie heard her words and understood what she was saying. She even maybe believed some of it, but she still felt as though there were some kind of trap closing around her. Or maybe an Acme brand anvil dangling by a rope above her head. "You mean, I should just lie back and think of England," she said, sighing.

"Oh, hell no!" Wynn scoffed. "I'm much more an advocate of sitting up and riding him like a cowgirl. I just mean that maybe if you just stopped fighting quite so hard and stopped trying to make everything make sense, things might fall into place without your help. You have to remember, Koyote girl, that life is not a program you can debug, or a line of code you can tweak until it all does what you want it to. It's a little bit more complicated than that."

Oh, how she hated it when other people made all the sense. She lifted her head and narrowed her eyes at her friend. "I still might stab you."

"Ha! I'd like to see you try. You'd have to get through my fiancé first, and he can't stand the sight of my blood."

And that reminded Kylie of all the things Wynn had gone through since she had been dragged into this mess well before Kylie had gotten involved. Wynn hadn't just been hurt, attacked, shot at, and nearly killed, she had lost a brother.

It all came back to Bran, and his loss was what had motivated Kylie to start digging around in the first place. She didn't want anyone else to lose their own family the same way, stolen from them by a group of people too greedy for power to see the lives of others as anything other than fuel for their evil fires.

Stopping the Order was the most important thing Kylie could ever do. Could she do that without the giant Guardian by her side?

Did she want to?

Chapter Twelve

Az dos harts iz ful, geyen di oygen iber.
When the heart is full, the eyes overflow.

Dag entered the room warily, nearly tiptoeing over the cool floorboards, entirely unsure of his welcome. A smart warrior, a cautious warrior, would have executed a strategic disengagement and given his mate the time she had told him she needed to sort through her feelings and the crucible of events she had already been through.

He wasn't that smart. Or maybe he simply wasn't thinking with his brain at that moment. Either explanation could be true. Possibly both.

He hadn't come upstairs for sex, though. At least, that hadn't been his primary motivation. He simply needed to see Kylie again, to be near her without the distraction of their temporary guests or the plans of the *nocturnis*. She had burrowed her way under his skin, and the only way to soothe the constant itch was to be near her, to smell her, to touch her, to feel the warmth of her small energetic body that somehow appeared restless even while lying still.

"I guess not growing up with a strict *bubbeh,* or you know, at all, means I shouldn't give you too much grief for not knocking."

Her voice floated out of the dark, quiet and relaxed, more amused than annoyed. Dag let out the breath he hadn't realized he'd been holding. "I did not wish to wake you if you slept."

"Yeah, not sleeping." She shifted, her skin shushing across the smooth sheets. He could see well in the dark, but she remained curled on her side, the puffy height of her covering obscuring her face from his angle near the door. "You might as well come in."

He crossed immediately to the bed and reached for the blankets.

"Whoa! Hold up there, Quick Draw," she said, holding out a hand to stop him. "I meant come into the room, not climb into my bed. I'm pretty sure we still have a few things to talk about."

Dag swallowed his disappointed sigh and sat on the edge of the bed, on top of the covers. He noticed the smaller size of this mattress compared to the one downstairs and couldn't help but picture how close they would have to curl together to both fit. His mate wished to talk, so he would talk with her. He just wished he possessed more skill at the activity.

"You have questions," he guessed.

She frowned. Now that he sat beside her, he could see her expressions clearly, and this one looked confused but not angry. He felt a stirring of hope.

"Actually, I'm not even sure I do," she murmured. Both of them instinctively kept their voices low, unwilling to disturb the intimacy of the quiet, darkened room. "I mean, I think I understand everything everyone has told me, so I don't need to ask how this all works, or what the legend says, or what my role is in all of this. My mind gets all those things. At least, it gets that they're things you all think are true, and I have no concrete evidence to disprove any of it."

Dag struggled to sit still and listen, to not lean toward her and try to make her see things the way he did. He might not have known this female for a long time, but he already knew that trying to rush her or pressure her would only result in frustration for him and more stubbornness for her.

"The only question that keeps popping into my head is why," she continued, tucking one arm under her cheek to raise her head on the pillow. "And it's not even clear to me which why I mean. Why me? Why you? Why would Fate care about the love lives of ordinary women and a bunch of stone statues? Why do men have nipples? Honestly, at this point they all seem equally relevant. So no, I don't have any questions, because I don't even really know what it is I want to know."

He tried hard to wrap his head around her words, which as usual she had strung together and knotted into sentences that took him time and effort to untangle. Finally, he said, "I cannot think any of those questions has an answer. Even if they did, I am unsure the answer would satisfy you."

She pulled a wry face and stuck her tongue out at him. "That big a *balagan,* am I? A big, crazy mess?"

"No." Dag shook his head. "But you seek answers that do not exist, because Fate does not operate in ways the living can understand. She has Her own rules and Her own agenda."

"Yeah, I think that's pretty clear."

He had to gather himself before he asked his own

question. "Do you object so strongly to me that you wish to deny our connection?"

She gave a long, heavy sigh. "That isn't it. There's nothing wrong with you. There's nothing wrong with Fate. There's not even anything wrong with the situation. I mean, if you take away the Demonic evil and its madcap minions. I'm not even sure what I feel is an objection to begin with. I don't really know how to articulate any of what I feel."

In the dark, his hand reached out and closed over hers. He rubbed his thumb over the back of her dainty fingers and squeezed gently. "Simply try."

Kylie looked away from him, turning her gaze to the shadows filling the room. "I think maybe I'm kind of hurt."

She spoke so softly, he had to strain to hear her, and when he did, he felt a jolt of shock and guilt. "I have hurt you?"

"No! No, you really haven't." The corner of her mouth hitched up just a tiny bit, and she squeezed his hand in return. "I was talking about Fate. It seems so strange to think that Fate could send me some perfect mate, some guy I'm destined to love and be loved by forever when it couldn't even be bothered to make my parents give a crap about me."

She tensed when she said the words, as if waiting for a blow or as if her own admission had shocked her. He suspected it might have been a combination of both.

Her hand tugged at his, trying to escape his grip, but Dag refused to allow it. Instead, he used the connection to pull her closer until he could scoop her into his arms and cradle her against his chest. She struggled half-heartedly while he settled himself in her bed, bracing his shoulders against her headboard and arranging her neatly in his lap. When she sniffled, he felt a crack run through his heart.

"I cannot explain the foolishness of your parents," he said, bending close to press his cheek to her curling hair. "It is unfathomable to me that a parent should treat their child so coldly, let alone that anyone should behave so toward one as good and precious as you."

She sniffled again, then followed with a laughing snort. "You're just saying that because you want into my pants."

"You are not wearing pants," he pointed out, running his hand up the smooth skin of her thigh beneath the overlarge T-shirt she wore as a sleeping garment. "And as I have already been inside them, the argument loses all meaning."

She gave another disbelieving snort, but then she let her head rest in the hollow of his shoulder and snuggled closer against him.

Dag continued, "You are precious to your grandmother, so much that she argued with her own child in defense of you, did she not?"

Kylie nodded with clear reluctance.

"You are precious to Wynn, too. Anyone can see the affection she holds for you. She claims you as her sister, in her heart even if not by blood." He had to clench his teeth to get the next example out without biting something. "And it is clear that you are precious to your other friends, if Victim was any example."

She slapped his chest lightly. "Vic*tor,* you big jerk. You know, you weren't very nice to him while he was here. I'm sure that's why he rushed off like that."

Not *nice* to the puny human? Dag had allowed him to leave with his head still on his shoulders and his intestines intact in his abdomen, hadn't he? He called that being very nice indeed, especially given the puppy-dog look of devotion the young male had turned on Kylie every time he glanced at her.

He swiftly moved to his next point. "You are precious to anyone who takes as much as a moment to get to know you, little one, because to know you is to see your true beauty." His arms tightened around her and he nuzzled the soft, fragile skin at her temple. "You are very, very precious to me."

She melted against him, which pleased him greatly, but he felt the hot warmth of tears on her cheeks, which made him want to kill something for daring to hurt her. Her relationship with her parents was clearly strained, but he sensed she might object if he tore their hearts from their chests and stomped on them.

He had to content himself with merely holding her, rocking her gently until her tears dried up and her breath went from uneven hiccups to a soft sigh. For a moment he thought she had fallen asleep until she raised a hand and laid her soft palm against his face. Unable to help himself, he turned into it and inhaled the sweet scent of her, loving the touch of bitterness that grounded her and made her somehow attainable for a monster like him.

Kylie threw her pity party for five more self-indulgent minutes. She wore the pointy hat, blew the noisemaker, threw the streamers, and ate the cake. Then she sat up and took a long hard look at the man sitting before her.

Dag looked back, his black eyes steady and unblinking, his expression calm and neutral. He didn't push, didn't withdraw, he just let her be.

How did he know to do that? Even she wouldn't have been able to identify that as what she needed, but Dag

knew and he gave it. Maybe that was why she trusted
him; even after only a week—and what a week it had
been—she knew that when he had sworn to protect her,
he had meant it. And she knew that when he had sworn
he was her mate, he meant that, too.

Did Kylie really want to fight him on it? After all,
what good would it do? The man's head had been carved
out of granite, more literally than most, so she knew
he wasn't going to change his mind. She didn't know if
she could change hers, either, but she knew she didn't like
the person she'd been on and off for the last couple of
days. She didn't like being confused, didn't like being
angsty, didn't like being a big, whining ball of "why me?"

Which meant that right here, right now, she was putting a stop to it. Time not just to nut up or shut up, but
to make the choice that no matter what the future held,
she would be fine just as long as she remembered to be
Kylie.

Squirming in Dag's embrace, she maneuvered herself
to straddle his lap, pressing her knees against his hips
and resting her hands on his chest. His own embrace
loosened but didn't fall away. His hands dropped to
lightly clasp her hips and his face lit with curiosity.

She grinned and stroked the hard muscle hidden beneath his gray T-shirt. She knew he'd put it on for her,
since he'd grumbled more than once that week over the
necessity of confining human clothing when not in his
natural form. Earlier, she'd been vaguely grateful. Now,
she wished he hadn't bothered.

"I'm done whining," she announced, finding the edge
of a pectoral muscle and tracing the curving line beneath the cotton covering. "I just thought you deserved
to know that. And I should thank you for putting up with
it. For that and for just now. What you said was really

sweet. And you're right. I'm a pretty lovable person, so I should get over myself and move on."

He blinked, his expression looking a little dazed and more than a little confused. "You owe me no apologies, little one, nor any thanks, but I am glad to hear you acknowledge the truth."

"That I'm lovable?" He nodded and Kylie let her grin turn wicked. "Yeah, I am." She leaned forward and let her unbound breasts press against him while she whispered into his mouth. "Want to love me right now?"

For a second, she wondered if he had turned back to stone, but then he shot forward in a burst of speed, locked his arms around her and flipped her onto her back. While he loomed over her, growling his arousal, Kylie tipped her head back and laughed with giddy pleasure.

"I'll take that as a yes." She giggled, loving the flash of mischief that glinted in his eyes as he relaxed and realized her blue mood had truly passed.

"Take this as well," he rumbled just before he dove into her mouth and dragged her into a riptide of desire.

She gloried in it, encouraged it, wanting to taste his wildness and the urgency of his need. When they had come together earlier, he had been careful with her, tender and seductive, until at the end when she had goaded him into letting go.

This time, she wanted him to hold nothing back.

She tried to tell him with the fervor of her response. She nipped at his lips, sucked at his tongue, and moaned at the rich, exotic flavor of him. She pressed herself up into his restraining weight, canting her hips to cradle his hardness, wrapping her legs around him and pulling him as close as she could manage. She twisted and writhed and dug her nails into his back, and all he gave her was the steady, smoldering heat of restrained passion.

Ha! She'd show him.

It would be great if she could pull off that trick of his and just make their clothes disappear with a thought, but she wasn't a Guardian or a witch. She'd have to drive him crazy the old-fashioned way.

Breaking free from their kiss, she turned her head to nibble her way from his jaw to the corded muscles of his throat. She heard his growl echoing in her ear before he dropped his head and began his own assault on her shoulder. He pulled the neck of her shirt aside and scraped his teeth across her pale skin before retracing the same path with his tongue.

While he distracted himself nicely, Kylie slipped one hand from its grip on his back and slid it sneakily between their bodies. Her fingers burrowed beneath the waist of his soft, drawstring pants. At the same moment that she closed her fingers around his straining erection, she twisted her head and struck, sinking her even white teeth into the flesh where his neck and shoulder met.

Dag howled.

He shuddered like a bolt of lightning arced through him, lit up with violent arousal. Kylie had the fleeting thought that she hoped he hadn't woken Wynn or Knox, before she decided to hell with it and stroked up his length with a tight fist. He muttered something sharp and guttural against her shoulder and half a second later she found herself imprisoned beneath more than two hundred pounds of male lust.

He had grabbed both her wrists, dragging her hands from him and pinning them to the bed above her head. While his own clothing disappeared with a thought, hers he dragged up over her head but didn't bother to pull completely off. Instead, he bunched the fabric in his hands, twisted and manipulated it until she discovered for the first time that a properly knotted and tightened T-shirt could make an effective pair of soft, abrasion-free shackles.

Who knew?

She mentally kissed her second pair of panties of the day good-bye, since he tore them from her with even less finesse than the first pair. She wasn't sure she'd be able to find all the pieces in the morning, but then again, she didn't really care.

She cared even less when he grasped both her legs just above the knees and leaned forward until he blocked the entire world from her view.

"You know, it is not nice to tease, little one," he murmured, his voice a rasping purr that raised goose bumps on her flesh and sent shivers racing down her spine. "Here. Let me show you."

Before she could even process the threat in his words, he wrenched her legs apart and covered her pussy with his hot, hungry mouth.

Her eyes rolled so far back into her head, she'd need surgery to get them out.

His tongue lashed at her like a tender, silken whip, flicking back and forth across her swollen clit until she actually begged him to stop. He did, sort of, abandoning her clit to explore the soft folds around her entrance and stab his tongue deep inside her. What on earth had she done?

Her hips writhed in a futile attempt to escape the relentless pleasure he forced upon her. Again and again, his mouth brought her to the brink of climax, then retreated, varying or dulling the stimulation until the pressure eased and she once again fell to breathless moaning.

The man should be outlawed.

"Dag, stop." She was panting, unable to draw in enough air for true coherence. "Enough. Just come inside me. Please. Fuck me."

He lifted his head just enough to meet her gaze, licked his lips and shook his head. "Mm, not yet," he growled and returned to his torture.

His lips closed around her clit and drew against it with soft, steady pulls that almost had her weeping. Her entire body felt feverish and aching, and she could feel beads of sweat trickling down her temples. She could only hope her heart was healthy enough for this kind of strain.

Desperate for relief, she brought her bound hands down and grabbed at his head, trying to pull him up and over her, but it felt like trying to shift a grand piano with her pinky finger. He batted her hands away and shoved them up out of his way before increasing the suction on her clit to something that tap-danced wildly across the line between pleasure and pain.

"Dag! Please!" she shouted, her voice hoarse and barely recognizable to her own ears. He responded by thrusting two long fingers into her soaked, empty passage and finding the spot on her inner walls that made her head explode.

The rest of her followed shortly after. The orgasm tore through her, taking her like a kitten in its teeth and shaking ruthlessly. Dag barely eased off the pressure, continuing to stroke and lick and torment until all she could do was shake and shudder and gasp for air.

Her pleas had dissolved into nothing more than a steady stream of whimpers by the time Dag lifted his head and stroked his hands soothingly across her belly and thighs. Her skin felt so sensitive that even the nonsexual touch almost set her off again.

"Such a good little human," he crooned, continuing to rub with firm, comforting pressure, avoiding her over-stimulated sex and her aching nipple until she finally felt like she could breathe again.

She forced her eyes open, surprised to realize she hadn't just closed them, but had clenched them so tightly that they didn't want to open. When she eventually managed it, she blinked up at him in a daze and found him watching her with that blazing black gaze.

"Good girl," he murmured, leaning forward to brush his mouth over hers. The simple touch made her realize that while the painful level of arousal had eased, her pussy still ached and pulsed with emptiness. She needed him inside her.

Kylie reached for him and he met her halfway, swiftly removing the T-shirt from around her wrists and bringing them to his lips for a rain of tender kisses. Then his hands clasped her shoulders, lifting her upper body from the bed and pressing her tight against his chest.

"I have but scratched the surface of how I wish to love you, little Kylie," he said, his voice a tender rasp. "I have so much more to show you."

"Good," she breathed and sank into his kiss.

He drew it out, deep and slow like all great kisses, the frantic pace of the last little while dissolving in a pool of languid heat. Then his teeth began to nibble, his hands stroked up her bare sides to close over her breasts, and the tension began to creep back into her muscles.

No way could she take another round of Dag's tender torture, but she still needed to feel him inside her. Pushing herself up onto her knees, Kylie tried to swing one leg over to straddle his lap, but his hands tightened, stopping her.

She felt a whine building, and had no problem with

telling him exactly what she needed, but he was already ahead of her. His hands urged her to twist until she faced away from him, staring through the darkness at the shadow of her headboard. Pressure on her shoulders eased her forward, while his grip on her hips held her lower body in place.

Eager for what was coming, she settled her knees under her and braced her forearms on the mattress, tilting her hips to offer herself to her lover. She shivered as his hands stroked across the round cheeks of her ass, and she couldn't bite back the moan of anticipation as his fingers closed around her hips. She needed him like her next breath.

He shifted behind her, his weight making the mattress dip. She had just an instant of warning as he set the head of his cock against her entrance before he thrust inside and filled her to the brim.

She didn't scream, but she did cry out, a long, low, trembling sound of surprise and pleasure. In this position, he felt enormous, his width stretching her tender muscles, his length seeming to press against her heart. Her pussy clenched, trying to grip and hold him in place, but he was already moving, setting a rhythm of deep, heavy thrusts that made her head whirl and her clit throb between her legs.

His harsh breathing sounded loud in the quiet room, and the slap of his hips against her ass made her blush even as it added to her arousal. She began to thrust back against him, reaching for the pleasure she could feel beginning to build low in her belly.

Dag grunted his approval and leaned forward, draping his chest over her and pressing their bodies together, drowning her in the slick feel of his skin, and his hot, earthy scent. The intimacy only drove her higher, and when he scraped his teeth over her shoulder, she shuddered and clenched around him.

"Give me your pleasure," he demanded, grasping her hip with one hand and sliding the other beneath her to press against the tight bundle of nerves he had already spent so much time tormenting. "Come," he said, tapping her clit with firm, deliberate pressure. "I want to feel you around me, little human. Now."

God, she wanted it, too. She reached for the climax, feeling it shimmer on the horizon. Then she felt his teeth close over the nape of her neck, digging in and holding her in place like an animal with its mate, and she lost it.

Everything went up in flames. Her body burned from the inside out, the orgasm like a wall of flames racing from the place where they joined through every inch of skin and muscle she possessed. She felt his hips bucking against her as he emptied himself inside her and wondered if he burned as well. Her arms and legs gave out, no longer able to support her, and she collapsed onto the mattress with a living blanket pressing her into the soft surface.

At least this time there was a sheet, she thought drowsily. As a couple, maybe they were making real progress. It was her last thought before sleep took her, but it took her smiling.

Chapter Thirteen

Az men hot a sakh tsu ton, leygt men zikh shlofn.
When you have a lot to do, go to sleep.

Kylie entered the fray with renewed energy and determination. After about twelve hours of recuperative sleep.
Ridiculously hot sex could apparently take a lot out of
a girl.

She had no illusions about a miraculous solution to
her issues. She wasn't naïve enough to think one conversation, one self-administered slap upside the head, and
one night of whew-boy-howdy sex meant that she and
Dag were now on the straight path to happily ever after.
She did, however, think that a more rational way to deal
with this relationship, as with any relationship, was to
take things as they came and to let it evolve into its own
thing.

Besides, she had other stuff to worry about. That end-
of-the-world nonsense just didn't seem to be going
away on its own.

Her bagels, however, were disappearing at an alarming rate. Apparently, gargoyles as a species got a real charge out of boiled and baked rounds of dough.

Everyone had gathered in the office, naturally, with bagels and coffee or tea (or soda) in hand to answer the day's burning question. Where the heck did they start?

"Okay, say I'm a psycho-killer Demon worshipper," Kylie threw out, bouncing lightly on her balance ball. "I want to make a big splash and raise a whole bunch of power in one fell swoop so I can feed it to my evil overlords. How am I going to do that?"

Wynn grimaced over her mug of tea. She perched on the arm of King David's chair, which was currently occupied. Not by the cat, but by her bagel-munching mate. "I'd like to say you're not, but then we wouldn't be here worrying about it."

Knox licked a schmear of cream cheese off his thumb. "Efficiency demands the *nocturnis* gather a crowd of humans together in one place. Once they strike, even if they are able to disguise the truth as some sort of natural disaster or terrorist action, the human authorities will descend and cut off their opportunity for another attempt. It must be all at once and quickly abandoned."

"Oh, crap." Kylie felt a quick clutch of fear. "What about Patriot's Day? It's coming up in just a couple of weeks, and there's the history there with the bombing."

Dag frowned. "What is Patriot's Day?"

"It's a state holiday here in Massachusetts to commemorate the American Revolution. It's the anniversary of the first battles of the war on April 19, 1775. The third Monday of April every year is the observance. There are historical reenactments, schools are out, and that's the day they run the marathon."

"With the bombing," Wynn said, her eyes widening.

When the Guardians continued to look confused, she clarified. "The Boston Marathon. It's an annual road race through the city. From what I understand, there are tens of thousands of runners entered, and several times that many spectators. A few years ago, a couple of terrorists set bombs near the finish line. Three people died and a couple hundred were injured."

"That is not the kind of death toll the Order will be seeking, not if they wish to raise enough power to summon the Unclean one, as well as to return the Defiler to full strength." Knox shook his head. "It is a brutal fact, but a fact. They will require dozens, or more likely, hundreds of deaths for that kind of black magic."

Now that she heard the facts, Kylie's stomach unclenched, and she nodded reluctantly. "You're right. Achieving that at an event like the marathon would be a massive undertaking. The route actually goes through like eight different towns. The runners will be scattered all over the course, and spectators are spread out all along it as well. It seems inefficient to try to strike in a place that will not get the results they want. Their best bet would be the finish line area, but the security there since the bombing is insane. I'm guessing the *nocturnis* are too, but that seems like banging their heads against a brick wall."

Dag grunted. "Agreed. We must consider other possibilities."

"I wish we even knew when they planned to strike," Wynn said. "Then we'd at least have a frame of reference."

Kylie frowned. "I've been through all of Ott's notes so many times, I can quote them by heart. He didn't know when the attack would come, but he knew it was in the works. He left the Order before the meeting where

Carver outlines the plan. His notes read to me, though, like he thought it was coming soon. There's a real sense of urgency in them."

"But does that mean tomorrow, or six months from now?" Wynn asked. "Remember, we're dealing with a cult that's been around thousands of years. Time means something entirely different to these people."

They all went quiet for a moment, each mulling over the problem for themselves. It was a few minutes before Kylie ventured, "You know, maybe we're looking at this from the wrong angle. Maybe our approach shouldn't be to try and pick a date or an event out of thin air. Let's try a little deduction."

Wynn laughed. "What did you have in mind, Sherlock?"

Kylie set aside her soda and turned to her computer. Her fingers flew over the keys as she typed and talked at the same time. "We need to start using what we already know about the Order and how they operate. I mean, the Guild has been watching them for, well, ever, right? And you've known about them your whole life, plus you've come up against them personally a couple of times recently."

"Yes, but I'm not sure I'm following you."

"Okay, let's think about what the Order wants." Kylie paused in typing and looked at her friend expectantly.

"You mean total global apocalypse."

"Well, sure, that. But *why* do they want it? Why enslave yourself to a bunch of Demons who see you as nothing more than a convenient tool or a late-night snack?"

"Power," Dag growled. "The *nocturnis* seek power, and they believe that if they remain faithful to the Seven, they will be granted power in the wake of their rising."

"Exactly," Kylie said, "but after reading Ott's notes, I have to say it's not just power. From what he wrote about, I think they want more. I think they want to be feared, and to watch the havoc they cause. It's sick, but I honestly believe they get off on it."

Knox nodded, his face grim. "That would not surprise me. Cruelty and sadism can be methods to raise power, but also to heighten the emotions of the victim. If the soul is in distress, it becomes a tastier treat for the Darkness."

"Right. So, if we operate on that understanding, it would make sense that whatever big bang the Order has planned, they're going to want to watch it happen. Especially the ones who planned it."

"Like the Hierophant."

"Yup. This is where we have to take a little leap of faith, so if we work for the moment on the assumption that Carver is the Hierophant, we could take a look at his public schedule and see if anything coming up looks like the kind of opportunity the Order would want to take advantage of."

Wynn looked dubious. "Do you really think he'd be so obvious as to pull that kind of stunt when the date and time are listed on his public schedule?"

"I think everything Carver does is listed on his public schedule. The man can't take a leak without reporters there," Kylie drawled. "The guy has made statements in the past that the constant media scrutiny is a burden he tolerates for the sake of the causes he supports. But no one can put up with that kind of twenty-four-seven attention without slipping up now and then, not unless they secretly like the spotlight. And Carver *never* slips up."

"It would fit neatly with the theory that the Hierophant will want to see the effects of his plan," Dag said.

Knox added, "And would point to the utter lack of conscience of the leaders of the Order."

"I don't think that was even in doubt." Wynn grimaced and drained her tea.

"It's also a great way to hide in plain sight. If the Order knows that the strike will happen at a public and highly publicized event, they can risk coordinating along public channels," Kylie said, pulling up Richard Foye-Carver's Web site and downloading his public events schedule. "All they have to do is keep the language neutral and they can skate by without notice as any other interested participants. Just leave out the words 'demon,' 'apocalypse,' and 'mass murder,' and they're golden."

Wynn frowned. "That sounds . . . disturbingly practical."

"It is an avenue we cannot afford to ignore," Knox acknowledged. "Without any idea of where and when the strike might happen, we are helpless to prepare even the most rudimentary defense."

Kylie let the others continue the discussion, the words droning on in the background, while she scanned the information on the screen. She couldn't put her finger on exactly what she was looking for, but she hoped she'd know it when she saw it.

It would have to be a large event, something open to the public. She suspected the Order would want large media coverage to up the fear and hysteria that would be generated, though the presence of reporters was never in question where Carver was concerned. She also had the niggling feeling that it was coming up soon, perhaps not tomorrow or the next day, but certainly within the next few weeks.

A jolt of something sizzled through her when she saw

it. Electricity, awareness, magic, she didn't know what to call it, but she absolutely felt it. All the way down to her bones. Maybe because she read it on the computer, her mysterious power made the seemingly innocuous information mean more to her, but whatever the explanation, she had no doubt that she had found the fateful day.

"It's not Patriot's Day, but it's close," she said, and felt all eyes turn her way. "The following weekend, in fact. The Carver Foundation World Congress on the Environment, Hunger, and Global Activism."

Wynn hurried to her side and peered at the screen. "Right here in Boston, April 23 and 24, at the Hynes Veterans Memorial Convention Center. You really think this is it?"

Kylie nodded. "I'm certain. Don't ask me why, but there's not a doubt in my head. It hits all the criteria—first, numbers. It says they expect more than five thousand people to attend from all over the world. All those people will be concentrated in one place for the event. The media will be swarming because of Carver, the topic, and the chance of other prominent world figures attending. The topic is so philanthropic that emotions will be running high, and there will be a huge outpouring from the public if anything tragic happens there. It both feeds the Demons and feeds Carver's need to appear in public and be adored. I *know* this is when they'll strike."

She met her friend's gaze and watched while Wynn digested her words and nodded. "Okay. I buy it."

Knox rose and began to pace. "It is a starting point. We should still perform our research to confirm." When Dag snarled at him, the other Guardian held up a calming hand. "I do not doubt your mate's sincerity, nor her intuition, but we cannot afford to be careless. I believe Kylie is correct, but we will use our research to verify and to gather further intelligence."

Kylie flashed the room a grin, a surge of energy filling her. She had a mission, a method, and a goal in sight. "Grab me a flashlight, boys," she crowed, cracking her fingers and settling in at her computer. "I'm going dark."

Kylie enjoyed the dark and dangerous aura of the deep Web as much as the next person, but the truth was most of what lurked out there was about as sinister as your average university bulletin board. A little sex, a lot of rock 'n' roll, and maybe one or two part-time pot dealers. The darknet, the dingiest corner of the deep, did play host to illegal activity and immoral adventures, just the kind of thing to interest the cultist who wanted everything.

Or, you know, a bored NSA agent with an arrest quota.

Its reliance on anonymity made the users of the darknet feel safe in doing things they wouldn't want to come to light (pun intended), but the rub was that as soon as what was discussed on the Net was put into action in the real world, that anonymity disappeared. When you actually started to do stuff physically, people got the chance to see you doing it and figure out who you really were.

Kylie was counting on that, and kept it as a mantra in her mind while she began to slowly and carefully follow the threads of the *nocturnis'* plans for the April conference.

Knox and Wynn elected to return to Chicago for a couple of weeks. With the group fairly certain that whatever was going to happen wouldn't happen until late in the month, hanging around twiddling their thumbs together seemed less than productive. Wynn could work more and better magic in her ritual room at home, and Knox could train and prepare from anywhere. They would return once they had all agreed on their plan to foil the Order, and in plenty of time to set themselves up.

Before leaving, Wynn had dragged Kylie away from the computer long enough to give her a few short lessons in what it meant to be a woman of power. Apparently, no one intended Kylie to get away with being a supernaturally gifted hacker and nothing else. Since she knew she had magic inside her now, Wynn fully intended to show her how to use it.

She had to learn to feel it first. Wynn showed her how to turn her attention inward and look for the spark of the power inside her, the little buzz that always lived in the corner of her mind. And here for all these years, Kylie had thought of it as the mark of undiagnosed ADHD. No, Wynn laughingly contradicted her; that was magic.

Once she found the spark, she got a lesson in how to nurture it. How to blow on the tiny flicker and bring it to a small, steady flame, then how to pull on it and let the power in it seep through her until it waited, tingling, in the tips of her fingers, ready to do her bidding.

Wynn, though, wouldn't let her bid it for *bupkes*. No, teacher witch told her that for now, she needed to concentrate on just learning to recognize the magic and calling it to her command. Anything more advanced would have to wait until they had some real time to concentrate and work together.

Just the idea made Kylie grimace. It was like those three horrible months when her mother had forced her to take piano lessons all over again. Kylie had wanted to rock a little ragtime and the stern, humorless teacher just had her practicing scales over and over and over until the very sound of them made her teeth ache.

At the time, giving up had felt like being released from prison, but to this day, she couldn't play more than "Mary Had a Little Lamb" on the piano. Wynn assured her that taking the same path with magic practice would undoubtedly lead her at some point to singeing off her own eyebrows. At the very least. So Kylie promised to practice.

Wynn and Knox's departure left Kylie and Dag alone in the house, which worked out better than she had expected. Her new live-in-the-now philosophy kept her from getting too worked up by analyzing everything that happened between them, and she had to admit the sex continued to rock her world.

That pun she had not intended, but she couldn't deny its applicability.

Trying to discern the details of the Order's plans proved to be slow going, but if nothing else, her crawl through the deep Web was turning up some really interesting reading material. She'd known about the deep forever, and used it herself for her more . . . well, actually, her *less* officially sanctioned projects, but she had never thought of what a perfect place it was for magic users.

Part of that probably stemmed from the fact that, like most people, she had never believed magic existed. Now that her eyes had opened to that particular world, she found that the anonymity and discretion offered by the deep allowed people all over the world to discuss something that users of the surface Web would have either mocked or tried to copy, with potentially disastrous results.

Kylie got to listen in on a group of ceremonial magicians in Europe discuss the effects of days of the week on the quality of raised energy. She watched a Yoruba priest from Benin counsel a young practitioner in South America on the basis of Oshun's passion for honey. She even saw a witch in Ireland sending out an enquiry on the sudden uptick in seismographic activity in her area and what magical causes might be underlying.

She freely admitted that she understood almost none of it, but just seeing it all fascinated her and opened her eyes to how much she needed to learn. Especially if she had any intention of sticking with this Warden gig for the long term.

Right. Still not thinking long term. Move it along, Kylie. Nothing to see here.

The problem she ran into fairly quickly was that the short term seemed to be taking. For. Ever.

Every day, she hunkered down in front of the computer and played cyberspy, taking short breaks here and there to run through the magical exercises Wynn had taught her. It quickly evolved into a routine that kept her semisane while still allowing the gremlin of tedium to niggle her brain stem. Meanwhile, Dag seemed to be turning her basement into some sort of arsenal-slash-dojo.

Where he was getting the weaponry she occasionally caught him hauling through her hallways she still hadn't managed to figure out. When she asked him about his pet project, he only told her that a warrior must train in order to keep himself prepared and ready for battle, and that a Guardian always had access to the tools he needed to perform his duty. From this cryptic nonanswer, she deduced that something about a Guardian's magic allowed him to create the weaponry out of thin air, the same way he seemed to be able to do with his clothing. Of course, when she asked for a model Millennium Falcon to add to her collection, all of a sudden his power had limitations. Sandbagger.

Actually, the way he explained it to her, and the way she pretended to understand, was that while each Guardian was in and of himself magical, a Guardian could not *work* magic. He could not wield the power in the way a witch or a Warden could. In other words, he had magic flowing in his veins, but he could not cast a spell the way Wynn could and the way everyone told Kylie she would eventually be able to manage. If she kept practicing.

When she told him that sounded like a cop-out and rolled her eyes at him, he retaliated by kissing her senseless, and she wound up being thoroughly taken on top of her own kitchen island. She enjoyed every darn minute of it, but *oy*! That granite was cold under her bare skin.

Every day or two, Kylie tore herself away from either her computer or her Dag to touch base with Wynn and share any details she had gathered on the Order's planned attack. So far, she had managed to narrow down the most likely time for the strike to occur at either the opening banquet on Friday night, at which Richard Foye-Carver would personally welcome attendees and outline the goals and structure of the weekend's events; or the keynote address, delivered of course by Carver, which would cover the topic of corporate responsibility for the climate changes now affecting so many of the world's people.

Carver and his speechwriters made it all sound so noble and altruistic. Frankly, it made her a little *blech-edich*.

Wynn, in turn, reported their findings to the other Wardens and Guardians, who had placed themselves on standby in case reinforcements were needed on the day of the attack. Kylie hoped that by the time the date rolled around, they'd have a much better handle on what needed to be done and why.

Finding out the nature of the attack was the problem currently driving her crazy. Her initial theory of some kind of a bomb had been dismissed by the others as unlikely, for the simple reason that it sounded too mundane for the *nocturnis,* who tended to favor dramatic acts of black magic, dark ritual, and supernatural chaos. Planning a mass murder cum Demon raising at a modern American convention center already stretched the boundaries of (im)propriety for them. Underground caverns, defiled woodlands, and abandoned buildings all ranked as much more traditional choices.

Knox had suggested an old-fashioned armed ambush, with *nocturnis* flooding into the convention center armed with cursed daggers and simply overwhelming the attendees with huge numbers and the element of surprise. To Kylie this sounded impractical. The welcome dinner was expected to draw about two thousand attendees, all of them the most highly visible and politically influential of the weekend crowd. To stab that many people before a whole bunch of them figured out a way to either escape or fight back would take way more physical numbers than they assumed the local sect could draw upon.

For her part, Wynn theorized a more magical offense, where the most powerful of the *nocturni* mages would seal the room and summon minor demons to slaughter the trapped humans. This seemed more practical to Kylie, if not equally as gory.

Dag had contributed the ever-so-uplifting suggestion of either the dinner or the keynote being merely a decoy. The Hierophant and other *nocturnis* would never enter the room, but would lure the attendees inside, seal the space, and then set the whole thing on fire. Demons, apparently, found souls equally appetizing after a little charbroiling.

Every day, Kylie kept the theories in mind as she dug deeper and spied harder, trying to sift through metric tons of data for the few little kernels of truth that might or might not be buried in the *drek*. It became the kind of mind-numbing, backbreaking work that she'd always sworn to avoid, the very idea of which had made her devote all her free time to her own interests and eventually drop out of college so she would never have to do the grunt work.

The fact that she'd taken this all on not only voluntarily but for free made her an extremely grumpy Koyote. More often than not, Dag turned out to be the thing that dragged her out of her moods and made her remember that grump was not her natural default setting.

Feeling the tension building to critical mass one Thursday afternoon, Kylie pushed away from her computer and went in search of a distraction. These days, nothing proved more distracting to her than descending the stairs to her basement and watching Dag swing giant pieces of medieval-looking weaponry around his sexy head.

When he practiced in his human form—shirtless, of course—was her favorite, because she wasn't stupid, and hello that was a pretty sight; but oddly enough, she found watching him train in his natural form equally compelling. It might not make her fantasize about sex the same way (no way was anyone that big getting near her with what she knew darned well was proportionally sized genitalia), but his lethal grace and immense power still left her in awe.

Deciding it would be unbecoming to have drool already drying on her chin when she got downstairs, she forced herself to think of work on the short trip to the basement. Fat lot of good it did her, because her dry mouth lasted less than five seconds.

Dag had already stripped off his shirt and worked up a fine sheen of sweat when he appeared in her line of sight. Sucking in a breath, Kylie let her knees buckle the way they wanted to and plunked her *tokhes* down on the bottom of the stairs to watch him train.

His muscles glistened under the fluorescent lights as he flexed and stretched and spun in an intricately choreographed dance of battle. His lean hands wrapped around the shaft of his favored weapon, a massive war hammer Kylie had been unable to move, let alone lift, when she'd curiously touched it.

Unlike other hammer weapons she had seen (yes, she had Googled the things after her first glimpse of Dag in action with one), this one didn't look like an ice axe with one blunted end. In fact it seemed to have more in common with the type of weapon Thor carried in those superhero movies. Its huge, heavy head was bigger than both Dag's fists put together, and instead of one end tapering to a point, this weapon saved its spearing for the end of its long handle. Kylie had seen Dag send the head swinging through the air with lethal force and immediately follow with a graceful twirl that had him burying the end of the handle in some imagined foe's black heart.

She had to admit, it might have made her panties a little wet. Did that make her a bad person?

Now she watched the Guardian move through his

paces in a warm-up routine he said helped to calm and focus him before his real training began. To Kylie, it looked like the katas she'd seen in movies and documentaries about the martial arts. Only, you know, with more giant iron weaponry.

When Dag finished his warm-up, he set the hammer head on the floor at his feet and turned to look at her, his expression intent and unexpectedly . . . hungry. She felt her eyes go wide.

"Um, I didn't mean to interrupt," she offered, trying to keep the squeak out of her voice. "I just needed a break. From the screens. You know. I, uh, I can go if I'm disturbing you."

She couldn't call his expression a smile, but his face shifted and his mouth eased at the corners, while a slightly softer light entered his eyes. Right alongside the glint of lust.

Ei! Ei! He'd already pounced on her once this morning, before she even got out of bed. Could he really think either of them had the energy for another round? Had he never heard of chafing?

She squirmed against the hard wooden stair tread, realized what she was doing, and bounced to her feet. "Right. I'll just, uh, let you get back to it."

He was on her before she could turn, closing the distance between them with a speed that only proved how inhuman he really was underneath all that yummy human muscle. His hand closed over hers and tugged her toward him. Standing on the bottom of the stairs, she didn't have to crane her neck, but she still had to look up to meet his gaze.

"You have no need to hurry away, little one," he rumbled in the voice she had come to think of as the big sexy. Ever since she slipped up and told him it made her shiver, he'd begun throwing it around with shameless regularity. "I have completed my warm-up, as you call it." He leaned down to nibble on her shoulder. "Should I show you how warm I am?"

She wasn't sure her heart could take it. She lifted a hand, intending to push him away. After all, she hadn't come down here for this. No, really, she hadn't. But her fingers ended up smoothing over his hot, damp skin of their own volition. Darned things could no longer be trusted. Traitors.

"I really don't think that's—ah!—necessary," she mumbled, gasping when he closed his teeth gently over the tendon in her throat and swiping her skin with the flat of his tongue. "I'm fine."

He leaned the handle of his hammer against the side of the stairs and wrapped both arms around her, trapping her against his bulk. One rough hand slid under the back of her T-shirt and rasped against the skin at the small of her back, causing an instantaneous reaction between her legs.

Sneaky male. He'd obviously paid attention recently and noted that the small of her back was an incredibly sensitive erogenous zone for her. The right caress there could have her begging in seconds. Especially when it came from his uniquely textured fingers.

She had become fascinated by his hands. Not only were they huge—more than twice the size of hers; she had measured—but they had a texture he claimed was unique to his kind. Instead of the whorls and ridges of a human fingerprint, the surface of his skin featured tiny microscopic pitting, like the surface of an unpolished stone. Not only did it make him immune to the identification procedures used by human authorities (which was handy when one occasionally had to kill people the human authorities didn't always know needed to die), but it provided the exquisitely abrasive tactile sensation that made Kylie squirm.

In fact, the man was making her squirm right then and there. "I thought you had to train," she half gasped, half moaned, as he shifted his grip to lift her off her feet and press her against the hard length of his torso. Things felt pretty hard slightly south of his torso, as well.

Kylie estimated she had approximately fifteen seconds to put a stop to his seduction attempts before they stopped being attempts and became a grand slam home run. Did thinking it in her head count as a college try? A kindergarten putsch?

"A Guardian is always prepared," he purred, "but what sort of mate am I to place your needs below my own."

Kylie tilted her head to the side, giving him better access to the sensitive skin underneath her jawline. "Trust me, my needs are doing just fine, big guy. In fact—"

Whatever she intended to say disappeared into the raucous chime of the doorbell. Wynn and Knox had suggested she add it before they left, just so that future knocks on the door didn't go unnoticed for long enough to encourage visual exploration.

Kylie knew Wynn was a witch, but was she a psychic, too?

Tearing herself from Dag's embrace, she backed up a step, nearly fell over backward, and righted herself with a blush of embarrassment. "Yeah, I'd better get that."

Dag replied with a low snarl and a flash of teeth.

She turned to jog up the stairs, throwing a hasty suggestion to him over her shoulder. "If you want to guard my back, you might want to put a shirt on first. You'll give my poor innocent mail carrier a heart attack."

Since her own heart still pounded in her chest, Kylie figured she knew whereof she spoke.

She hurried along the hallway to the front door and pulled the panel open to receive whatever package the mail carrier couldn't fit through her door slot. That smile froze then fell into a gape of surprise when she saw who really stood on her front stoop.

"What? No hello? You were raised by wolves?"

"Bubbeh!" The word squeaked out from paralyzed vocal chords as Kylie looked into her grandmother's weathered and wholly unexpected face. "What are you doing here?"

Chapter Fourteen

Far vos hot Oden un Khave tsugedekt di mayse mit
a blot, ven keyner hot zey nit geyzen?
*Why did Adam and Eve cover their business with
a leaf if there was no one to see them?*

"I sensed a disturbance in the force," Esther Kramer
said, stepping inside and depositing her archaic brocade
carpetbag on the entryway floor. "That's how that saying of yours goes, right?"

Kylie closed the door slowly behind her grandmother
and surreptitiously leaned back against it for support.
Shock had turned her knees into chopped liver. "Um,
yeah. That's right. But *bubbeh,* I wasn't expecting to see
you. How did you even get here?"

Esther leaned back from the embrace she'd already
pulled her granddaughter into and gave her a stern look.
"I'm seventy-eight years old. You think I don't know
how to ride a train and hail a cab?"

"No, of course, I know you can do that." Kylie attempted to soothe her. "It's just that it's such a long way.
Did you come by yourself? All the way from Westport?"

Her grandmother reached up and gave her cheek a
forceful pat. Just a reminder that if she needed some

sense slapped into her, Esther was the woman to do it. "All the way? You live in the next state over, and you make it sound like I wandered the desert for forty years. What? Are you not happy to see me?"

Uh-oh! Minefield ahead! "Of course I'm happy, *bubbeh*. I love you. But—"

"Because you could forgive a person for wondering." Esther unbuttoned her long, rose-colored wool coat and handed it to Kylie, following it with her smart black hat, gray scarf, matching gloves, and her small, much beloved Chanel handbag. "I mean, when your only grand-daughter calls you on the telephone and tells you in a voice message that she won't be coming for Passover seder, what do you think this does to a woman's heart?"

"Bubbeh—"

"But we can talk about that later. First you can show me this beautiful home you bought for yourself and haven't invited me to yet."

Oy.

Vey.

Esther Rachmann Kramer was on a roll.

She sighed. "Yes, *bubbeh*."

"Or, on second thought." Esther looked over her granddaughter's shoulder, her hazel eyes going wide and her lips curving in a smile that spelled nothing but trouble for Kylie. "Maybe first you should introduce me to the young man standing in your hallway. I'm guessing this is why you took so long to answer the door, with your hair all mussed and your cheeks red like borscht."

Zol Got mir helfen! Oh, God help me, she thought, squeezing her eyes shut for a brief moment and wishing she'd just wake up in the ICU at Mass General. That coma theory simply kept sounding better and better.

The elbow in her ribs, however, told her it was not

meant to be. She had to suffer through this. People thought it was so nice that Jews didn't believe in hell; they didn't have to. Hell was right here on earth. In Kylie's front hall.

"Bubbeh," she said very carefully, gesturing Dag forward. He was lucky she didn't gesture for him to lift her up and fly out the nearest window. "This is my friend Dag. Dag, this is my grandmother, Esther Kramer."

Esther held out her hand and looked from Dag to her granddaughter. "What, he's like that Prince singer? He doesn't have a last name?"

Before Kylie could manage to swallow her panic, Dag stepped forward and gently clasped her grandmother's delicate, wrinkled hand in his own. He shook it carefully while simultaneously making a sort of abbreviated bow that on him looked not pretentious, but sort of old-world and chivalrous. "Dag Steinman, Mrs. Kramer. I am honored to meet you. Kylie speaks of you often and with great warmth."

Stone man? Kylie nearly choked on her tongue.

"Steinman," Esther repeated, eyebrows rising toward her hairline. She looked him over more deliberately, not bothering to hide her interest. "Are you Jewish? Or just German?"

"Bubbeh," Kylie groaned.

Esther didn't even bother to look away from the current target of her interest. "What? I'm just curious."

Dag barely hesitated. "I am sorry, I am not Jewish. My, ah, my ancestors did spend a great deal of time in Germany, though. In the fifteenth century, I believe."

Meaning Dag had lurked on the battlements of some castle there, no doubt. Desperate to change the subject, Kylie carefully linked elbows with her grandmother and attempted to guide her to the open doorway to the living room. "Come on, *bubbeh.* You said you wanted to see the house. Let me give you a tour."

"All right." Esther waved her free hand to Dag. "You can join us, Mr. Steinman. It looks like you've spent plenty of time here. You can help show me around."

The older woman let Kylie lead her into the living room, took one look around, and dug in her heels. Then she threw up her hands and turned on her granddaughter like a rabid ermine.

"This is how you live?" she demanded, the New York accent she had sublimated with the softer tones of Connecticut after fifty-odd years reemerging with a vengeance. "And you invite people over to see you living like a *vilde chaya*? No curtains on the windows, no rugs on the floor! You have that gigantic television on the wall, and all the furniture you can manage is a single sofa and one measly table? Who exactly raised you, Kylie Tsifira Kramer? Because I know I did not teach you anything like this."

"Bubbeh—"

"No!" Esther slapped her hands against the air, closed her eyes, bowed her head, and drew a deep breath. "Don't speak. Just show me the rest. Go on."

So Kylie did, wincing every time her grandmother hissed air in through her teeth and muttered under her breath in Yiddish. Since Dag didn't speak the language, it went against Esther's fundamental beliefs about good manners to use it in his presence, which only served to emphasize how heinous she considered Kylie's transgression. She inspected the house top to bottom, mercifully leaving the attic and basement off the list, since no one outside of Kylie needed to see those.

When the tour concluded in Kylie's bedroom, the old woman pursed her lips, drew a cleansing breath, then turned a steely gaze on her granddaughter. "Coffee," she said flatly. "Then we can discuss this."

"Yes, ma'am," Kylie said meekly, and followed the woman back to the kitchen.

Dag had watched the entire event quietly and with deep apparent fascination. His gaze moved back and forth between the two women like a spectator at a tennis match, even though neither spoke much after the first two or three rooms. At first, Kylie had been grateful to him for not calling Esther's attention to himself, but gradually she had begun to pray he would do something drastic to save her from the obviously growing disapproval. Heck, if he'd stripped her naked, thrown her to the floor, and proceeded to ravish her in front of God and everyone, at least it might have made Esther think about something other than Kylie's utter lack of home-making skills.

At least his manners remained impeccable. When they moved up or down the stairs, he gallantly offered his arm to assist with the older woman's balance, and as soon as he returned to the kitchen, he pulled out one of the chairs at the small table Kylie never used and helped Esther to her seat. Climbing onto one of the tall counter-height stools at the island would have been awkward for her.

She remained silent, but her sharp gaze watched Kylie's every move as her granddaughter scrounged through cabinets looking for the cups and saucers and other hostessy items that she would consider necessary to properly receive a guest. By the time Kylie had brewed the coffee and set a tray with cups, saucers, cream, sugar, and the leftover almond cookies she had squirreled away after the Chinese feast (the only cookies she had in the house), she felt like she had just run a marathon.

On one leg. With a stab wound to the kidney.

Very carefully, Kylie poured her grandmother's coffee, then turned to offer some to Dag. He shook his head, and Esther seemed to take that as some sort of signal.

"Pardon me for being unforgivably rude, Mr. Steinman—"

"Dag," the Guardian insisted.

"Dag," Esther conceded. "You're very gracious. Forgive me, but I was hoping I might have a few minutes alone to talk to my granddaughter."

"Of course," Dag said at the same moment that Kylie's internal voice screamed, *"Noooooooooo!!!!!!"* like a character in a bad horror movie who had just stumbled on the first mangled body.

She knew she couldn't say anything, though. Not to the woman who had kept Kylie secure and grounded and seen that she knew what it meant to have a family when her own parents couldn't have cared less.

"Well, miss," Esther began, slowly stirring a spoonful of sugar into her black coffee. "I hardly even know what to say to you."

"Bubbeh, I know the house isn't finished, and—"

Esther gave her head a sharp shake. "That is not the problem here."

Kylie felt the dagger in her kidney move up to her stomach and twist. "Dag? *Bubbeh,* you don't know him. He's really the—"

The old woman snorted. "That wonderful young man? I grant you, he's a little too quiet for my taste, but my Ben was a talker. No, he seems like a fine man, polite, respectful, and the way he can't take his eyes off of you shows me he at least has good taste. It would be nice if he were Jewish, but I gave up on that idea years ago. That is not what we need to discuss."

Kylie shook her head, utterly confused. "Then I don't understand."

"Kylie." Esther stretched out her hand and laid her fingers over her granddaughter's, squeezing with surprising strength. "There is something that is not right with you, *bubeleh*. I could feel it before I even got here, and now I can see the evidence with my own eyes. So I'm here, and I'm asking you. What is going on with my only baby girl?"

Dag had left the room at Esther's request, but he hadn't gone far. Just far enough that his keen Guardian hearing could pick up their conversation while remaining concealed himself.

He had scented Kylie's distress the minute he emerged from the basement and saw her open the door to an elderly woman in a black hat and a pink coat, but when she had turned to face him, he hadn't needed his nose to discern her state of panic. It was written all over her face.

For a moment, his instincts had urged him to throw himself into the fray and place his body between his mate and the danger that threatened her. His instincts, however, had a hard time reconciling the idea of the small, wizened, and obviously aged woman in the doorway with an assault on Kylie's physical well-being. He quickly realized that the only weapon Esther Kramer carried was guilt, but she wielded it like an expert swordswoman.

Standing barely an inch over Kylie's four-ten frame, and although her spine might have begun to curve, Esther still carried herself with the straight-backed pride of a much younger woman. Her skin had taken on the faint translucence of age, but the color reminded him greatly of her granddaughter. The women also shared the same curve of the cheekbone and that distinctively stubborn chin.

Esther's hair had gone gray, strands of steel and iron lightened by the occasional thread of silver, but it appeared to curl much like Kylie's, though she wore it in a much shorter crop that had obviously been styled with care. The same attention to her appearance showed in her clothing, all well tailored from fabrics of obvious quality.

Everything about her stated that this was a woman to be reckoned with. He imagined that in fifty or sixty years, his Kylie would look much the same. He looked forward to seeing her mature into an equally formidable matriarch.

In that moment he realized the true importance of convincing her to accept their mating. Only a true bond between them could free him of his duty and allow him to share a natural human life span with his mate. If she were to reject him and their relationship, he would be condemned to another long slumber and an eventual awakening to a world with no Kylie in it.

The thought made him clench his fists until the knuckles ached. He could not survive in such a future. He needed her too badly.

A grunt of satisfaction escaped him when he heard his mate's grandmother express a positive opinion of him. He would not have stepped away from Kylie even had the old woman commanded it, but he was glad not to be the cause of tension in their family. As he understood, Kylie had too few family members she could rely on as it was.

But it was the old woman's softly voiced question that really got his attention.

What is going on with my only baby girl?

He heard Kylie's tired sigh.

"*Bubbeh,* it's nothing," Kylie said. "I'm just tired. I guess I've been working too hard."

"Du kannst nicht auf meinem rucken pishen unt mir sagen classe es regen ist."

Dag frowned even as Kylie laughed weakly.

"I'm not pissing on your back and telling you it's raining, *bubbeh.* I really have been working hard."

"On what?" Esther demanded. "You made enough money with that big-time program you wrote that you never have to work another day in your life. And before you interrupt to tell me you like to work, I'll remind you that in all of your years, you have never missed coming home for Passover. Not while you were in college, not while you were in negotiations for your business, not even the year you had a broken leg and mono all at the same time. Busy does not keep my *ainikl* from home on the holiday."

"*Bubbeh,* please. What if I promise I'll come for Shavuot instead? I know it's not Passover, but we can light the candles together and—"

"Is it this man of yours? He doesn't want to come with you? He doesn't want you to go? Because I thought I already made up my mind to like him, but it hasn't been very long. I can change it."

"No. No, it's not that. It's just—"

Dag hated hearing her struggling for words that would pacify her grandmother's fierce curiosity and determined persuasion without giving away the secrets she had so recently become privy to. Part of him wanted to race in and show the woman what was at stake if he and Kylie should fail to thwart the plans of the Order, but he knew his duty too well.

He also knew Kylie tended to get testy with him when

she thought he was being overprotective, or behaving as if she could not take care of herself.

There was a stretch of silence before he heard Kylie shift in her chair and sigh. "*Bubbeh,* I can only apologize for not visiting you for Passover. Believe me when I tell you it's not what I want either, but you raised me to keep to my principles and to always remember my duty to my fellow man. I can't tell you exactly why I can't come, because it's a story that isn't all mine to tell. But I can tell you that someone will be in danger that weekend, and they'll need my help to keep them safe."

Another brief silence. When it finally ended, he expected the same kind of insistent demand for answers he had come to expect from Kylie. The same trait that he had begun to suspect she had inherited directly from Esther.

Instead, the old woman said, "Is this going to put you in danger yourself?"

"I don't know. But I can tell you that I'll have friends looking out for me. Dag will be there. So will my old friend Wynn. You remember her. Bran's sister? She'll be there with her fiancé and maybe others. But this is too important to leave to just them. I need to be here, and I need to help."

Esther harrumphed. "Well, I probably don't have to tell you that I don't like this."

"No, *bubbeh,* you don't."

"But you're right. I did raise you to know what is right and to do what is right when you're the only one who can. We should all be loving and kind to each other."

"That's what I'm trying to do. Thank you for understanding."

"But I still don't like it!"

"I know, *bubbeh*. I'll come for Shavuot. I promise."

Dag heard movement and the rustling of fabric and the soft sound of patting hands and knew the women shared an embrace. Relief washed through him.

"Yes, you will come," Esther said, her voice slightly muffled by the hug. "And bring your boy. I'll make blintzes."

Kylie chuckled. "We'll see, *bubbeh*."

"Now, since I'm already here, and there's no way I'm getting back on that *farkakta* train tonight," Esther said, her voice coming clearer as she pulled back from her granddaughter, "why don't you tell me what you have planned for your birthday tomorrow?"

Shock propelled Dag forward and out of hiding. Unable to stop himself, he stared at Kylie in offended shock. "Your birthday is tomorrow? But you never mentioned this to me."

Esther looked from Kylie to Dag and back again. "*Bubeleh,* you never told your boyfriend about your birthday? How is he supposed to get you a present if he doesn't even know the date?"

Kylie looked as if she couldn't decide who to glare at, so she settled on staring at the ceiling. "Dag doesn't have to get me a gift. And I've had a lot on my mind. It just hasn't been a priority."

"I don't care how important this work of yours is! You have to take the time to celebrate your life." Esther patted her granddaughter on the cheek and stepped back. "Go put on some lipstick. I'm taking you out to dinner. Both of you."

"That's really not necessary. I don't even—"

"Lipstick. Now." Esther pressed her lips together in a stern expression and pointed to the stairs. "And maybe a dress. Or at least a blouse that doesn't have some smart-mouthed saying on it. And a little perfume never hurt anybody!"

She had to raise her voice on the last suggestion, because Kylie had already given in and marched obediently—if with obvious reluctance—toward the stairs. Dag watched, then turned toward the woman.

"That is an impressive feat, gaining her compliance so readily," he observed, feeling slightly dazzled. "Perhaps later you could show me how you achieved it?"

Esther turned and eyed him with speculation and a glint of humor in her dark hazel eyes. "Come with Kylie to Shavuot. If you do that, then we'll talk."

"Very well. I will look forward to it." He nodded his promise.

"So will I, Dag."

Before he could say another word, the small, elderly woman took him completely by surprise. Stretching to the top of her toes, she reached up and patted his cheek, much as she had done to Kylie. The tap packed a surprising sting coming from such a small, frail-looking human female. He found himself blinking down at her in astonishment.

"Just so you know, however," she said with a smile. "If you hurt my little girl, I'll make you wish your mother had died a virgin."

And with that, Esther Kramer turned on her heel and headed for the powder room, snapping the door closed behind her.

Bemused, Dag stared after her, one hand lifting to rub his tingling cheek. Yes, he did look forward to seeing Kylie grow and develop over the next sixty years.

He looked forward to it very much, indeed.

Chapter Fifteen

Az men vil nit alt vern, zol men
zikh yungerheyt oyfhengen.
If you don't want to grow old,
hang yourself when you're young.

Dag found Esther's short visit with them both refreshing and entertaining; Kylie found Dag fundamentally and certifiably insane. However, she also found the pair of *Star Trek* original series Tribble bedroom slippers he managed to locate online and give her as a belated birthday present adorable, so she was willing to overlook it. Especially given the effort he'd had to go through to call up Knox and get a crash course in online shopping, and probably a loan, because what supernatural defender of humanity carried plastic? That doubled the gift's *awww* quotient, easy.

What she could not overlook was the mounting evidence that the strike the Order of Eternal Darkness had planned for the Carver conference over Passover weekend would be one of the most hellish events in modern history. Provided, of course, that the Guardians and the Wardens failed to stop it, which Kylie already knew was not an option.

Really, though, she needed to start a conversation with the others about their group identity. Calling them "the Guardians and the Wardens" was just so cumbersome. They needed a collective name for themselves. Something like "the Avengers." Though less taken, obviously. Although Kylie would totally dig being the Black Widow. That character kicked ass!

If Kylie's research proved correct, it would take the kicking of hundreds of asses to keep the attendees of the Carver conference safe. A lot of what she had begun to suspect was speculation, because even on the darknet, the *nocturnis* appeared to be operating with an abundance of caution in order not to arouse too much suspicion regarding their plans. Still, she had gathered enough data by the middle of April to warrant not just a routine call with Wynn, but a videoconference with all the currently known Guardians and Wardens at once.

It took a couple of days to put together. Kylie arranged it all, of course, but she had to talk the others through the process of installing the necessary software on their computers. Thanks to everything holy that none of them had required system or hardware upgrades to make it possible. Once she had insured everyone was online, Kylie drew her office chair in close for Dag and perched on the edge of her balance ball.

"I'm glad you guys are all here," she began. "I know we're still ten days out, but I wanted to make sure we had enough time to not just put together a plan, but to get everyone in place where they need to be."

"Hey, don't worry about us." Fil—short for Felicity—Shalvis was a no-nonsense woman with pale blond hair and an attitude more like a cop or a biker than the artist Kylie knew her to be. "Spar and I have been waiting for this. We missed all the fun in Chicago, so if you guys need physical backup, we call dibs."

"Um, I have a feeling you might want to dig out your suitcase."

"Just lay it on us," Wynn suggested, motioning with both hands in front of her. "What's going down?"

Kylie tried for a wry smile. "Remember when we first talked and you said, 'How about the end of the world?' You may have hit closer to the bull's-eye than any of us really want to contemplate." Dag laid a hand against her back, lending his support and reminding her that she was not in this alone. None of them were. "If I'm right, this is going to be really, really bad."

She took a deep breath and started walking them through her findings. Since the conference expected to draw more than five thousand attendees from all over the world, it represented a veritable Demon's smorgasbord of souls all gathered in one place, ready to be consumed. The only thing Kylie and the others could be grateful for is that at almost no point would that number be gathered in one place within the convention center.

"That makes me twitchy," she told the others. "It seems to me that part of the appeal of hitting an event this big is the ability to harvest so many souls at one time. But if they're not all in one space, does that mean they're intending to hit a whole bunch of different spots simultaneously? That would be a nightmare for us."

Most of the time, she explained, attendees would be spread out among a number of smaller sessions, with each discussing an aspect of the overarching issues the conference was intended to address. There was an extensive schedule of these sessions for attendees to choose from and some were expected to draw larger crowds than others. That was the nature of these kinds of meetings. Unfortunately, Kylie didn't know enough about the topics or the attendees to determine which of the sessions would likely draw the largest crowds.

"Am I wrong in thinking that coordinating so many simultaneous attacks would be too big a headache even for superpsycho demon worshippers?"

"No, I do not think you are," Kees said. Ella's Guardian looked like some kind of rogue angel, with features almost too handsome for Kylie to believe he was a real Guardian, but Spar, Knox, and Dag all accepted him at face value. Plus, he did have that gravelly Guardian voice, and the look that said he could rip off heads if suitably motivated. "That number of coordinated strikes would require hundreds, if not thousands, of *nocturnis* in order to achieve success. We have never seen a single sect with anything even close to those numbers. Coordination between sects is always a possibility, but Ella feels that, for now, it remains unlikely."

"The 'for now' is a point worth stressing, though." Ella, a quiet woman with brown hair and unique gray eyes, sounded wary but certain. "I think it's inevitable that as the Order gains in strength, they will need to begin coordinating their efforts to bring about the apocalypse they're all dreaming of. But at the moment, every time we've run into an active sect, it's been headed by a big ego. That alone makes me think that until the Seven are awake and aware enough to force the groups to work together, they're just all too power hungry and full of themselves to pull off working together in any kind of direct way."

"Okay, that's a little bit of good news," Kylie said. "it also adds some weight to my theory. Now mind you, it is just a theory, and I'm not sure that what I found out is going to be enough to substantiate it for you guys, but—"

Wynn interrupted gently but with a steely smile. "Just spit it out. You're one of us now, and in order to be one of us, you have to have power. That means that if your intuition is telling you something, we're all going to believe it unless something pretty solid points us in another direction. So, spill."

Dag slid his hand around and squeezed her hip. Kylie took a deep breath. "Okay. Sorry. I think it's going to happen at the keynote address. That's on the schedule for first thing on Sunday morning, right after breakfast. Eight-thirty. It won't draw in every single attendee, but the room will be set up for three thousand people, with overflow standing room for at least a few hundred more."

"That's a pretty impressive crowd," Fil said. "I think that would count as a pretty filling lunch, even for two greedy demons."

"It is enough power to return Uhlthor to strength and to free Shaab-Na from its prison," Spar added grimly. "I fear it may even be more than enough."

Kylie nodded. "I was afraid of the same thing. But what tips it over the edge for me is that Richard Foye-Carver himself is giving the keynote address. He'll be right there, in the room, when it happens. And not only that, he'll be up on a stage getting the best view in the house."

She frowned and took a deep breath. "I know we don't have definitive proof that he's the Hierophant, but my gut tells me he is, and my gut also says that if he could, he'd bathe in the blood of those people himself."

She exchanged glances with Dag, and he nodded encouragement. Last night, in preparation for this call, she had stared at the enhanced photo of Carver for what felt like hours. Every single hair on the back of her neck had stood up, and the pit of her stomach had descended into her Tribble slippers when she looked into the man's smiling blue eyes. What looked back at her was not right; it was evil pure and simple.

Hierophant or not, if Richard Foye-Carver had ever possessed a soul, he must have sold it to the Seven a long time ago. How he managed to pass himself off as an activist and a philanthropist she couldn't understand for a minute. Every time she looked at him, she got sick to her stomach. If she were Catholic, she'd have crossed herself. As it was, she couldn't stop herself from mentally pronouncing *kaynahorah* to ward off his evil eye.

"Like I said, you don't need to convince us," Wynn said. "But if we're going to come up with a way to stop him from doing just that, we need more information about their actual plan. We need details."

"Full details I don't have, and trust me, I wish I did. But you all know more about the way the Order operates than I do, so let me tell you what I found, and maybe you can piece it together better than I can." Kylie looked at her notes on an adjacent computer screen. "I found chatter on the darknet about something called *oblatio*."

"It is their ritual of sacrifice that is demanded by the Seven," Kees reported grimly.

"Okay, context here paints a disturbing picture that *oblatio* is something pretty ordinary for them and that whatever is coming up would be more appropriately referred to as a *molkh*."

"Oh, crap, that's bad," Wynn breathed.

Dag snarled, baring a fang when Kylie glanced at him. "*Molkh* is what you envision the Hierophant wants.

It is a bloodbath, where both the souls and the blood of the victims are offered to their unholy masters."

"It also implies that my mate was on the correct path with her theory of the plan," Knox said. "*Molkh* traditionally involves the summoning of lower demonic creatures who murder the victims and feed on the flesh while the released souls are then consumed by one of the Seven."

Kylie closed her eyes and swallowed back bile. "I was really hoping you weren't going to say something like that. That clarifies my next item, though. The chatter indicated that there would be four 'doormen' serving inside the room, and that they'd be in charge of who got in, not who got out. I'm guessing those are the summoners?"

"Yes. Not only will portals need to be opened to allow the creatures into the space, but if they hope to target that many victims, the gates must be held until sufficient numbers pass through."

"That's got to be our biggest concern, then," Fil said. "We need to keep those doors from opening. That's our plan."

Spar picked up his mate's hand and brought it to his lips, blocking his small smile. "Perhaps we should work out a small number of additional details," he suggested.

"Yes, like how we're going to do it," Ella offered.

Fil sent her a teasing glare. "Nitpicker."

"Listen, Rembrandt—"

Wynn cut in. "Excuse me, children? I think the obvious solutions all involve us being present, in the room, for a coordinated counterstrike. And that means we need to decide which of us is going to Boston and how soon we can get there."

"I already told you that Spar and I are there, and I meant every word. Just try and keep us away."

Wynn nodded. "I wouldn't dream of it. Which makes Dag and Kylie, Fil and Spar, and me and Knox."

"You wish to exclude us from the fun?" Kees growled, his eyes glinting with both humor and bloodlust. It made for an interesting expression.

"Actually, I was just thinking about how synchronous it all seems," Ella said, leaning into the camera. "Four *nocturnis* attempting to open four portals to the demonic planes. Four Guardians and four Wardens. Doesn't it just seem like Fate?"

To Kylie it seemed like something that fit way too perfectly to be true. It made her want to look over her shoulder and spit.

"Ella and I will come as well," Kees proclaimed, and Kylie sighed.

"Looks like I'll be furnishing those extra bedrooms sooner than I intended," she said. "Just wait till my grandmother hears. She'll be so pleased."

"You got a doorbell!" Wynn beamed at her the minute Kylie opened the front door. "And look! You answered it and everything. Wearing clothes, no less. It's so sweet."

"Get inside, you smart-ass," Kylie grumbled, stepping back and waving in the onslaught of houseguests. "If we're going to turn this place into a barracks, we might as well get on with it."

"Did your grandmother bake while she was here? Please tell me she did. I've been dreaming of her *kichlach* since we booked our plane tickets."

Kylie gave in to the urge to give her friend a hug while the circle of hulking males hauled in luggage and exchanged greetings in the form of grunts and nods. "She tried to teach me how to make them. Again. Ten minutes later, she was on her way to the closest kosher bakery to buy me a gift certificate."

"Yes, but did she leave any behind?"

Kylie laughed. "She put them in the freezer. Her subtle way of reminding me not to have any leavened food during Passover."

"Score!"

While Wynn scampered into the kitchen, quiet Ella stepped forward and took her turn for a hug. "It's so nice to meet you in person," said the art historian and the first one to be dragged into this big mess. "Wynn's been talking about you for weeks now."

"Yeah, when she hasn't been talking about your grandmother's cookies." Fil flashed her a grin and offered a brief one-armed embrace. "I've been fantasizing about stuffing so many in her mouth at once that she'd finally be forced to stop speaking for five minutes."

From the pile of testosterone near the bottom of the stairs, a deep voice emerged. "Did someone say cookies?"

Ella shook her head. "Kees has a bit of a sweet tooth."

Kylie laughed. "Okay, everyone in the kitchen. We'll have a nosh and get settled in before we get down to business. Remember, we've only got four days to pull this thing together."

"Yes, but the cavalry has arrived." Fil swung her arm over Kylie's shoulder and half dragged her down the hall after Wynn. "Everything will be fine. Just wait and see."

Oy. Kylie knew famous last words when she heard them. She just hoped the reality check wouldn't hurt as bad as a hockey check. Maybe she could find some pads, though. Just in case.

For a short while, they gathered in the kitchen over

kichlach and coffee, tea, or soda like a group of friends who didn't often get the chance to spend time together. They laughed and joked, teased and shared gossip, but the constant undercurrent whispered of the coming danger, and the interlude couldn't last long. They all knew too well what they faced and how many lives were at stake. They also knew that they stood as the only defense between humanity and the Darkness.

Yet more evidence they should have a cool Avengers-style nickname, Kylie concluded. And capes. She would definitely be needing a cape for this.

Soon enough, the group migrated to the living room, which sported a second sofa, two new chairs, and a couple of end tables hastily ordered and delivered to accommodate the influx of guests. Kylie had even remembered to buy lamps so that when they sat down to talk, they didn't have to do it in the dark. Go her.

Kees immediately claimed the end of the older sofa and pulled his mate down beside him. "We must get down to business," he said in his gravelly, rasping voice. "Kylie, you will fill us in on the most recent developments."

Recognizing the order as a personality trait of the gigantic, dominant Guardian, Kylie managed not to get her back up and to reply civilly. Hey, look—personal growth.

"The darknet has gone quiet," she said, settling down on the floor while Dag took the chair behind her. There were enough seats to go around now, but she was accustomed to the floor and found it perfectly comfortable. Especially with the new rug softening the hardwood surface. "I think they must be under orders to keep quiet now that the event is getting so close. I haven't heard anything new in the last two or three days."

The others nodded, looking unhappy but far from surprised.

"On a more positive note," she continued, "I managed to get us all registered for the conference. When I first called, they told me it was closed and that next year I should be sure to keep an eye on the deadline." Her smile, all teeth and no humor, showed what she had thought of that brush-off. "But when I told them my name and mentioned the possibility of a substantial donation to Carver's foundation if the conference program impressed me, the organizers did manage to squeeze out a few badges for myself and my entourage. So, you guys get to be my entourage."

Fil bounced in her chair and sent her pale blond ponytail flying. "Ooh, ooh! I want to be the one who mouths off to the paparazzi and gets your name splashed all over the tabloids!"

Wynn snorted. "Fine. I think we can handle being your plus seven if it means getting us into the event."

"Actually, I didn't just get us into the event," Kylie qualified. "I got four of us seats at the opening dinner."

Dag scowled. "You did not mention this to me."

She shrugged. "I'm mentioning it now so we can figure out who should use the tickets."

"Did you not initially speculate that the Order's strike could come at this event almost as easily as at the keynote address?"

"It was a possibility, but I really think they'll go for the keynote. Bigger audience, more attention, and doing it on the final day of the conference is a lot more theatrical."

"But you could be wrong," he snarled, baring his fangs at her. She found it totally unfair that he could call those up when not in his natural form just for the intimidation factor.

Of course, the fact that she knew he would rather gnaw off his own arm than actually hurt her kind of balanced out the added threat. But still.

"I could be," she admitted, "but I'm not, so rather than waste time, let's just move on and decide which of the three of us will attend."

"The four Guardians will attend this dinner event," Dag decreed, leaning back in his chair and crossing his arms over his chest to denote he would listen to no arguments. "If you have mistaken the target of the Order, it would be too dangerous to allow the females to attend."

Said females turned four disbelieving gazes in his direction. Even the other Guardians had the good sense to wince and hang their brother out to dry. He'd put himself in that position, their expressions seemed to say, and he would need to dig his own way out of it.

"Oh, no, he didn't," Ella breathed.

Fil elbowed her in the ribs. "Shh! Do you think there's time to make popcorn?"

"To 'allow' us to attend?" Kylie scooted across the rug until she could turn around and look her Guardian full in the face. Or rather, look *the* Guardian full in the face, because no way in hell was she putting her claim on anyone who spewed that kind of sexist *meshugas*. "Since when did a single one of us 'females' stop to ask your permission, Goliath? Because I don't remember this conversation. I hope I was funny."

"Damn," Fil muttered from the sofa. "No popcorn."

"The idea of four frail females in a room full of *nocturnis* with the threat of demons entering at any moment?" Dag leaned forward in his seat until he could nearly press his nose to Kylie's. "It would indeed make me laugh if such a thing were a remote possibility, but as I will turn back to stone before I allow it to happen, it is not worth so much of my energy."

The fist Kylie swung at that arrogant, testosterone-poisoned face never connected. Some kind of force field flung itself between knuckles and nose the instant before impact. Startled, Kylie looked around the room to see Wynn with her fingers pointed at them and an unhappy expression on her face.

"Not that he doesn't deserve the hit," the witch said, "but I refuse to waste time on his bullshit attitude. Especially since I think it's better if *none* of us attend the dinner."

"Why not?" Kylie snapped the question and reluctantly dropped her hand into her lap. Then, she scuttled across the floor to the opposite side of the coffee table from the sexist Guardian.

Wynn explained. "Because I think it's a bad idea to put the Order on their guard. Magic recognizes magic. If we plunk two Guardians and two Wardens down in the middle of a dinner the *nocturnis* think they control"—she did not even pause to acknowledge Dag's snarl of protest—"they'll be able to sense our presence. And if that happens, then they'll know we're onto them and they'll have to suspect we figured out their plan. The only logical reaction to that is to either change the plan or abandon it."

The witch shook her head. "I'm sorry, but after all the time and energy we've invested in figuring this plan out, the last thing we want is for them to change it. If they do that, we're back in the dark, and the chances of us coming up with an effective counter to the new plan become almost nil. And abandoning the plan altogether? That just means they'll strike at another time and place, and we won't have a warning."

Ella nodded. "She's right. The element of surprise is one of the biggest advantages we have going into this. If we lose that, our chances of success go way down. Yeah, they'll sense us at the keynote address, too, but we'll have a much bigger crowd to blend into, and by then, it will probably be too late to change their plan. They're a lot more likely to go through with it at that stage even if they know we're there."

"Okay, all that makes sense," Kylie acknowledged, "but us staying away until Sunday and then just strolling in blind does not. We need to get an idea of the layout of the room, the entrances and exits, where the stage will be set up, what pathways will be laid, how traffic will flow. All of that will not only help us figure out where they're most likely to set the portals, it will also tell us the best ways to get people out quickly if we need to do that."

"Which means someone will have to take a look around at some point," Fil said. "I'm thinking Saturday afternoon or evening. For an early Sunday event that large, the convention staff is going to want to set up the room the day before at least, to give themselves plenty of time."

"And this risks the same problem of detection as attendance at the dinner," Dag grumbled.

"Not necessarily," Spar said, his gaze turning to Kylie. "While I do feel a small aura around your Kylie, she has not yet been Warden long enough to read as one. Her magic has such a unique flavor to it that it does not make one think of the Guild at all, especially not from any distance. I think she might pass entirely undetected, or if not, as merely an untrained human with potential. Someone might target her for recruitment, but I doubt they would perceive her as a threat."

Kylie thought of the possibility of a *nocturni* attempting to lure her to the dark side as they had with Dennis Ott and his girlfriend. "Yeah, that would go well for everyone."

"Wynn is the other logical choice," Knox growled, not sounding happy with his own conclusion. "As much as I dislike the idea of sending you into such a nest of vipers without me by your side, you are the most likely to pass beneath their notice. Your magical energy still reads at first glance as witch, not as Warden. You should be able to pass as nothing more than a witch with a strong interest in the environmental actions the conference will be espousing."

"I agree." Wynn smiled and leaned over to kiss him lightly. "But you get special brownie points for figuring it out on your own and not pouting about it too much."

Fil stifled a smirk. You know, eventually. "Alrighty then, so if Kylie and Wynn are going to be our advance team, when do we send them in to reconnoiter?"

"The conference opens Friday afternoon, with the welcome dinner that evening. Since we've put the kibosh on attending the dinner, we definitely have to be there on Saturday, preferably early, or after the fuss I made getting on the list, it's going to look weird."

"Well, nothing says we have to spend the whole day there," Wynn said. "We can show up early to check in, disappear for a while, and go back when we think we have the best chance to get a look at the keynote room setup. At an event that big, it's easy for people to assume you're just at one of the other sessions if they don't see you in theirs."

"Yeah, that could work in our favor."

"Gathering our information on Saturday will not allow us a great deal of time to set up our defenses," Kees observed. "We will need to strategize the best method to deal with the attacks we expect and make plans that require only fine adjustments to the details in order to operate successfully."

"Agreed. And you in particular have a lot to learn," Wynn said, fixing her gaze on Kylie. "Have you been practicing the things I showed you?"

"Me?"

"No, the other brand-new Warden in the room." Her tone could teach dry to a desert. "Ella, Fil, and I have all experienced battle with the *nocturnis*. We know what to expect, but you don't. Those exercises I taught you are going to become really important really fast."

"Yes, I've been practicing. Every day even."

"Good." The witch pushed to her feet and motioned for the other women to join her. "Because the girls and I are going to have to teach you a few tricks. The *nocturnis* fight dirty, and they like to fight with magic. We're going to give you a crash course in self-defense and show you what you need to know to help us either stop those portals from opening, or take them out fast, if they do manage to form. Got it?"

All at once, the reality of everything they had been talking about for the past month came crashing down on Kylie's head. She felt a whole lot like her cartoon namesake right after the Acme contraption blew up in his face. She wondered vaguely if her ears were smoking.

But Kylie also knew that defeating her adversary meant a lot more than roast Road Runner for dinner. If she and her new friends failed to counter the Order's planned attack, people would die. Hundreds of people, if not thousands. How could a person live with herself if she didn't do every single thing in her power to prevent such a tragedy from happening?

She didn't know, but she knew that she could not. She hadn't been raised that way, she wasn't built that way, and she wasn't going down that way. Not without a fight.

Taking a deep breath, Kylie pushed to her feet and squared her shoulders. "Well, then, let's get started."

Oy vey iz mir!

"Now I know the real reason why they call Wynn a witch." Kylie groaned and collapsed back onto her mattress way, way, *way* after she would have preferred to appear there. "She's like the Genghis Khan of teachers. I swear by all that's holy, I wasn't this tired and sore after the one time I let Bran talk me into that fitness boot camp class. In fact, I think if that instructor met Wynn, he would have run away screaming."

More than six hours had passed since the kaffeeklatsch in the living room, and Kylie was really regretting those *kichlach*. Her stomach had been roiling since twenty minutes into Wynn's magical workout and showed no imminent signs of stopping. Everyone was waiting downstairs for dinner, and just the thought of food made Kylie close her eyes and swallow hard.

She felt the bed dip as Dag settled on the edge beside her and fought not to groan. Maybe she should have collapsed on the bathroom floor. Sure, it was hard, but it didn't move, and if worse came to worst, she would be a whole lot closer to the toilet. Much less chance of a mess.

"Poor baby," he murmured. She felt a huge, rough hand settle gently on her forehead, and she had to admit the sensation was soothing. The initial coolness of his skin quickly faded into a comforting heat that made her relax almost against her will. "Did you learn anything useful?"

"You mean aside from the fact that Felicity *really* hates being called Filly-Willy, Wynn is a secret agent for the Spanish Inquisition, and Ella packs a hell of a magical punch for such a sweet-looking person?" She sighed. "Yeah, I learned that I really might not be cut out for this woman-of-power stuff. If those three chicks downstairs are like the high-powered rifle of magical offense, I'm like a squirt gun. Not a Super Soaker or anything cool, but one of those old-fashioned water pistols that barely get your target wet and yet manage to leak all over your hand every time you pull the trigger."

She heard—and felt, *oy!*—Dag chuckle beside her, but she just didn't have the energy to hit him. All she could manage was to flip him a very small bird. Like the hummingbird of middle fingers, only a lot less energetic. A dead hummingbird.

"Do not worry, little one. I have every confidence that you will prove most adept as a Warden with a bit more training and a little practice. You forget, this is your first real attempt at using magic. Every new skill takes time to learn."

Forcing her eyelids open, she looked up to eye Dag suspiciously. "That's a very mature and rational statement from a hunk of rock who came within a flea's whisker of calling me 'the little woman' and ordered me into the kitchen a few hours ago."

Dag heaved a great sigh and shifted to stretch out on the bed beside her. She noted how carefully he moved to keep the disturbance to her to a minimum. Not that it got him off her shitlist, but she noticed it.

"Yes, I have thought over what I said to you earlier," he admitted, "and I have come to regret my words."

"Really? Do tell."

"I owe you an apology. By attempting to forbid you

from attending the conference dinner, I insulted you deeply. I belittled your abilities not only to take care of yourself and defend your own safety, but even your ability to assess a situation and to decide for yourself the inherent risks, the possible rewards, and the weight of one in relation to the value of the other. For this, I am sorry."

Pushing to her elbows, Kylie looked at him with her skepticism sitting right on the tip of her nose. "Who told you to say all that? Did they make you practice?"

Dag gave a rueful chuckle and tugged her to his side. Carefully. "They did not. It is true that the others did initially point out that my attitude may have offended you. They also let me know that they had learned very quickly from their own mates that human females are both sturdier than they look and fierce in their independence, which I should have recognized on my own. But once I grew calmer, I not only saw the reason for your anger but the justification for it as well. I reacted badly to the idea of sending you into danger, and I allowed my fear to control me."

She kept her narrowed gaze on him, but felt herself softening. "When did you become so enlightened?"

He grinned and leaned close to kiss her. "When I feared that your anger for me would lead you to keep me from your bed this evening."

Kylie scoffed. "Typical." Settling once more onto the mattress, she allowed herself to snuggle against her Guardian's side. "You know, right after I recovered from Wynn's school of magical suffering, I was planning to come find you and skin you alive for the way you acted."

"I know. This is why I came to you and commenced groveling with all due speed."

"Groveling?" She tilted her head to look at him. "I heard an apology, but I don't recall any groveling."

Dag shifted to one elbow and loomed over her, resting his other hand on the mattress beside her head. "Oh, no? Then what is it that you consider to be groveling, little human?"

His smoke-and-stone voice rasped against her like a caress, sending shivers straight through her to pool low in her belly. "Well," she purred, fighting a smile, "it usually starts on your knees . . ."

His grin turned wicked as he began to crawl down her body. "If you prefer to see me on my knees, I am happy to oblige you. Just let me get these jeans of yours off, and I can kneel before you and show you how very sorry I am for upsetting you."

Just as her breathing began to speed up, the loud peal of the doorbell shattered the moment.

"Pizza!" a loud female voice shouted from the stairwell. "Dinner's here, you guys, so get your stinking clothes back on and get your butts downstairs. If I have to come up there, I'm afraid I'll be struck blind or something!"

Fil's footsteps drifted away from the stairs and Dag groaned, collapsing to the mattress beside Kylie. "Can you remind me of the reason why we invited these nuisances into our home?"

Kylie pushed aside the rush of warmth she felt hearing him call the house "our home" and threw her arm across her eyes. "I plead insanity. What's your excuse?"

"I'm eating all the extra cheese and mushroom!" Ella's voice drifted up from the hall and Dag swore before shoving to his feet.

He reached down to pull Kylie up behind him and

dragged her toward the stairs, mumbling, "I have no excuse," as he went.

Kylie laughed. "There *is* no excuse, but we'd better go. I want those mushrooms."

Chapter Sixteen

Shlof gikher; men darf di kishn.
Sleep faster; we need the pillows.

Three days later and Kylie still couldn't be certain she had recovered from that first lesson in magic. Not that it mattered, because the Terrible Trio of Trainers, as she had dubbed them, hadn't let up on her for a minute. Every day, they had dragged her into the empty dining room (nothing valuable to get caught in the crossfire, Wynn explained) and put her through not just her paces, but the paces of several world-class athletes. At least, that's what it felt like.

The first thing they insisted she know was defensive magic. After they made her demonstrate how well she had learned her lesson about calling the power to her fingertips. Once the magic tingled in her hands, Wynn explained, sending it out into the world with intent was what made for a spell, and a darned effective one. The witch demonstrated with a very cool cone-of-silence trick that ticked Fil off to no end (she'd been in the middle of a sentence when Wynn bespelled her) and yet that she refused to teach to Kylie.

"First off, you just want to use it on Dag. And me," the witch added, noting her pupil's glare. "And second of all, it's not going to be much use against the *nocturnis*. You need to learn the important stuff first. We don't have a lot of time."

Sighing, Kylie had gotten back to work. Wynn was right. They didn't have a lot of time.

When they entered the convention center on Saturday morning to pick up their badges, Kylie's new bag of tricks included a personal shield spell that helped to deflect magical attacks (it would get stronger the more she practiced, Wynn assured her), a kind of magical mirror that bounced a spell back toward the one who had cast it, and what Ella called her bad-guy bubble spell, a favorite of hers. That one trapped whoever it was directed at in a giant bubble of energy that both kept the target contained and prevented him from casting magic outside its confines. Apparently, any spell he attempted just bounced off the interior of the bubble and ricocheted around inside. Very messy, Ella had noted with a grimace.

Messy, but effective, Wynn assured her.

Tonight, they would continue to work on the most important spell—the one that sealed portals and prevented what was on the other side from making its way into the human world. It was a tough spell, and not one Wynn would normally have taught to someone so inexperienced, but it was the last measure they would use if the Order succeeded in getting the portals open. Hopefully, the Guardians would stop them before that happened, and the spell would never be needed.

Az a yor af mir. I should be so lucky, Kylie thought. She refused to hold her breath.

In the meantime, Wynn and Kylie had reconnaissance to collect and *nocturnis* to avoid.

"Ms. Kramer," the woman who provided their badges gushed, a bright smile on her face that went nowhere near her eyes. Or, you know, near sincerity. "We missed you at the dinner last night. We were afraid you might not attend our event after all."

Kylie flashed a toothy smile of her own. "Oh, you know, business first," she said breezily. "It's how we can afford to help these little causes, isn't it?"

As she guided Wynn away to find lanyards for their laminated conference badges, the witch laughed. "Wow, I've never heard you use your multimillionaire tech guru voice on anyone before. That was impressive."

Kylie rolled her eyes. "Just wait till you hear my 'pissed off woman with a nagging Jewish grandmother' voice. It'll knock your socks off."

Esther had already left three messages of good luck on her voice mail, each one with the implied threat that if Kylie wound up getting hurt, Esther would be coming up to Boston personally to kick asses and take names. Kylie wouldn't put it past her.

"Oh, trust me," Wynn assured her, "I'm already familiar with your earlier body of work. Now come on. Let's get programs and stand around leafing through them and talking earnestly about the most important use of your time before we disappear."

Kylie readily agreed. After all, the plan was to make their appearance and then leave, waiting to return until they had a better shot at getting a glimpse of the setup in the auditorium for Richard Foye-Carver's scheduled speech.

After retrieving programs from a bored-looking intern at the welcome table, they chose a conspicuous spot next to a pillar so they could be stared at and identified by the masses. Kylie had gone out of her way to make it easy for people, dressing in ripped and battered jeans, cherry-red canvas high-top sneakers, and two T-shirts. The long-sleeved red shirt provided the perfect contrast to the short-sleeved black one worn on top, which spelled out the word "genius" using elements of the periodic table.

She could have tattooed the word "SUPERGEEK" on her forehead and not looked more the part. That, plus all the publicity generated by her high-profile sale to a gigantic tech conglomerate a couple of years ago should take care of getting her recognized and firmly implanted in the minds of attendees and organizers alike.

When she had spotted enough stares and whispers, she checked the clock to be certain the next session was about to begin before she tapped Wynn's arm. "I think we're good. Let's get out of here."

"No, wait." Wynn continued to face her, smiling, but her gaze was fixed over Kylie's right shoulder. "I just saw a couple of guys take a cart loaded with electrical equipment toward the sign pointing to the auditorium. It looks like they may already be setting it up. Maybe luck is actually on our side."

Kylie made a noncommittal sound. She didn't plan on counting any chickens, personally. "All right. What's the closest minisession to the auditorium?"

Wynn flipped through her program. "Let me see. Um, it looks like 'The Technology of Social Justice' with Armand DuClare."

"Perfect. It sounds like something a techhead would go to, but I've never heard of the presenter. That means there won't be any need to meet and greet, and no one to contradict me if I have to say I was there. Let's go."

The women strolled through the convention lobby with their complimentary reusable canvas tote bags on their arms. Kylie kept a discreet eye peeled for anyone who might know her well enough to waylay her, but honestly she tended to steer away from the do-gooder philanthropical crowd. Not because she didn't support philanthropy and doing good, but because she kept her head in the bits and bytes and let her accountants worry about making her contributions. To her, it was just another form of point and click while she got on with her work.

Which reminded her, she didn't think any of Richard Foye-Carver's little projects was on her list of approved charities, but she thought it might be a good idea to call someone and double-check. Just to be safe. Wouldn't it suck large to find out she'd been unknowingly financing the very people who were trying to kill her and as many other innocent people in this world as possible?

Ick.

Wynn and Kylie lingered in the hall while the crowd slowly began to thin out as people and groups disappeared into the various meeting areas for the breakout symposia. When the area outside the auditorium was clear, Kylie waved her friend to follow and chose the farthest door in the corner to ease open and peek inside.

No one even noticed.

The floor of the auditorium hosted huge racks of chairs ready to be unloaded and placed in rows and aisles according to the markings taped to the polished concrete. Around the perimeter of the room, balconies on three sides boasted permanent theater-style seating. At the far end of the room, workers and technicians scurried around erecting a long low stage and rigging lights and screens for what would obviously be a multimedia presentation. Didn't want anyone thinking Richard Foye-Carver might be behind the times.

A sharp finger in the back forced Kylie into the room. Wynn followed right on her heel. "Ouch! What the heck was that for?" Kylie hissed.

"Standing in the hall with the door half open and your butt hanging out is a heck of a lot more conspicuous that just coming inside and taking a look around. Like actual conference attendees can't be curious?" Wynn took out her cell phone and began snapping pictures. "Besides, I wanted to get this on camera."

"Excuse me, ladies?"

A man's voice carried toward them through the nearly empty auditorium. Just what Kylie had been afraid of— ten seconds inside the damned place, and already they had called attention to themselves.

A man in his thirties wearing a loose-fitting gray suit approached them at a fast clip, with a patently false public-service smile on his face. "I'm so sorry, ladies," he said, arms out to herd them through the door, "but this part of the facility is off limits at the moment. We're setting up for tomorrow's event, and insurance won't allow us to have the public around all the heavy lights and electrical equipment. You understand."

His tone said he didn't care if they understood or not, he was making them go. Glancing at the pin on his lapel revealed that he worked for the convention center, though, not Carver or his foundation, so Kylie relaxed a little. Chances of him being *nocturni* at least had gone down a few notches.

She was about to order him to take a chill when Wynn opened her mouth and played dumb.

"Oh, I'm so sorry, I'm being such a tourist," the witch gushed, painting a little bit of Chicago into her voice. "I'm making my friend here show me everything. But we totally understand your concerns. I mean, I wouldn't want one of those great big light boxes falling on my head, that's for sure. We'll just get back to our session."

The member of the convention staff offered them another fake smile and an instruction to enjoy their day, then snapped the doors closed approximately three inches from their faces.

Wynn looked at her, one eyebrow arched. "Why do I feel like he just told us no one gets in to see the Wizard?"

"Yeah, well, the wizard can *kish mir en tokhes*. Let's go show the boys what we found."

"Do you think what we got is enough?"

"I think it's the best we're going to get. Between the photos you took and the plans and photos I should be able to dig up, I'm sure we can figure something out. Besides, we left four Guardians alone with Fil. I'm afraid to stay away too long."

"True, but Ella's there, too. She should be able to keep the peace. Maybe."

"That's the only reason I have hope that the house is still standing." Kylie led the way to a less frequented stairway and back toward their parking spot. "Plus, if there's something else someone thinks we really ought to know, we can always come back later this afternoon like we originally planned."

"True enough." They climbed into Kylie's car and Wynn threw her a grin. "Five bucks says someone back at the house is missing their eyebrows."

Kylie snorted and pulled out into traffic. "Do I look like that kind of sucker?"

* * *

As it turned out, no one had any less hair than they had when Wynn and Kylie left, facial or otherwise, but the house had significantly less food in it. Wow, could Guardians eat!

They had to call out for Chinese. Again. And this time, they got free General Tso's shrimp, free spareribs, and a free six-pack of Chinese beer. There might even have been mention of naming a new baby after Kylie. Or maybe they said a boat. It was hard to hear over the cheering in the background.

When she finally crawled into bed beside Dag, Kylie was stuffed and her fridge boasted of one measly container of leftovers. A swarm of locusts couldn't have eaten as much.

"Next time I invite this group over, remind me to buy a supermarket first," she griped, collapsing back onto her pillows. "I swear to God, I think Spar ate an entire pig. I've never seen that much twice-cooked pork in one place, let alone seen it disappear into one mouth like that. I don't even keep kosher, and still I felt a little guilty just watching him."

Dag chuckled and drew her close. "He claimed he needs plenty of fuel in order to be ready for tomorrow's battle."

"He'll be lucky if he can haul his *tokhes* out of bed in the morning, much less do battle. I'm just glad there's antacid in the guest bathrooms. I have a feeling they'll be needing it."

They lay in the darkness for a few minutes, listening to the house and the houseguests settle in around them. Kylie knew she needed to sleep. Today's magical workout had been the most intense Wynn had led yet, and tomorrow was the big day, but her eyes refused to close.

"And how are you feeling, little one?" Dag asked softly, his voice rasping across the silence like a work-roughened hand over sheer, smooth silk.

"Nervous," Kylie admitted, letting out the breath she hadn't known she was holding in a rush. "All of a sudden it feels like I have hundreds of people's lives in my hand. Oh, wait, I do!"

"Our hands," Dag corrected, squeezing her gently. "The weight of this is not something you carry alone, sweet Kylie. We all know what is going to happen, therefore we all share the responsibility to stop it. In fact, according to the traditions of my kind, you and Wynn, and Kylie and Ella, none of you need to put yourselves at risk. This is why the Guardians were summoned. It is our duty to stop the Seven, not any of yours."

"Is this you getting ready to forbid me to go again?"

He laughed. "No, that is one lesson I believe that I have learned. I will forbid you nothing." Swiftly he shifted, his hands clasping her waist to lift her and set her down on top of him. "Have you not realized it yet, little human? I cannot, because I can deny you nothing. Whatever you ask for, I will give you. Whatever you need, I will provide."

She gazed down at him silently, reading the sincerity in his voice and the love in his eyes.

Yes, love. How had she missed it before?

Her mouth began to curve. "And what if I need you, big guy?"

"Kylie. I am already yours."

She leaned down to kiss him, and he shook with the need to seize her. Instinct rode him hard, urging him to take control, to claim, to plunder, to mark his woman

forever as his. The need was fierce and dark and prim-
itive, but then, so was Dag.

He had entered the world as a warrior, in a time when
wars raised kings and toppled empires, when men who
fought ruled and the men who ruled never stopped fighting. Summoned into being for one single purpose, he
had been created not to evolve but to defend and to destroy, or so he had thought.

Now, he believed that perhaps he had been summoned for this purpose, for this woman, to exist wholly
and solely for her. It hit him like a revelation, and it felt
like a blessing.

Grasping hard on his control, he forced himself to remain still beneath her, flexing only his fingers as they
caressed the soft, tempting skin at her waist. That, he
couldn't help. He could no more stop touching her than
he could stop needing her. Neither was an option.

He concentrated on the kiss, on the feel of her lips
moving soft and warm against his, on the teasing strokes
of her clever little tongue, on the sweetness of her taste
and the whisper of her breath against his skin. It helped
for a little while, but when he began to feel the heat of
her pussy dampening the skin of his abdomen he could
no longer hold back his growl of need.

Pushing herself into a sitting position, Kylie smiled
down at him and ran her tiny hands over his bare skin,
taunting him. Her short, neat fingernails scraped over
his nipples, making him hiss, and her fingers kneaded
his muscles like a kitten arranging its bed. He hoped by
the Light that sleep was not the first thing on her mind.

"I like that you're mine, Dag," she whispered, leaning down to rain kisses along his collarbone. "I like
being yours."

He stiffened, hardly daring to breathe. Was she finally admitting the truth? He was afraid to let his hope soar too high.

Her soft little body wiggled atop him, making his jaw ache and his fangs intrude on his human form. Then she reached back and closed her hand around him and he forgot about human and Guardian, about hope and duty, about everything but his mate and the need to be inside her.

He growled her name and caught the white flash of her smile in the darkness. A moment later, she rearranged herself slightly and positioned the head of his shaft against her entrance. Then she sank down and he hissed at the sharp, sweet pleasure.

He both heard her sigh and felt the rush of her breath against his skin. He felt the muscles in her thighs and her belly tighten and she enveloped him in her slick heat. A shiver rushed through her from head to toe, and the feel of her shaking above him and clamping down hard around his erect cock nearly made him howl. He controlled himself, barely, if for no other reason than that he refused to share one second of this experience with anyone else. To be overheard even by their friends would steal a particle of the pleasure that he meant to hoard greedily for them alone.

Dark eyes stared down at him as she began to move, her hips twisting and rocking in a sensuous rhythm that stroked and squeezed each hard inch of him without mercy. He watched her breasts shimmy as she moved and lifted his hands to cup the soft mounds, teasing the hard nipples with flicks of his thumb and quick pinches that made her hum and gasp.

Ignoring the tingling at the base of his spine and the pressure building in his groin, he savored every soft sound she made, every shift of her body, every flush of her skin. He wanted the moment to last forever, to never have to rise from this bed, to never have to slip from her body, to never have to see her look into the face of evil and know fear.

"Dag."

Her hoarse whisper drew at his soul, made him croon soft nonsense even as he increased the force of his hips thrusting upward to meet her. He heard her breath catch in her throat and then the change in her ragged breathing and knew her climax was close. Shifting his grip, he slid one hand between their bodies and teased her sensitive clit while his other palm cupped the back of her neck and drew her down toward him.

"You are mine, sweet Kylie," he whispered, knowing the words sounded rough and possessive, more like a snarl than the promise he intended. "And I am yours."

She didn't seem to mind his tone, because she shuddered and tightened, and cried out, her breath hot and damp against his skin. "Yours," she panted. "Mine."

Her body strained above him, hips flexing, thighs gripping, pussy clenching as she fought for her pleasure. Determined to give it to her, to give her everything, he drew his finger in swift hard circles around her little bundle of nerves, then suddenly struck, pressing directly over it, hard and deep.

She cried out and shattered, the rapid spasms of her channel around his cock pulling him over his own edge. He emptied himself into her, gasping her name, but all he could hear was her raspy, beloved voice reaching out to him through the darkness.

"Dag. I love you."

Chapter Seventeen

Der ergster sholem iz beser vi di beste milkhome.
The worst peace is better than the best war.

Kylie really thought there ought to have been a film montage, one of those scenes where the grim-faced heroes and heroines buckled themselves into tight garments of canvas and leather, and then armed themselves with unwieldy arsenals of high-tech weaponry in preparation for the ultimate battle. It would have been so cool.

Instead, she got seven ordinary-looking humans (well, as ordinary as Guardians could look in their human forms) dressed in average if casual clothing carrying nothing but their cell phones. Well, in Wynn's case she had added a messenger bag that Kylie was convinced held not only the kitchen sink, but a bathtub and washer-dryer unit as well.

That was it. No machine guns, no big black knives with wicked blades and grips meant to stay grippy even when covered in the enemy's blood. Not one single lousy hand grenade. How was a girl supposed to go to war without hand grenades? Honestly.

The closest she had were two small pouches Wynn had pressed into the hands of each of the Wardens on the way out the door. "Drive-away salt," she told them. "Fil has used it before. If you get cornered by something nasty, use it. It won't destroy anything much bigger than a *hhissihh*, but it will give you some room to maneuver out of a tight spot."

Which was all well and good, and Kylie made sure to thank the witch, but it still wasn't a grenade.

Since she had pouted about it all the way to the convention center, Dag didn't need to read her mind to know what to say to her as they parked and climbed out of her car, followed by Wynn and Knox. Ella, Kees, Fil, and Spar had followed in a rental.

"I told you, little human, any weapons the Guardians require we will summon when the time comes," he said, patting her hand. "Cease your worry."

"It's not worry," she grumbled. "It's disappointment. I was promised a battle royal, and now I just feel let down. You guys wouldn't even let me dress all in black."

Wynn sent her a look. "We need to look like all the other attendees, Kylie, not ninjas. And I mean attendees at *this* event, not Comic Con."

Kylie stuck out her tongue. Childish? Yes, but satisfying.

Thinking ahead to the possibility of collateral and structural damage to the facilities, they had parked the cars not at the convention center itself, or even at the attached hotel, but at a public lot a few blocks away. No one wanted to believe it would come to that, but things happened. Either way, the parking situation meant they had to hoof it to make the meeting on time.

Kylie couldn't help noticing the incongruity of the day. It had turned out to be one of those rare moments

of early-spring perfection that occasionally settled over
New England like a blessing from above. The clear blue
sky seemed vast overhead, with the warm sun shining
down and tempting humanity out of houses and busi-
nesses, urging the shedding of thick winter layers. A
fresh breeze teased through hair and picked at light fabrics with just enough nip to remind everyone to enjoy
the interlude while it lasted. The day was just too beautiful to believe that so much death and destruction lurked
just around the corner, but she supposed that was what
made evil *evil*—it didn't care what it had to destroy, it
just wanted the destruction.

The group entered the convention center and blended
with the crowd of other attendees. Polite chitchat created a little blanket of sound as bodies milled in the hall
outside the auditorium, plenty of coffee cups in evidence, waiting for the big event.

Kylie had to bite back a laugh that owed more than a
little bit to hysteria. The "big event." Ha. If only they
knew.

A hand landed on her shoulder and squeezed. Looking up, she caught Dag's reassuring gaze and tried to
relax. It didn't go very well, but she made the effort.
Maybe if she'd gotten that cape, she'd feel differently.

She almost expected to hear tense, slowly building
music in the background, like a movie sound track.
Every one of her senses had gone on high alert, making
her simultaneously jumpy and strangely numb, as though
nothing around her were quite real; it all seemed too
overamped, as if it were actually playing out on a movie
screen.

Maybe she needed to take a break from her film ad-
diction, Kylie told herself, trying to keep her actions
casual as she glanced around her. At least for a while,

until she could stop comparing her life to a Marvel Studios production. It might be the healthy thing to do. Put down the remote; step away from the Netflix.

"Everyone, remember the plan," Kees said, as ushers opened the auditorium doors and attendees began to flow into the room. "We must wait until they make their move. If in doubt, look to Wynn or Ella. They will be monitoring for a buildup of energy that could signal the moment."

Kylie nodded and tugged at the hem of her T-shirt. This one read ALSO, I CAN KILL YOU WITH MY BRAIN, partly in homage to one of her favorite television shows and partly to remind her that she could do things she had never before thought possible. As Wynn had told her, she just needed to concentrate and try not to get in her own way.

With Dag's hand at her back guiding her through the aisles, she made her way to the spot everyone had decided on last night. The four couples would split up, with each one choosing their seats in one of the four corners of the room.

They had theorized that the most likely scenario for the Order's plan was to open the four anticipated portals at the edges of the room around the four corners. This would effectively surround the audience, blocking them from the exits, and trapping them inside the room. Dividing up along similar lines would allow the Guardians and Wardens to launch the quickest possible response, and hopefully put them physically close to their targets.

You know, maybe.

It drove Kylie's analytical, scientific soul bonkers that with all of their research, all of their preparation and strategizing, they still found themselves walking into the lion's den with nothing more than a "best guess." She felt pretty confident that best guesses were one of the main ingredients in lion chow, and she really didn't want to have to explain to her grandmother why neither she nor Dag had managed to show up at Shavuot dinner.

Of course, if they didn't show up, no explanation would be necessary, because *bubbeh* would be sitting shiva over her mangled corpse. As excuses went, it was about the only one Esther would accept.

Kylie settled into a seat at the end of a long outer aisle in the rear right corner of the room. Then she had to slide over a seat as Dag insisted on putting himself directly on the aisle. With the threat expected to come from the outer perimeter of the room, he had already told her he would expect her to let him stand between her and danger. She had initially rolled her eyes, but when he pointed out that she was so much smaller than him that she couldn't effectively shield him anyway, she had to concede to his logic. She'd need three of her to block him from attack.

At least their assigned seats kept her from having to crane her neck to look around her. She had a decent view of the whole room, although the balcony had given all of them cause for grief. They couldn't be certain that the *nocturnis* would not choose to open the portals up there rather than on the auditorium floor, but they were not able to effectively cover both levels so they had to work with the highest probability. Opening portals on the balcony would be more discreet, but it would also delay the moment when the demonic attack could begin, and it might give some of the crowd time to escape in the initial moments of violence.

Gee, wasn't this a fun topic to muse on?

Turning her attention to the stage, she took in the

elaborate curtained backdrop, the projected images of the Carver foundation's logo, and the silent slide show of all the good work the group was doing. In a good number of the photos, Richard Foye-Carver posed with shirtsleeves rolled up and battered boots on his feet, helping African farmers in their fields, listening to the concerns of poor women, even playing with dusty urchins and their underinflated soccer ball. It was enough to warm the coldest heart.

Provided you didn't look closely enough to see the dead, flat, empty void behind the man's smiling eyes.

Kylie shifted in her seat and glanced down at the time displayed on her phone. T-minus eight minutes. She wondered if her nerves would survive the wait.

"Relax," Dag whispered, leaning down to place his lips near her ear. "Your worry will only slow your responses. Do as Wynn advised you and breathe slowly."

"Easy for you to say, Goliath. You were made to fight Demons. I was made to eat latkes and kvetch about the state of the world. There's a big difference."

"No," he disagreed, brushing his mouth against her temple. "You were made to set me free, little love, and to spend a lifetime by my side. Never forget that."

Well, when he put it that way . . .

It didn't do away with Kylie's nerves, but it allowed her to press them back enough to manage a deep breath. The feel of his huge, warm hand enveloping hers didn't hurt, either. Both gave her courage, and if all else failed, she would do the one useful thing her father had taught her—fake it with authority.

When the lights dimmed and music began to hum through the loudspeakers, she felt every muscle in her body go tense and had to force herself to shake off the instinctive reaction. Adrenaline, Wynn had taught her, could be her friend or her enemy. Enough of it would sharpen her senses and hone her reflexes, helping her out in tight situations, but too much could make her freeze and leave her vulnerable to attack.

Fight or flight. Kylie sure as *shudden* intended to fight.

The focus in the room turned to the stage where a small, portly man in a wrinkled pair of khakis and an ill-conceived shirt-and-tie combination appeared behind the podium to introduce the keynote speaker. With a forced-casual glance she saw the ushers who had manned the doors step inside the room and pull the panels closed behind them. All perfectly innocent actions to ensure privacy and minimize the chances of outside interruptions and distractions, but to Kylie it smacked of sinister intent. The ushers to her appeared more like guards, stationed at the exits to prevent any attempt at escape.

She forced her attention back to the man speaking at the front of the room. Kylie barely heard a word he said. While the music had gradually lowered and then turned off, the buzzing in her head had quadrupled in volume. She felt as if a swarm of bees had nested in her ear canals and settled in for a long honey-making chat. She couldn't seem to sit still, either. Her habitually bouncing foot shook so fast her eyes could barely focus on the movement.

Beside her, Dag shifted, his gaze moving over her with obvious concern, but she couldn't do much to reassure him. She couldn't even reassure herself. Something was so very, very wrong. She felt it in her bones.

Obviously, they all knew something was wrong with this meeting; the eight of them wouldn't be here otherwise. But this was a wrongness that didn't quite fall in with the kind of wrong they were expecting. Something else was going on, something that seethed beneath the surface of the room's energy, like a great dark snake stalking its prey. If she listened closely to the sound waves beneath the buzz, she swore she could hear it hiss.

She laid her hand on Dag's leg, trying to think of what to tell him, how to describe the sensation crawling under her skin, but he had his gaze focused on the stage like most of the others in the auditorium. She wanted to shout to get his attention, but she couldn't even manage a whisper. It was like her voice had become locked inside her and she couldn't find a key.

"And so without further ado, ladies and gentlemen," the man at the podium intoned, "it is my pleasure to introduce the organizer of this event, the inspiration for good works around the globe, and today's keynote speaker, Mr. Richard Foye-Carver."

The audience stood to applaud. The move should have made it impossible for supershort Kylie to even see the stage, let alone the tall, fit man currently striding across it, one arm lifted to wave to the crowd. Providence, though, had carved a path through the bodies, leaving her a perfect sight line to the man of the hour.

She could see every detail as if she occupied a much closer spot than her seat at the back of the room. She saw his perfectly coiffed, elegantly graying hair and his expertly tailored suit. She saw the healthy tan of his skin and the flashing white of his disarming smile. She even saw the way he leaned down to shake hands with a few attendees who approached the stage for the chance to bask in the fame and glory that surrounded his noble acts.

She saw all of that, but beneath it, she saw something else.

As if she viewed a data construct or a hidden code,

Kylie stared at the man with a hazy green veil before her eyes. The filter seemed to blur his outer appearance, make it vaguely translucent, and show her an image of what rested inside.

The sight made her want to scream.

Her hand flew to her mouth, instinctively protecting against the quick rise of nausea. Bile choked her and her mouth flooded with sour saliva as the thing seethed and writhed beneath the skin of the man. She had no words to describe it, nothing to compare it to, no frame of reference for the mass of rotten, festering evil that hid within the photogenic masculine exterior. She couldn't name it, but she knew instinctively what it wasn't.

It wasn't human, and it wasn't something they had been prepared to face.

Clinging to Dag's hand, she used every bit of strength she could muster to pull him down to her. Of course, she couldn't force a Guardian to move, so she had to wait until he turned his attention toward her and leaned in close, a clear mask of concern molding his features.

"What is it?"

Kylie lifted a hand and pointed to the stage.

"Demon."

Chapter Eighteen

Got zol af im onshikn fun di tsen makes di beste.
God should visit on him the best of the Ten Plagues.

Dag's first reaction was denial, simple and instantaneous. He and his brothers had discussed the Seven at length. They knew Uhlthor had been freed but lacked the strength to take his full form, and they knew the goal of this action by the Order was to free Shaab-Na from its prison. Neither of them could have entered this room without the power of a major sacrifice.

And Kylie did not know what a real Demon was. She had thought the lowly *drude* qualified, when it was barely more than an unthinking insect compared to the evil of the Seven. She could not know the reality of a Demon.

Yet she stared at the stage as if the gate to hell itself had opened before her. Her skin had paled to a hue so white, he feared she might faint at any moment. She shook from head to toe, fine tremors he didn't believe she even noticed, and her dark eyes had gone stark and wide, her pupils so dilated he could barely see the chocolate brown of her irises.

She looked as if she had seen . . .

A Demon.

Scowling, he turned his gaze toward the front of the room and opened his sight to the man on the stage.

"Nazgahchuhl."

He spat the name and looked immediately to his brothers. This event they had not prepared for. Another of the Seven had been freed from his prison and had hid among the humans while awaiting his moment to strike. The Corruptor had been using the body of the Hierophant to walk among humanity and the Guardians had not seen the truth.

Shame and rage flooded through him. He and his brothers had failed to respond to a Demon's rising, had allowed one of the Seven to gather its supporters and arrange this complex and massive strike against humanity. And now his own mate was in danger.

At the center of the stage, the Demon in the man's body spread his arms to encompass the entire audience and raised his voice to allow every word to reverberate through the sound system. "Thank you, friends, for the enthusiasm of your welcome, and allow me also to thank each and every one of you here in this room for the enormous contribution you are about to make to the future of this world."

Dag tensed, ready to leap forward, when the lights blinked out and everything descended into hell.

This is. So. Not. Good.

Kylie saw the lights blink out and instinctively dropped to the floor. She couldn't have explained why, because it wasn't like she suddenly came under attack from a flock of pigeons, but her butt hit concrete a split second before Dag roared out his battle cry.

She felt the rush of air under his wings while her eyes tried to adjust to the dark and realized once and for all that the excrement and the bladed wind machine had just become very close acquaintances. She and the rest of the humans in this auditorium had just come under attack from a Demon.

She knew Dag had doubted her at first, but when he'd seen what she saw, he'd spat out a name that made her skin crawl. She had no doubt she'd been correct, and no idea how this changed their carefully laid plans.

Who was it who had come up with the whole "splitting up" part of the plan? Because right at that moment, she wanted to give that person a good, swift kick in the *tokhes*.

Built like a theater, the convention center auditorium lacked windows, so when the lights went out, it became black as pitch. Kylie could literally not see her hand in front of her face, not even when she waved it around close enough that she could feel the breeze it stirred on her skin.

She shouldn't have worried, though, because a source of light presented itself soon enough, in the form of the sickly, putrid red light of the energy four robed *nocturnis* directed into four corners of the room. Well, it looked like they'd been right about one thing.

Patsh zikh in tuches un schrei, "hooray!" Slap your butt and yell, "hooray!" It might end up being the only thing they got right, but it could prove to be the most important.

Gathering the slightly bent and worn edges of her courage, Kylie pushed herself to her feet and faced the *nocturni* in her corner of the room. He stood perhaps twenty feet away, his face illuminated by the light of his tainted magical energy. She could see the malevolent

excitement in his eyes and the cruel line of his mouth
as he chanted something she didn't understand and had
no desire to translate. She just wanted it to stop.

She inhaled deeply and reached inside herself, finding the spark of magic at her core. This time it leaped
immediately to life, going from ember to blaze in a
blinding flare of pale green light. She accepted the surge
of energy with gratitude, letting the magic flow through
her, under her skin, and down her arms until her fingertips itched like a thousand bug bites.

Then she raised her hands and let it loose.

It struck the *nocturni* in the side, catching him off
guard and making him cry out not in pain, but in anger.
His gaze swung toward her, but his hands remained
pointed at the swirling vortex of darkened energy at the
end of his stream of magic. Instead of responding to her
attack he shouted something and another robed figure
rushed out of the darkness toward her.

Kylie yelped and dodged, managing to put a row of
chairs between her and her attacker, but it interrupted
her concentration, and her hold on the casting *nocturni*
broke apart. Damn it. She had to stop that portal.

Unable to see in the dark, her attacker ran right into
the row of chairs and tumbled head over heels into a
tangle of plastic and metal. Chairs slid and skittered
across the floor, giving Kylie enough time to run to the
end of the seating area and into the open outer aisle. It
made her more vulnerable, but it also gave her a lot more
room to maneuver.

Her gaze zipped around the room looking for Dag,
finally catching sight of him at the front of the room.
He and Kees seemed to be attempting to catch the
Hierophant/Demon host in a pincer move, approaching
the inhuman entity with wary caution. She didn't want

to distract him from an enemy she knew was a lot more powerful than the one she faced, but darn it, she could use a little help here.

Apparently, she wasn't the only one. The initial buzz of confusion caused by the loss of light had turned into widespread panic when the magic had begun to fly. People screamed and shouted, pushing and shoving as they tried to rush toward the nearest exits. The ushers continued to block the way, erecting some kind of magic barricade that contained the audience to the center of the room. Like cattle in a pen.

She pressed herself against a concrete wall to avoid the pushing and shoving of overwrought conference attendees. It really seemed like that was something the Wardens should have planned for a little better. She'd give up any one of those defensive spells Wynn had taught her for something that would just freeze the mass of humanity in place.

And make them stop screaming. Do not forget to stop the screaming.

An odd, low popping noise reverberated from the far corner of the room. Immediately, Kylie's gaze swung in that direction in time to see another swirling vortex of energy splinter open like a miniature star gone nova. A moment later, deformed figures sprang forth into the auditorium, long, claw-tipped arms swinging out to catch human prey, huge maws opening to show rows and rows of dripping, threatening teeth. They looked like sharks and gorillas and psychopathic dust bunnies all rolled up into one slavering, grasping bundle of evil.

And they kept coming.

She heard Ella scream, a sound of mingled pain and frustration, and knew she must be hurt in order to have allowed the portal in her quadrant to open. She needed help, but first Kylie would have to ensure her own area didn't add to the nightmare.

Screams of panic had turned to abject terror and agony as the demonic minions began to feed. She could hear the crunching of bones and a wet, sucking, tearing sound that she didn't even want to know the source of. Keeping her eye on the prize, she quickly found the *nocturni* she had already jolted once and began pushing through the crowd to get to him.

She could see the edges of the vortex before him begin to glow, and she knew she didn't have much time. Raising both hands, she began casting as she ran, concentrating on forming the bubble Ella had said would trap a fellow caster and turn his own spell against him. For a moment, she thought she saw a shimmer begin, but then someone knocked into her from the side, interrupting her concentration and snapping the spell in two.

Well, fuck it, she thought. She didn't know enough about magic anyway. She'd had less than a week to practice the easiest of those spells, and Jews weren't supposed to be doing magic, anyway. As a half-Jew, she shouldn't be surprised if her magic turned out to be half-assed. Luckily, her brain was her most potent weapon, and it was still working at full capacity.

Pouring on a burst of speed, she flew toward the portal-opening *nocturni,* hands outstretched as if ready to trap him in a renewed burst of magical energy. He looked at her briefly and bared his teeth in a taunting smile, but Kylie had her own kind of magic. At the last moment, she dropped her hands, grasped the back of a hard, molded plastic and metal chair, and swung it with all her might at the *nocturni*'s head. There was a satisfying crack just before he crumpled to the concrete.

The vortex winked out with a shriek of protest. She

didn't know if the sound came from the aborted portal itself, or from whatever had been waiting to cross through it, but either way, it gave her the willies.

Dropping the chair, she looked around, trying to judge a path to Ella's side. Unfortunately, a multiplying sea of demonic minions stood between them.

What was she supposed to do now? She'd try blasting the portal closed, but clearly magic was not the way she was going to win this fight. What other tools did she have in her little bag of tricks?

She still had the drive-away salt in the pocket of her jeans, but no way did she think the two small pouches' worth that Wynn had provided would be enough to get her through all those monsters. She'd have a better chance with a handy trailing vine, a leopard-spotted loincloth, and a ululating cry. A better plan must be had.

The scent of blood had begun to taint the air, and although the back of the room remained safer than the front where Ella had been stationed, the murderous creatures had begun to push away from their portal and deeper into the room. This seemed to be keeping Knox and Spar busy, as they tried to take out the demonic minions while avoiding the innocent human bystanders who kept getting in the way. The poor clueless audience members just didn't know where to run and a few of them inevitably ended up throwing themselves between a Guardian and his prey. Only quick reflexes and solemnly sworn vows kept those fools alive.

Maybe she would have to resort to her half-assed magic after all.

If there was one thing Kylie could do better than almost anyone in the world, it was tweak code. She could always seem to find the subtle little glitches in a string of computer commands that kept a system from operating the way she wanted it to, and she had become renowned for finding the simplest, sneakiest little twists that got her the perfect result. If her magic had first shown itself in this ability, maybe that meant she could turn it back onto the magic itself.

Narrowing her eyes, Kylie reached once more for her magic, letting it fill her up and tingle in her fingertips. Then she brought to mind the shield spell Wynn had hammered into her brain and looked for the code.

It almost jumped out at her. She felt like she had just landed in the Matrix, seeing data scrolling before her in endless streams. She could see the code of the magic and knew exactly where it needed to change to perform her will. A quick twist of her mind, and the spell that flowed when she raised her fingers was something a little different from Wynn's protective shield. Instead, it became a battering ram of vivid, living energy that she held out before her and used to slice through the crowd.

Everything it touched slid away and to the sides. She felt a little like Moses parting the Red Sea, only she didn't have the entire nation of Israel at her back, and she only needed to get as far as the other side of the room.

Not understanding exactly what she had done or how long it would last, Kylie held tight to her magic and ran. She didn't bother to test herself too rigorously, ducking and dodging around the largest and hungriest-looking of the monsters and taking the path of least resistance to Ella's side. That still amounted to a lot of resistance. Luckily, for the moment, nothing seemed able to cut through her supershield.

She took a detour to edge around the still gaping portal. The only mercy about the thing was that it remained its original size and shape, meaning only one entity could pass through it at a time. Any more and they'd end up clogging the drain, like some kind of preternaturally evil hair ball. Still, not something a living person wanted to get in front of. So far, everyone who had was dead.

Kylie averted her eyes and pointedly ignored the sticky slickness under her feet as she finally set eyes on Ella. The Warden lay under a row of chairs, unmoving, and bleeding sluggishly from a wound in her side. Luck had stuck with her, because without the chairs making her difficult to spot, she'd have wound up brunch for the forces of Darkness a long time ago.

Hurrying to her friend's side, Kylie reached down to feel for a pulse, just to be certain. It beat strong and steady against her fingers, but that left their little army of good guys down one valuable soldier. And that *farkakta* portal to Demonland was still wide open.

Maybe it was time for a new plan.

For once in her life, being small was turning out to be a big advantage for Kylie. It made it a lot easier for her to hide and scurry and escape notice than most of the other people in the room, not to mention the ginormous winged Guardians who currently dove in and out of the fray, ripping apart any demonic creature they could lay their claws on. The continuously replenishing horde kept them so busy that no one had yet noticed Ella had fallen.

Certainly her mate, preoccupied with the big Demonic kahuna in the front of the room, had not. If he had, he'd have been at her side by now. That was a good thing, because Kylie and the rest of the innocent people here really needed him and Dag to keep Nazgahchuhl occupied, otherwise this battle would already be over, and Kylie would not have been on the winning side.

At the moment, she still wasn't certain she was on the winning side, but she definitely wasn't ready to give up.

A survey of the room showed only the one active portal, so that was a heck of a lot better than the alternative, and it indicated that Wynn and Fil had fared better with their opponents than Ella had with hers. Go, team.

Right, a new plan, Kylie reminded herself. Number one had to be to close that portal. Cutting off the flow would mean Knox and Spar could concentrate on really taking out the summoned creatures, allowing Kylie, Wynn, and Fil to figure out a way to begin getting the survivors to safety. At least the ushers had abandoned their posts at the doors. Kylie had a feeling they had not been cult members, but staff bespelled to follow commands. Once a demon creature had taken one of them as a little snack, the rest had scattered into the crowd, leaving the doors locked, but unattended.

Kees and Dag would stick with the Demon she was really trying not to think about. With the other Wardens currently helping on the opposite side of the huge auditorium, that left Kylie to deal with the portal.

Easy-peasy, right?

Wynn had told her that while the *nocturni* mage would need to cast a spell that opened the portal and continue to channel energy to hold it open for a while, after a certain amount of time, it could stabilize sufficiently to remain for an unknown duration. Which meant that even if she took out the caster, the portal might remain open even after he was out of the picture. Double trouble. Always fun.

Oh, well. Sometimes it was better to just swallow the medicine and worry about the aftertaste later.

Rising into a low crouch, Kylie took aim at the back of the casting *nocturni*'s head and let 'er rip.

She knew none of the spells the others had taught her had enough juice to stymie one of the Order's most pow-

erful magic users, but once again she found the code in
the spells she did have to work with and tweaked. This
time, she didn't bother with finesse, just grabbed, twisted,
and plunked in her own addition and then sent the energy
winging through space.

The little ping of green light hit the robed figure on
the back of his hooded head and then exploded like
a firework. Unlike a firework, however, these trails of
sparkling light expanded outward and fused together to
form a bubble just the way Ella had described. Or almost the way Ella had described. The bubble that Kylie
created enveloped both the *nocturni* and his portal to
hell, and it didn't take the emerging creatures long to
recognize there was only one food source available inside the magical trap.

Kylie looked away when blood splattered the inside
of the bubble like water on a windshield at the car wash.

She looked around and saw Fil headed her way at a
jog. The blonde looked bruised and bloody but intact
and Kylie had never been so happy to see anyone.

"Ella's down, but okay," Kylie said, the minute she
thought Fil could hear. "I cut off the portal for the moment, but I don't know how long my bubble will last,
and I don't know if I can close the portal myself. That
is one spell I do not want to try tinkering with. If I take
down my spell, do you think you can blast the portal
closed?"

Fil nodded, already turning her attention to the problem at hand. "Yeah, I'm with you. That was some nice
work, though, Koyote. Very innovative. On the count of
three."

They ran through the numbers aloud, and on three,
Kylie reached out, grabbed her magic, and yanked,
flinging it down into the earth. Sort of like pulling the

tablecloth off a table and hoping the place settings stayed where they were. In the same instant, Fil threw a bolt of bright light at the portal. It hit with a shower of sparks, and then the whole thing collapsed in on itself like a dying star. Minus the black hole, which was kind of the point.

She flashed Kylie a cheeky grin. "Hey, Wynn was right. Practice makes perfect!"

"Duck!"

That was all Kylie had time to say before the two creatures released from the bubble came flying at them like ravening wolves on tasty-looking elk. Once again, Kylie went the old-fashioned route. She lifted another chair and swung for the fences, knocking the first creature into the second and sending them both skittering across the concrete floor. An instant later, a huge shadow passed over them and Spar dove on top of the monsters, grabbing them in his enormous talons and literally ripping them to shreds.

Kylie had to look away, but next to her, she heard Fil heave an exaggerated sigh.

"My hero," the blonde teased, then yelped out a muffled laugh as her Guardian dragged her close for a brief fierce kiss before wading back into the fray.

"Oh, get a room," Kylie mumbled.

"Oh, we will. Just remember you said that. After all, we're staying with you."

Kylie rolled her eyes and tugged her friend's arm. "We need to either get Ella back on her feet, or find someplace safe to stash her. She's over here."

The pale brunette was already stirring when they reached her side, and Kylie heaved a sigh of relief. Maybe the tide was finally turning in their favor.

"Don't sit up!" Fil warned as Ella began to stir. "You're

lying under a chair, and the last thing you need is to give yourself a concussion."

"I think I already have one." Ella groaned, lifting a hand to her head and wincing. "Concrete is really hard."

"We've still got stuff to do, Ellabella. How are you doing? Can you stand?"

"Give me a hand and let's see."

They each gave her one, first sliding the chairs that had concealed her out of the way to make room. Then they grasped the woman from either side and swung her to her feet. Ella swayed for a moment, then smiled wanly and gave them a thumbs-up. "All systems are go. Go slowly, but go."

"Good," Kylie said grimly, "because Fil was right. We do still have a lot to do."

She nodded toward the front of the room where the two Guardians and the Demon on stage had been joined by a slightly battered and wholly defiant witch. A witch who currently knelt at the Hierophant/Demon's feet with a pissed-off expression on her face and a short, sharp knife to her throat.

Chapter Nineteen

A finstere cholem auf dein kopf und auf dein
hent und fiss.
A dark dream on your head, hands, and feet.

Dag had approached the Corruptor with rage and with
caution. The one he could not help, but the other he had
to work hard to remember.

Every instinct he possessed wanted him to throw
himself on the vile Demon and rend it limb from limb,
but he recognized the impossibility of victory. The body
of the Hierophant was simply the host for Nazgahchuhl,
not the Demon itself. Destroying the host would merely
inconvenience the Demon, and with all the death already
filling the hall, that action might provide the last bit of
strength needed to return the Demon to its natural form.

Knowing this, he forced himself to stay back, to give
the Demon a wide berth even as his claws stretched and
ached to feel the tearing of muscle from bone. Out of
the corner of his eye, he could see Kees approaching as
well. The other Guardian moved in from the opposite
side, keeping the Demon in front of and between them
as they closed the distance across the stage.

Dag did not fool himself that the Corruptor didn't feel his presence, didn't know down to the last inch where each Guardian in the room stood or flew at that very moment. It knew Dag and Kees approached from the sides; it knew Spar and Knox waded through the bodies on the floor of the auditorium while battling the evil creatures that had poured through the portal, the *nocturnis* had managed to open.

It knew where the Wardens stood, knew how fiercely they fought to vanquish the cult's magic users and turn the tide of the battle. It knew about Kylie.

"Yes, Guardian, I know all sorts of interesting things," the Demon purred, its voice reverberating in a range a human could never have achieved. The host's vocal cords would never be the same. Not that it mattered; no human could survive the taint of hosting one of the Seven for more than a moment. "I know you and your brothers think you can win this little war of ours, so of course I know that you have found these females you call mates."

It laughed, a sound that scraped against bone and tooth, pinging against exposed nerve. "Poor fools. Do you not see that the thing you so value is your greatest weakness?"

"Weakness?" Kees hissed, baring his fangs. "Our Wardens are standing against your precious servants and fighting the battle we all know we *will* win. You cannot triumph, Demon, not while the Light exists."

"Oh, your precious Light is already growing dim," the Demon said dismissively. "In the end we will devour it, just as we will devour this pitiful little world and every soul in it."

It lifted its head, stretching the human neck to unnatural lengths, then closing its eyes and sniffing the air like a pig scenting truffles. "Mm, so many tasty, tasty souls, falling like a banquet before me. I must remember to thank my servants for the feast."

Suddenly its eyes snapped open and its head whipped around to stare at Kees with a malevolent smile. "Though what was that you said about your Wardens 'standing,' Guardian? Because I think that if you'll care to look, you'll see one of them very much off her precious little feet."

Kees looked immediately to the floor, his black eyes searching for the petite form of his mate. Dag looked as well. His gaze flitted over Fil, her pale hair easy to spot in the crowd, and he thought he saw Wynn as well, but the glimpse was fleeting. He told himself not to worry because his gaze failed to find Kyle; she was so tiny, she could easily become lost among all the taller and larger humans. And Ella might be a bit larger, but her sweet, unremarkable looks could also get lost in the chaos below.

Kees growled, and Dag turned to glare at him. "Calm yourself, brother. You know better than to listen to a filthy, lying Demon. Your mate will be well. They will all be well."

"Such optimism, Guardian," the Demon taunted. "Are you so certain your own *little* female is not one of the souls that already fills my belly?"

"I am certain," Dag snarled. "Her power is such that it would catch in your accursed gullet and choke you, filth of Darkness."

"Ooh, that flavorful, is she? Maybe I'll save her for dessert, then. I could even let you watch while I suck her body dry."

Kees thundered, "Shut your mouth, Demon scum. My brother is right. Our Wardens are too much for you or any of the loathsome pit crawlers called the Seven to deal with. In fact, if I were you, I would turn my attention away from baiting the ones who will destroy me and fix on the depletion of my forces by the little females you choose to dismiss."

For a moment, the Demon's smile slipped and his gaze flew to the floor of the auditorium.

Dag had heard a shift in the chaotic noise of battle, but he stood angled too far away from the floor to see what had happened. Kees had a much better view and had begun to appear grimly satisfied.

"I believe I see your little Warden, brother," Kees said, satisfaction ringing in his voice. "And I believe she has just managed to ensure that no more demonic scum will be joining us for this morning's festivities."

Dag felt a surge of relief and renewed purpose. He knew his Kylie was strong and more powerful than she believed, and he couldn't wait to rub her nose in the evidence.

For a moment rage and disbelief flashed in the Demon's stolen eyes, but it was quickly masked behind another taunting smile. "Oh, don't worry, Guardians. The fun isn't over. I still have a few tricks up my sleeve, if you will. In fact, let me show you one of them."

Lifting its fingers to its lips, the demon whistled shrilly. All at once, the chaos in the room went silent, like a television turning off. A glance showed that every remaining living human in the room had frozen like a statue where they stood. A moment later, Dag heard the sound of wings cutting through the silence. Not Guardian wings, but something smaller and faster, something that stirred the air with the scent of old blood and rotted meat. Just as the smell registered, a thump shook the stage to his right and a snarling, cursing witch appeared at the Demon's feet. Immediately, it grabbed her by the hair and hauled her close, and a small dagger appeared in the hand pressed to her throat.

Kees immediately leaped high and dragged the winged minion out of the air, snapping its spine and tearing its heart from its chest with his bare fangs. As it dissolved into ash at his feet, he roared his displeasure into the Corruptor's laughing face.

"Tsk-tsk," the Demon chided. "That temper could get you into trouble one of these days, Guardian. You wouldn't want that, now would you?" The hand at Wynn's throat shifted and a thin line of red appeared, drops of blood welling to the surface.

"UNHAND MY MATE!"

The thunderous roar shook the stage and rattled the lights in the rigging. Knox swooped in from above like death, covering the distance from the back of the auditorium in two beats of his powerful wings. He landed on the edge of the stage in a crouch and let out another cry so loud and so fierce that even Dag felt the need to bow to his fury.

"Careful, Guardian," the Demon said, smile tightening and eyes flashing red. Its hand pressed tighter to Wynn's throat. "Make me nervous and I might just slip. No one wants any accidents."

"I'm fine, big guy," Wynn reassured her mate. Her voice shook, not with fear, but with anger. "Don't worry about me. Just stick to the plan."

The Demon chuckled. "Oh-ho, there's a plan, is there? That just sounds so precious. Would anyone care to enlighten me on the details?"

"There really aren't that many."

Dag's heart stopped in his chest as his tiny mate climbed up on the stage at Knox's side and stood facing the ultimate corruption of Nazgahchuhl with nothing but a few feet of space separating them.

Kylie stood as she always did, with her head high and her shoulders back, looking like nothing so much as a bored college student facing off against an arrogant professor. He wanted to grab her and kiss her and tell her how proud she made him; then he wanted to turn her over his knee and beat the stuffing out of her for putting herself in danger and scaring millennia off his life.

"Not that many details, I mean," Kylie continued. "Mostly it was just a matter of come here, kick your ass, then go home and eat babka."

Nazgahchuhl turned his attention to Kylie, and Dag rumbled a warning. He couldn't help it. It escaped without his permission, but at least he maintained enough control not to leap at the Demon's throat, thus jeopardizing Wynn's life.

"So you're the little thing my servants were trying so hard to find," the Demon mused, tilting his head as he gazed at her. "I can see how they overlooked you. You're quite insignificant, aren't you?"

"Short jokes? Really?" Kylie scoffed, which made Dag twitch. "You're, like, as old as time, and the best you can come up with are short jokes?" Kylie looked at her mate and jerked a thumb in the Demon's direction. "Is this thing for real?"

"I can assure you I am very real," the Demon hissed, leaning forward over Wynn's captive head to glare at the Warden. "If you don't believe me, I'm certain your friends can share with you a few of my greatest achievements."

While everyone concentrated on the conversation between the Demon and Kylie, Dag became aware of more movement. From the floor of the auditorium, Fil approached with Spar by her side. They climbed onto the stage between Kees and Knox, providing the last pieces in a wall of opposition to Nazgahchuhl and his plans.

The Demon saw them—everyone saw them—but its reaction was not what Dag had expected. Instead of growing more tense in the face of the combined power of four Guardians and three Wardens, the Demon smiled and seemed almost to relax.

"Well, now, I see the gang is finally all here," it said, sounding almost cheerful. "Excellent."

Once again, Kylie's mouth took off. "What? You were waiting to ask for our autographs?"

Fil snorted and this time the Demon just smiled.

"Oh, no, nothing like that," it said dismissively. "But now I have the chance to tell you all how much I appreciate your kind assistance."

Dag's gut clenched as he realized something was very, very wrong.

"Assistance?" Kylie demanded, fisting her hands in the front pockets of her jeans. "You think we helped you out today?" She looked at Dag. "He's a *meshugener*."

"Oh, no, I can assure you I am quite sane," the Demon practically purred. "Quite intelligent, too. I had to be in order to plan out this little distraction so convincingly."

"Distraction," Dag snarled. He had a bad, bad feeling.

"Oh, I'm sure you'll read all about it in the news, but I really couldn't have done it without you."

Kylie shook her head. "*Zayn vort zol zayn a brik, volt ikh moyre gehat aribertsugeyn.* If his word were a bridge, I'd be afraid to cross it," she muttered. "You're trying to tell us that you didn't really set this up and attempt to massacre all of these people because you wanted to. You just thought it would keep us busy while you did something more important. You couldn't have just sent us to the movies?"

"I never said this little event wasn't fun," the Demon taunted. "And delicious." It licked its lips, and Kylie made gagging noises. "I'm merely saying that this is not the only city in the world, and that death tastes sweet all over." It gave a sigh of pleasure that raised growls from all four Guardians. "But enough chitchat. I'm afraid I must be going."

Dag tensed at the statement and leaped, forgetting the knife at Wynn's throat, forgetting the poor odds, forgetting everything but the need to seize the Demon before it could escape.

He was too late.

They all were. The Guardians crashed together in the spot where Nazgahchuhl had stood, nothing there but an empty space and an extremely ticked-off witch who told them all in no uncertain terms to get their fat asses off her.

Knox scooped her up in his arms and cradled her to his chest, crooning reassurances at her until she slapped him upside the head and demanded to be set back on her feet.

"I'm fine," she insisted, loudly, as the others gathered around in concern. "The scratch on my neck doesn't even need a bandage, and that flying monkey barely dropped me six feet. Quit worrying. About me, anyway. If anyone wants to worry about what the Demon meant by his psychotic little spiel, I'd be happy to join you."

Suddenly a scream rang out from the middle of the auditorium floor, and Dag turned to see that the spell the Demon had cast to freeze everyone in place had ended as abruptly as the creature had disappeared. Instantly, he and the other Guardians shifted to human and looked to their mates.

"Anyone know how we're going to explain this?"

They all turned their gazes to the room filled with dazed and injured humans, as well as the bloody remains of the dead and the scattered ashes of destroyed demons.

Kylie sighed and pulled out her cell phone. "I have no idea. But you know what? That's why we have mayors, and why mayors have public relations specialists. I'm calling 911. We did the hard part, now someone else can clean up the mess."

Chapter Twenty

Az der soyne falt, tor men zikh nit freyen
(ober men heybt im nit oyf).
*Rejoice not at thine enemy's fall
(but don't pick him up, either).*

That night, over Indian takeout, they watched the news. The lead story on the local station was of the terrorist attack at the John B. Hynes Veterans Memorial Convention Center.

According to eyewitnesses, a hallucinogenic gas had been deployed in the auditorium during an important speech by noted philanthropist Richard Foye-Carver. Assailants had then stormed the room, killing seventeen people and wounding more than a hundred others. Carver's representatives assured the media that his security team had gotten him to safety, but that he would be canceling his public appearances for the near future out of legitimate concerns for his safety.

"I'll give them concern for his safety," Kylie mumbled before biting savagely into a hunk of naan.

Beside her Dag chuckled. "Down, girl. We still need to see what the Demon was really up to. Then we will decide how you are going to kill it."

That pacified her for the moment. Barely.

It also helped mellow her homicidal tendencies that she was frickin' exhausted. The events of the morning had led to five more hours at the convention center talking to police, talking to the FBI, giving statements, giving more statements, getting checked by paramedics, and giving yet more statements. By the time their group had finally returned to the brownstone and collapsed in the living room, she'd barely had the energy to call the restaurant and have the food delivered.

Seriously. She and the other Wardens had played rock-paper-scissors to decide who had to answer the door when it arrived. She had suggested rock-paper-scissors-lizard-Spock, but had been vetoed. Apparently, she was just "a big ol' geek."

Pshaw.

They all perked up, at least mentally, when the television transitioned to the world news. There, the terrorist attack in Boston took second fiddle to the news of a much greater disaster in Ireland.

"More than seventy people are dead, and authorities warn that the numbers may continue to rise as they sort through the aftermath of this afternoon's tragic events in Dublin, Ireland. Sources in the capital city are calling this attack 'an utter and complete surprise,' as well as 'one of the worst terrorist attacks in the history of the Republic.' Coming on the one-hundredth anniversary of the Easter Rising, Sunday's bombing and riot shocked authorities who claimed to have had no prior warning leading up to the event."

The station cut to film of an Irish official looking shocked and devastated as he delivered a statement to the press. Kylie felt a knot of dread in her stomach as she turned toward her friends.

"I think we know now what the Demon was really up to."

Fil looked blown away. "I can't believe they could do this. I mean, I can't believe they managed to coordinate across two continents to create simultaneous events. And to use one as a distraction for the other? That is way more sophisticated than we've been giving them credit for."

"Not to mention that we've been so busy concentrating on the things happening here in North America that we've completely ignored the rest of the world," Wynn said with a troubled frown. "I don't know what else we can do, though. We're already spread out between here and Canada, all the way from the East Coast to the West. Now we need to be worried about the British Isles and Europe, too?"

"Should we always have been worried about Europe?" Kylie asked. "I mean, that is where the Guild was based, and where the Order started, right?"

"Are you trying to make us cry, Ky?" Ella teased weakly. "I don't know about the rest of you, but I'm already feeling overwhelmed. I don't know if I can take on another continent right at the moment."

Kees hugged her close to his side. He had barely let go of her after hearing how she had been hurt attempting to prevent the portal from opening. A knife to the side had taken her out of commission, but had thankfully deflected off a rib before it could do much real damage.

"No one expects any of you to take on all of Europe," he reassured them. "You have enough on your plates as it is. This simply means that we must redouble our efforts to find the remaining Wardens and Guardians as quickly as possible. I have to believe that some of our brethren remain overseas. To have moved us all to the New World would make no strategic sense."

"That is assuming that the *nocturni* infiltrator did not arrange for our assignments," Knox growled, holding Wynn tightly on his lap. If Kees had been overprotective since this morning, Knox had been nearly feral. The sight of a knife to his mate's throat had thoroughly shaken him.

"Do not give in to paranoia," Spar advised. "To do so only weakens us. We must keep clear heads and trust in our Wardens until we have evidence to the contrary."

Dag sighed. "I trust *our* Wardens implicitly. It's the ones who came before that I wonder about."

Kylie pushed aside her plate and climbed onto her mate's lap. He looked surprised, but welcomed her with open arms and settled her comfortably against his chest.

"We can't give up on them all," she said, leaning her head against his shoulder. "The ones who've gone into hiding? They're probably on our side and are just as much opposed to the Order as we are. If we find them and share with them what we've learned, I'm sure they can help us. And at this point, we need all the help we can get."

She had to stifle a yawn with a fist to her mouth.

"You're right," Wynn said, "but that doesn't make finding them any easier. The three of us have been trying for months."

"Not on the deep Web."

"What do you mean?"

Kylie explained. "Before I knew magic existed, I never thought about where people would be able to safely discuss it without freaking out the public and shit. I mean honestly; you put that stuff on the surface Web, and someone is either going to burn a cross on your lawn, or send the men with the white coats to talk to you about it."

They all eyed her with various levels of confusion.

She sighed. "The average person on the street, or on the Internet, doesn't believe in magic, guys. When they hear people talk about it they either think they're a Satan worshipper or a lunatic. So where can people who *know* magic is real go to connect with each other? The deep Web. In fact, I found some interesting conversations on the darknet while I was searching for *nocturnis*. If any of the missing Wardens are even remotely tech savvy, that's the place where you should be looking."

Ella started to look excited, and by "excited" Kylie meant "awake." "Oh, wow, that makes perfect sense. If even a few of them are on the darkwhoosie, if we contact them there, then they can spread the word to others they might already know of. I mean, it's not a guarantee of anything, but I think it's the best lead we've had in a while."

Fil nodded. "Agreed. Can you show us how we can get hooked in to the 'darkwhoosie' there, Koyote?"

"Only if you all swear never to call it the 'darkwhoosie' again. At least not in my hearing."

"Deal," Wynn said firmly. She flashed her old friend a smile. "We really lucked out the day you became a Warden, Kyle E. Woyote. I don't even know where we'd be right now without you. We wouldn't even know that a third of the Seven had been set free, let alone about the attacks here and in Dublin. You've helped us save some lives."

"Not enough," Kylie said.

"It's never enough."

Kylie felt the sad silence stretch between them, but Dag let it go for only a moment before he hugged her tightly.

"You Wardens might be lucky to have Kylie join your

ranks," he said, smiling down at his mate, "but none of you have half my luck, for I have had Kylie join my heart."

Kylie returned his smile and added a roll of her eyes. "Yeah, yeah. Back at you, big guy. You know, for such a tough Guardian-type dude, you can be a real sap, you know that?"

The others laughed while Dag tickled her in retaliation.

"This is perfect then," Wynn said, snuggling against her mate's chest and nodding to the rest of the group. "Kylie will get us on the darknet, we'll intensify the search for the missing Wardens, and continue to dig up everything we can on those last three Guardians. I think Ireland is as good a place to start as any. And who knows? Maybe we'll get lucky again."

Kylie grinned and leaned in to whisper in her mate's ear. "I know what would make me feel lucky. Having the house all to ourselves again."

Dag laughed and whispered back. "At least we have the third floor to ourselves. Perhaps we should be thankful for small mercies."

Looking up into his flaming black eyes, Kylie felt her heart melt and the rest of the world recede. This Guardian, this mate, this man had burst into her life in a shower of stone and violence and changed absolutely everything. He had opened her eyes to an entire world she had never known existed, and opened her heart to feelings she had never thought were possible.

Really, the only thing she had to be thankful for was him.

And she would be, for the rest of her life.